Indivisible

*It's been a
lot of work.
Thanks for the
help, Linda.*

Blair

Blair Smith

PublishAmerica

Baltimore

First printing

ISBN: 1-59286-421-X
PUBLISHED BY PUBLISHAMERICA BOOK PUBLISHERS
www.publishamerica.com
Baltimore

Printed in the United States of America

Chapter 1

Random sunbeams popped through the forest canopy making the water from the cascade sparkle and dance as it plunged over rocks and logs at the upper end of Mohawk Creek. Light green, algae-coated stones lay beneath the water in quieter side pools. And above the surface on rocks or stumps, darker shades of moss added another green hue to the forest tapestry.

Barry jumped to a boulder in the middle of the stream and yelled at Thad and Butch to follow. Only his lips could be seen speaking; tumbling water drowned out the words. Barry stood daringly on the rock, his face shadowed by his oversized Scout hat. Chestnut hair and hazel eyes his trademark, he stood four-six at eleven years of age and looked out over the torrent from a delicate face with long eyelashes. Damp fragrances flowed up, and like the sound, were absorbed by the greenery of the forest.

Barry was a Christian boy. Baptism at birth saved him from eternal fire. His mom, a solid Congregationalist--his father too, before the divorce. Barry was honest, or at least tried to be, and swore very little, certainly not as much as other boys his age. Today, he took off on a Scout Troop adventure with the Rousell brothers, Thad and Butch, ages eleven and twelve.

The Rousells, on the other hand, were French-Canadian. Catholic. Butch, pug-faced and stocky, thought they were part Indian but he hadn't said so openly because he wasn't sure who their real father was. The two boys lived a half-mile down the road from Barry in a rundown mobile home along Mohawk Creek. The Rousells didn't go to church. Their mom never told them when to wash or go to bed; the two fixed their own meals. Butch and Thad would often sleep in a hut they had made in the woods if whoever their mom was sleeping with at the time wasn't of their liking. They were survivors.

Their friendship with Barry developed out of convenience. They grew up together, explored the woods together, rode to school together. They started out in Cub Scouts, then Webelos; Butch would be a Boy Scout in the fall. Their favorite caper was to get up early Saturday morning and fish, or catch crawdads, in the pond of an exclusive resort near their homes, the Balsams.

If you asked Butch what he wanted to be when he grew up, he would tell you: an Eagle Scout. Though he didn't do so well in school, Butch excelled at what he loved. The Scout Manual had become his textbook. He couldn't recite the state capitals but he knew the Scout Oath, Law, and Motto by heart. Bold, and at times bombastic, Butch often got in trouble at school. If caught, he always told the truth.

Scout Pack leader, Mr. Ronolou, was the reason the boys loved Scouting. He led New Hampshire's Pack 220 from Colebrook, the best Scout Pack in the region. Mr. Ronolou pushed the boys and insisted they do their best. As a seventy-year-old man, Ronolou had little patience for foolery. Through the tone of his voice and his stern look, he insisted on respect. His name was Mr. Ronolou, or Sir; no one called him by anything else.

Thad was small, and slender as a sliver. More timid than most boys, he followed his brother without question. Butch, being the oldest, set the pace. He never led them into any really serious trouble--nothing that needed parental intervention or payment of fines. Butch jumped to the rock. Then Thad leaped from the bank to a stone, then leaped again to Barry's boulder where they stood grasping one another for balance. The three of them jiggled and grabbed and laughed.

They spoke loudly to one another. Even though other Scouts in the Pack surrounded them, none heard. "Do you believe this shit," said Butch.

"We're standing in the middle of the river. You won't see anyone else gutsy enough to do this shit," Thad piped in with a broad smile on his face.

"My Mom says I can't say 'shit' anymore or I can't hang around with you guys," Barry stated to his friends. They still clung to one another on the rock. Spray from the rushing stream misted them. It felt good after the long hike. "She said my soul might go to hell, or something like that."

Thad laughed, "So you can't say 'shit'?" Butch repeated the jibe, chuckling as well.

"That's right, I can't say, 'shit.' At least not in front of Mom."

Charlie Ronolou watched it all as a shepherd would. Cub Scouts often taunted injury by climbing boulders, ledges, and the like. Charlie didn't mind; the boys of Pack 220 had hiked for over an hour; it was their time to cut loose. And if someone did get hurt, the troop might get some hands-on experience at first aid. Charlie cared all right, but to suppress the boys constantly was not natural.

Charlie had been the Akela of Pack 220 for almost twenty years, long after his sons had grown up and left Scouting. Now, despite his arthritis, he still made the traditional climb up Dixville Notch.

Scouting wasn't always popular in Colebrook. During the 1980s and 90s, Pack 220 had dwindled to as low as seven boys. Previous Akelas had attributed the downturn to a new karate school in town, or sports. Then Charlie Ronolou took over and stuck with it, giving the Cubs the consistency they needed from the ranks of Bobcat to Bear, on up through Webelos. He had initiated the annual Dixville hike and turned Scouting in Pack 220 from meetings in civic halls into an outdoor adventure. It paid off. Colebrook's Pack 220 was 66 members strong, outnumbering local bands at Memorial Day parades, Veterans' Day parades--even the Fourth of July.

Ken Minsen, a parent volunteer for the day, turned and looked at the boys. Then he spoke to Charlie, "Someone's going to hurt themselves. Those Rousell boys are pushing the limit."

"Don't worry about them. Those kids have gotten more bumps and knocks than you and I combined."

Minsen didn't comment but he could hear the fatigue in Charlie's voice. "Why do you run the Pack year after year, Charlie?"

"I would like to give this up but I haven't found anyone to take over. I'll be quite honest," Charlie continued with a sigh, "I'm getting too old to be doing this anymore but it's too important to drop. The oath these boys take about honesty and duty to parents and country; I think it becomes a part of them, if only a small part. You've got to build character early in boys, or the man in them only looks out for himself. Now look at Barry over there. I think he's a good influence on those Rousell boys. That's another part of Scouting; the boys have an impact on one another. Barry's influence might save those boys, might pull them out of this imp phase they're in."

"Sounds like you're in it awhile longer."

"If I could convince someone to take up the job of Pack Leader, I'd be gone tomorrow." Charlie waited for a response from Minsen.

Minsen understood the implication, "I couldn't put the time in. I'm struggling now to make ends meet with two jobs."

The nation had been in economic ruin for a decade. Fighting terrorism throughout the world strained the nation's treasury, so much so, that the standard of living America once enjoyed was no more. This nation continued to maintain her military strength, but at an extreme cost. Like the Soviet Union in the 1980's, America now experiences ideological, racial and eithnic strife.

It had been a bad year for his family. In these times, parents often had several part-time jobs to pay bills. "You gotta make time," said Charlie. "Gotta make time."

Minsen took the lead and headed up the trail toward the summit. He called back to the pack to get started again; some of them heard over the rushing water, others straggled behind as they noticed boys leaving around them. Charlie took the rear, coaxing dawdlers, preferring the slower pace.

Barry, Thad, and Butch leaped off the rock. Though Butch was the largest of the three boys, all but Thad caught the water with a foot. With his tight, wiry physique Thad could outrun anyone in the Pack.

The three had their disagreements of course, but they always reunited at Pack meetings or special Scouting events--too innocent to carry a grudge for long, too childlike to get into foolery without a supportive audience.

They relished the outdoors and attacked every aspect of boyhood with disregard to etiquette, making spears and bows, throwing knives and hatchets. They even killed a groundhog together. Barry's dog Tater caught it away from its hole and blocked the groundhog's retreat while the boys punctured it with spears and threw kitchen knives at it. It was a frenzied bloodletting. The wooden-tipped spears did a poor job of penetrating the thick hide, killing the animal inhumanely. Ultimately, the three boys pummeled the creature with dull tips that bruised and broke bones inside. The passion of the moment wouldn't let them stop. When the thing sat up on its haunches to face Tater's snarling teeth, Butch caught it with his throwing knife in the soft underbelly. It fought and crawled after that, but Butch's tossed blade signaled the end. Five minutes later the animal lay convulsing with body shakes, urinating, and defecating involuntarily. The three of them stood silently around the beast with bloodied spears and blades in hand, wondering why they did it. Only Tater knew.

Tater gnawed on the carcass at the boys' secret hideout for three days that summer until Butch finally buried the smelly remains. Though they hadn't talked about the event since that day, they wouldn't consider killing another groundhog.

Despite their introduction to death, today it didn't stop Butch from using a stick to scoop up the dried skin and bones of a squirrel carcass. He tossed it onto his younger brother's back.

Charlie saw it and called from the back of the line. "Get back here, you boys. Butch, Thad, I want you boys back here, now!" Barry was off with the other Webelos to continue up the trail without his cohorts.

Butch and Thad came to the back of the line like scolded puppies. Charlie dropped back from the Pack to talk to the boys privately. "You know, boys, I've had it with you two and your tomfoolery. I bend over backwards for all my boys but you two are always into something. I gave you guys time back at the falls to let loose and you're still pulling pranks on the trail. There are ledges and loose stones around here; someone could get hurt. Butch, I've never kicked anyone out of the Pack before but this can't go on."

Butch's eyes widened when he heard that, "Kicked out? Am I kicked out?" He stopped breathing for a moment, waiting for a response.

"You're not listening. I said this foolery can't go on. You're not kicked out, but you could be. Now, you boys follow me for the rest of the hike."

Charlie's sermon got Butch's attention; he lived for Scouting. Usually, he defiantly endured the lectures of his teachers, his mother, and Charlie. It always passed, and things continued on as before. But his life would not be the same without Scouting: the hikes, the camp-outs, the secret codes, the Pack. Butch knew that. He and Thad shut their mouths and didn't do anything unless told to.

The trail wound up the mountain, taking short detours around gullies and boulders, all through a thick pine forest with wide tree trunks. Tall conifers canopied the open, sunless underworld. Needles from those trees carpeted the ground with an aromatic layer that smothered other plant life on the forest floor. Life seemed to cease in the undergrowth. Small birds that usually fluttered brazenly about from branch to branch sat motionless in their nests.

Near the summit, Minsen emerged from the forest into daylight and led the Pack through a clearing. A Scout leading the group noticed a red light flash among the dead branches of a brush pile. "Hey, look at that." He walked toward it and stopped. "Come look at this. There are two red lights. Another one just popped on."

The whole Pack stood in the clearing, a few boys lingering near the trees at each end of the opening. A fourth red light popped on. An explosion of gunfire cut through the Pack, single bullets, often burst through several boys aligned with one another, the bullet continuing through trees deep in the wooded surrounding. The auto-gun strafed the group through their midsections. Multiple bullets passing through younger boys nearly cut them in half. The machine whirled from the front of the Scout pack to the back, shooting boys at both ends first, spraying bullets through the pack in its sweep. Minsen died instantly. A bullet to the ribs brought Charlie down; as he fell he snatched Butch and Thad's clothes, yanking the Rousell brothers down with him behind a boulder.

Most of the pack bolted for cover but the shooting happened so suddenly that some boys froze in horror and watched. The gun would rotate from one end of the clearing to the other, stopping at each end to sputter single bullets as though pausing to aim and fire at individuals. Every bullet seemed to hit someone. The few that froze in horror stood miraculously unscathed. When they moved, the horror left them quickly and with little pain. The entire pack lay bleeding, some boys with viscera strewn on the ground beside them. Some tried to put their intestines back, but movement only drew the auto-gun's attention; those boys received another fatal round to the gut. Boys who made it behind thick trees for protection were still detected by the gun; the bullets streaked through trees like tissue paper, splatting the Scouts behind them.

Charlie noticed the pattern of the auto-gun from his position behind the boulder. Everyone was hit at least once except for the Rousell brothers. Charlie knew he couldn't stay conscious for long. *I have to do something!*

Barry stirred behind another boulder. He looked down at his legs, both shot to a pulp and streaming out blood. A numb realization swept over him that life was temporary, "Oh God, someone help me!" His wasn't the only cry of dismay; screams and groans came from everywhere.

Butch recognized Barry's voice and got up to help. Charlie grabbed the boy's belt and yanked him down before the gun began shooting at their movement. Rock fragments jetted everywhere, eating away at the boulder the three hid behind.

"Don't move!" Charlie yelled to the pack. "Nobody move! You hear me." Pleas and whimpers continued--occasional bursts popped the kids who moved. But the cries from the boys . . . Charlie couldn't feel his own pain because of it. He could see boys off to the side and wondered why they were still alive, so mangled and all--or how so much blood could come from such small bodies.

"We gotta get Barry," insisted Butch. Thad looked at Barry with a frozen stare. "Next time it shoots over there, I'm going." Butch was crouched and ready to go.

"No you're *not* going!" Charlie replied.

"Why?" asked Butch.

"Because, I'm the Akela," Charlie insisted to Butch. "You *do* as I say!" He put his hands on Thad's face and turned it away from Barry's direction. "Do you hear me?" Thad, wide-eyed and anxious, nodded yes. "Now, when

I get up and go, you two haul-ass over to that boulder," Mr. Ronolou pointed, "and then crawl on your stomachs to the roots of that uprooted tree end. The boulder will block the gun's line-of-sight." Charlie paused to get his breath. "Dig a hole and stay there. You hear me? Stay there no matter what. Whoever set up this thing will be back. You boys have to keep yourselves alive if you're going to get help."

Charlie's face was fish-belly white; he drew a deep breath and struggled up to a squatting position and tossed a stone.

The auto-gun traced the movement but didn't fire. He lit a pack of matches and tossed it out in front of them. The gun blasted the flaming pack of matches. A ball of dust exploded into the air where the burning pack had been. *So, this cold-blooded machine detects heat and motion.* Now, Charlie knew what he had to do. He turned to Butch, "Get Thad turned the right direction and when I take off, you two go!"

Butch shook his head. "But, Sir. I'd like to say--"

"No don't. Just get ready." Charlie shook his head to try to stay conscious. The Scout leader didn't want the boy to say something that would make him feel guilty. Charlie couldn't return the admiration; he had never cared for the Rousell boys and didn't want a lie to be his last word. "Ready?" The man got up and ran out to latch onto a dead tree stump. The gun turned and popped him with one shot to his chest.

At the same moment, the Rousell boys sprinted toward the boulder in the other direction. Driven by fear, Thad's quick, lightweight frame darted yards ahead of his brother. Butch dove to make it behind the boulder in time. Thad bounded on like a deer, lightly jetting across the span toward the roots of the toppled tree. The auto-gun pivoted from Charlie to Thad and began firing; Thad outran the bullets' dust plumes that followed him, diving into the hollow pocket of dirt at the wall of tree roots. Bullets raked the edges of the uprooted tree end, throwing dust in all directions. But part of the roots were blocked by the boulder in front.

Charlie waved an arm and the gun turned on him again, shooting twice to the chest in exactly the same spot it hit before. Then, it pivoted back toward Thad's direction and waited. Charlie slumped from the tree stump and fell to the ground. The gun turned and shot through the top of his head as he lay dead; it rotated 180 degrees to shoot a boy who moved on the other side of the clearing--and mystically turned its aim back to the roots again.

Butch watched it all from behind the boulder. What was once a thick clod of dirt giving life to a fallen tree, now looked like a spiny-faced creature with a mouth that had gulped his brother. He didn't see Thad in the cavity. "Thad? Thad? You there?" Butch turned back to see Barry behind the edge of the rock. "Barry, don't move a muscle! Just don't move!" The gun detected Butch at the side of the boulder; bullets raked the rock's edge, tossing a chunk of stone into Butch's forehead and gashing it open. He sat dazed behind the stone holding the sticky blood in. The plaid Webelos neckerchief that seemed to be a part of his daily attire came off; Butch wrapped it around his head. If the injury hurt, he didn't feel it.

He crawled on his belly to the base of the roots as Charlie had told him. Thad wasn't there. "Thad!" Butch dug around and found a foot and followed it up to the head: Thad had buried himself all right. His face was completely mucked with black soil, his body rigid. "Thad, you all right? Say something!"

Thad's bulging eyes had seen it all: He could still hear his friends' pleas for help, he could still smell the bitter scent of gut; all this, Thad relived in his mind's eye.

"I'll get us out of this. Don't worry, Thad." Butch found a flat rock and began digging a tunnel out the backside of the roots. He figured if they kept the boulder between them and the gun, they could crawl out the back and down the hill.

Thad's look of terror only changed when a moan floated up from the pack. The auto-gun shot occasionally if a body rolled from its original position or a corpse slumped. But it always turned back to the roots--as though it knew they were still there.

Butch dug frantically. He had no idea how much time had lapsed from when the shooting began to now. He hadn't tired yet. Instead of sitting still as Charlie had said, Butch felt compelled to get out and go for help; Barry was still alive. The parking lot where parents would be waiting for them was just down the mountain. He could send Thad, the fastest runner in Pack 220.

"What the hell's that?" Butch looked back. A tandem helicopter hovered above the clearing and churned up leaves and dust; some of the Boy Scout hats went spinning through the air to the heavens. The copter landed.

Both boys looked out the hole. "Those are Federal soldiers," said Butch in amazement. "We've got to do as Mr. Ronolou said." Both boys feverishly pushed dirt up from the inside to fill the opening until only a peephole remained.

Troops jumped out both sides of the helicopter and flopped belly down with rifles readied. A technician, who carried a remote controller, punched a few buttons. He then darted to the auto-gun, threw off the cover, and flipped mechanical switches in the innards of the thing.

The weapon, called an AutoMan, sensed motion, heat, and target mass. The device was designed to target armored vehicles and soldiers over a particular weight who carried weapons. An electronic program memorized and tracked victims for "neutralization." It could strafe a crowd, then come back and neutralize individuals with single shots.

The technician waved all clear to the squad. The soldiers scattered out to the tree line, securing their unit's position. Additional Rangers jumped out of the copter and took positions with the troops. They were ready but didn't expect any fighting.

Captain Edward Thomas, an African-American, jumped off the chopper as the props coasted to a stop. A veteran of numerous campaigns in the Middle East, Haiti, Africa, and the Carolinas, he had become conditioned to the gore of battle. This was different. He looked at the child faces, the hats, the Scout uniforms. "Oh God." He had expected to find the bodies of men, part of a smuggling syndicate.

"I don't understand it. They're all gut shots, Captain. Gut shots." The technician came up behind Captain Thomas and spoke rapidly, not really looking at any of the faces for fear of losing his composure. "I think it must have something to do with our disarming the metals sensor. I don't know why but it's the only thing I can think of."

"The targets were children." the Captain whispered in horror.

The technician looked around more closely. "This is terrible!" He started walking through the carnage. Vapors rose from opened abdomens and hovered aimlessly above the corpses. The technician found an open spot and vomited on the ground. He stumbled back to the gun turret to help with its disassembly.

"Get three soldiers to check for any survivors," Captain Thomas told a private. The Captain started toward the tree line where it seemed the Scout troop had entered the clearing; he tried to look at bodies, not faces. He found Barry behind a rock; the boy's legs were shot up. Massive hemorrhaging still oozed from both legs. "Medic, here!" The boy was breathing, his face scrunched into distorted shapes to hold back pain. "You hear me, boy? Can you speak?"

"Yeah. Mom can help." Barry's mother was a nurse. As he spoke, scenes of childhood raced through his mind . . . the cuts . . . the bruises; his mom could fix anything.

Two soldiers jogged over with a stretcher and medical kit. "Hold him together the best you can. I'll call it in," said Thomas. On his way to the chopper, a private told him about two remaining targets locked into AutoMan's memory. "One target must have been the boy," the Captain concluded. "Just take the thing apart. I don't think we have to worry about smugglers jumping us, trooper."

"Here you go, sir." The pilot handed him a radio headset.

"Hawk's Nest. This is Sparrow. AutoMan hit a Cub Scout Troop. Out."

"What?" replied General Beaudock. "Repeat that. I said, repeat that. Out."

"A Cub Scout Troop of about sixty boys were hit, sir."

"Fatalities, Captain? How many dead? Out."

"All but one. We're patching him up and bringing the boy into Hawk's Nest. Out."

"Hold on, Sparrow. We'll get back to you. Out."

The radio fell silent at the Hawk's Nest end. It was a scrambled channel so they spoke freely. Unable to focus on the carnage, the Captain walked back over to watch the medic prep the boy. When the medic finished the initial prep, Thomas signaled him over to the chopper. Ducking the props, he crawled into the craft. "What's up, sir?"

"I don't know. Hawk's Nest is getting back to me. How's the boy?"

"Real bad."

The Captain dropped his face in his hands, "This is a nightmare."

"Sparrow. Come in."

Captain Thomas lifted the headset, "We're back, Hawk."

"What's the status on the boy?"

"I'm putting the medic on," the Captain handed the headset over.

"Sir, Corporal Jim Mathers. The boy's condition is critical. We've bound him and have him prepped for transport. Must move out as soon as possible, sir. I repeat, as soon as possible."

"Can you guarantee the boy will make it back alive?"

"Well, no."

"Put the Captain on," ordered General Beaudock. He handed the headset back to Thomas. "Captain, abort the mission. Disassemble AutoMan and return to Hawk's Nest *without* the boy."

Thomas looked at Corporal Mathers. "They want us to leave the boy." He asked Beaudock, "Repeat that, sir."

"You heard me, Captain. Leave the boy and come back to the nest. Now!"

To Mathers, "Do you think he has a chance at all, Corporal?"

"I don't know, but we can't just leave him here."

Thomas lifted the headset, "Sir, we can't leave the boy."

"Leave the boy or your asses will be mine, Captain! That's an order!" The General screamed over the radio.

Captain Thomas slammed the headset down. "Son-of-a-bitch! I can't believe this." He jumped from the copter and yelled to the technicians. "Breakdown AutoMan, we're out of here. Leave everything here as it was. He followed the medic to the boy at the top of the ridge. "Take the boy off the stretcher and put him back where he was."

Three young men, who were prepping Barry, looked up at Thomas in disbelief. One of them spoke. "Sir, we got him to talk to us."

"It's not my decision, Private. The fat asses on the other end of the radio gave the order, and they don't have to see this shit. Now, do as you're told."

The Captain turned on his heel and went to AutoMan. "Where were those recorded targets?"

The technician pointed in the direction of the large boulder and the spiny roots. Thomas walked between the boulder and the uprooted tree and found a fragmented rock with blood on it. Fresh dirt from where Butch had crawled, led to the base of the tree roots; loose dirt had recently been heaped at the root's base. Thad's footprints also led to the same spot. Captain Thomas looked right in the hole.

Butch leaned back from the opening. "Thad, don't say a word," Butch whispered. "The guy is right above us." Thad began to whimper. "Shhh." Butch put a hand gently over his brother's mouth.

The Captain stared at the hole, looked back at the blood-splattered rock and noticed the alignment of the boulder to the tree roots. He circled the roots through the woods and came back to the AutoMan turret. "A bullet hit the kids behind the root cluster," he told the technical team. "How soon before you're ready to go?"

The medic approached Captain Thomas one more time: He was distraught. "Leaving that boy is wrong and you know it."

"I know it. But we have our orders." Thomas paused. "But leave the boy prepped." Corporal Mathers was going to ask why, but years of training stopped him.

Thomas turned to his Sergeant, "Pull the troops off the perimeter and have them scoop up any vomit from our people and put it in a bag. Brush any boot prints." At last he spoke to the technician, "This was a terrible mistake and the top brass want it to go away."

Ten minutes later they hovered above the landing zone. Captain Thomas looked down to the pocket of dirt at the base of the roots and murmured to himself through the racket of the Mitsubishi engines, "Good luck, boys." The chopper spun and headed southwest.

Chapter 2

Butch clawed out of the hole first. He saw it all from the peephole and couldn't understand why they left Barry. Butch had considered coming out if they began to put his friend on the helicopter, but they didn't. They just left him there. He found Barry with his legs wrapped and tourniquets on. Thad followed with trepidation. "Get that duffel over there," Butch told his brother as he pointed.

Thad, still in shock, could hardly function. He looked around, but saw only carnage as he grabbed the duffel and gave it to his brother. In a sitting position, he rocked back and forth, breathing rapidly.

Butch placed the bundle under Barry's head and lowered his ear to his friend's chest. "I'm having trouble hearing anything. We've gotta get him home. We gotta make a stretcher." He looked about. "I'll pull the shorts off the others. You get some long sticks; we'll string 'em through." Thad rocked in a daze. "Do you hear me, Thad?" He went over and carefully took his younger brother's face in his hands. "Thad, I can't do this alone. Barry needs us. Can you get two strong limbs? Do you understand?"

Thad shook his head yes and sprinted for the brush at the tree line. Butch frantically cut shoelaces with his Scout knife and yanked the shorts off several of his dead friends. Thad returned with two thin saplings.

"Those won't work," Butch stated. "Here, hook these belts together, Thad, I'll get the wood."

"Thad," Barry whispered. Thad turned around like he had heard a ghost, then bent over close to his friend's mouth. "I'm scared. Is this real?"

Thad shook his head yes. Tears began streaming down his face, along his nose, across his tight-lipped mouth.

Butch returned. Thad took the limbs from his brother and frantically began constructing a stretcher.

Butch didn't understand the change in Thad; he just pitched in. They threaded the poles through five pairs of shorts and strapped Barry on top of the makeshift stretcher with the belts. The boys trotted across the clearing with stretcher in tow and headed down the steeper trail on the other side. Butch took the back of the stretcher as they started their descent. Though a strong boy for his age, Butch had trouble holding back the downward rush of the stretcher from behind; adrenaline drove the frantic boy. Rocks and trees whizzed by in their desperate race. Only footsteps and heavy panting resounded through the shadowy pine underworld, as woodland creatures paused to watch from their hideaways.

A two-mile stint to the base of the mountain and they were nearly there. Butch cut a corner around some brush; an inclined log, sticking up from a thicket caught Thad in the stomach, punching him to an abrupt halt. The sudden stop sent the older brother headlong down the hill. Butch continued holding on to the litter as he fell on his face and skidded down the trail; Barry's stretcher finally came to rest.

Butch got up, woozy. He spit blood and dirt before yelling to his brother, "Are you all right?" Thad had the wind knocked out of him, but rose to his feet and nodded his head yes. Butch put his ear on Barry's chest. He sat back. His pug face looked beaten, "I don't hear nothin'."

In dismay, Thad staggered to his friend and also put an ear down to his chest. He jerked up excitedly like he heard something, and scrambled to the end of the stretcher. Butch sprang up and grabbed the front. By the time they arrived at the parking lot they had fallen two more times, the second time gashing their legs and knees on a stony ledge.

Middle-aged parents stood around the vehicles chatting. One man had brought a large thermos of coffee he shared with the others. An overweight woman passed out cookies.

Thad lost his footing and tumbled forward down the last steep grade to the parking lot. He'd lost all strength in his legs. Butch dragged the stretcher into the gravel lot as onlookers watched the boy with blood-soaked scarf and red-streaked legs stumble to the middle and drop to his knees. Gravel was embedded into the puffy flesh of his kneecaps. He bowed his head and waited.

It took a full four seconds for the scene to register in the minds of the parents. Finally, the group dropped what they held and rushed to the boys. "What happened, Butch?" asked Mrs. Larson, the heavy woman.

"The Feds did it." Butch could hardly talk. Mrs. Larson helped him stretch out on the ground and took off her jacket to put under the boy's head. "A machine killed everyone," Butch claimed.

"Did he say everyone?" another mother blurted out with a horrified look.

Mrs. Larson leaned close to Butch. "Now take your time and say what happened."

Butch took several breaths, "Everybody but Thad and Barry and me got killed in an ambush. Then the Feds came in a helicopter and took the machine away. It killed *everyone!*"

Parents looked to one another in astonishment. Four thick-middled men sprinted up the trail into the woods. Two mothers followed. Mr. Larson rushed back to his truck and yanked a rifle from behind his seat; he grabbed a box of shells and loaded the weapon en route.

Mrs. Larson checked Barry's vital signs and found none. "Oh God, is Helen here? I think its Barry!" She looked at Butch, "Was he alive?"

"He was alive a minute ago. He spoke to Thad just up the trail."

Without hesitation, Mrs. Larson began CPR on the boy. Her tears dropped on Barry's soiled face as she cried with the realization of her own boy still on the mountain. The drops blotched and smeared, transforming Barry's angelic face into a streaked warrior, fighting a battle to survive. Everyone watched as Mrs. Larson struggled to move blood and air through the boy's fading, limp form.

Butch pushed away any help for himself, spellbound by the events unfolding before him. "It was just a few minutes ago he said 'Mom.' Watching Barry lie limp dropped Butch into a hopeless despair, as he personally realized the death of a friend.

Thad felt it too. Though others pawed him, checking his injuries, Thad's eyes never turned from his friend's face, peering past the adults who surrounded him, listening for some sign of life.

Max, Helen's older brother, had given her a lift to the Notch to get Barry. Tater's enthusiasm for truck rides made it difficult to leave the dog behind; she rode in back under the cap. As they pulled in, Helen knew instantly something had gone wrong when she saw the circled group in the parking lot. She recognized the Rousell brothers off to the side, bloodied and bruised. A wave of panic swelled inside her as she scanned the group for her son. She opened the door and began running before Max had even stopped the truck. Helen slipped on the gravel and caught herself with her hands on the jagged stones.

Tater sensed her distress. She pushed up the truck's back lid with her nose and bounded to the ground. In four bounds, she was in the thick of the crowd staring down at her lifeless master.

Helen pushed her way through the group. "Oh God, is that my son?" Mrs. Larson stopped doing CPR and looked up with tears in her eyes nodding.

"Don't stop!" said Butch. "He was just alive on the trail. Don't stop!"

Helen crowded the woman aside and took over mouth-to-mouth ventilation. Mrs. Larson continued on heart massage. Between breaths, Helen asked, "Did anyone radio the hospital?" Someone in the group said they had. After a few more breaths she blurted, "We've got to take him to the hospital. Now!"

Still performing CPR, three women and Max reached under Barry and carried him to the back of the pickup. Tater followed, prancing and whining. As Helen and Mrs. Larson crawled in, Tater jumped in the back with them. "Get out, you damn dog!" Larson yelled. Another woman tried to grab the dog's collar to pull it out, but Tater snarled and flared teeth.

"Just go! Just go!" yelled Helen between breaths.

The tailgate and back door stayed open as Max sped off down the hill, leaving the anxious parents behind with a glimpse of their own boys' fates.

Tater, perked ears and motionless, gazed longingly at her pallid companion and whined. When Helen came up for air, Tater dipped down to lick the boy's face to wake him as she had every morning. Helen pushed the dog back. "Stay, you mutt." Helen paused, "Barry, you can't die. You can't." She turned and gazed at Tater; the distressed animal had a look of confusion.

Helen shared that anxiety. Her son was her life. After her failed marriage and the illusion of true love shattered, she clung to the hope that her son would not be deprived of a happy childhood. Her ex-husband Bradley, rarely paid child support and didn't visit his son for months at a time. She struggled to make payments, cleaning rooms for the Balsams Resort after she had lost her nursing job due to Federal cutbacks. In her youth, Helen had been smart and attractive, grades came easy in school, boys crowded to be near her. All that had changed, she learned what it was like to struggle; she had discovered failure. Helen had been determined not to let her fate affect Barry's happiness. Now, the life she gave breath to was her own.

Her face streaked with tears, Mrs. Larson squeaked, "My boy was up there too." Her sizable frame quivered as she said it.

Helen wiped the tears from her cheeks and continued resuscitation.

Max opened the back window of the cab, "Holler if it's too rough back there." Uncle Max had raced stock cars in his younger days; he was a mechanic now. Today he raced for life, accelerating out of corners faster than he went into them--using his horn as a siren. Whining the Nissan to an extreme rpm, he jettisoned in front of other cars just before oncoming traffic whisked by. Trees, farms, and fields of wildflowers zipped by in an undefined mass. And the stunning red sunset they raced toward went unappreciated because of its blood-like hue.

"There's a dog trying to get into the hospital," said an orderly, entering the emergency room. "It bit a guy."

Mrs. Larson relinquished her spot on heart massage to a nurse, and found a man at the hospital to take her back to Dixville Notch.

"Somebody get the defibrillator and prep 1cc of adrenaline for injection!" Helen ordered. "And where's the damn doctor? Who's on duty?" Helen insisted on staying at her son's side, even though she no longer worked at Upper Connecticut Valley Regional Hospital.

In a two-patient room on the ground level, a nurse delivered dinner to Margaret Bouvier. Mrs. Bouvier was raising a spoon of green gelatin to her mouth just when Tater dove through her screened window and bound out the other side of the room toward the hallway. Gelatin on Margaret's spoon flew into the air; her tray landed on the floor. The nurse ran into the hall after the animal. Undaunted, Tater's paws clicked on tile as she slid around corners.

"What the hell's wrong? Where's the hypo? Where are the damn paddles to jolt him?" Helen used a mechanical ventilator now instead of mouth-to-mouth. The young doctor she was addressing stood aloof with the boy's statistics chart in hand. Deb Philbin, Helen's best friend and former coworker, was on duty and worked the heart compressor--but out of courtesy; Barry felt cool to the touch.

"Helen," said the doctor, "I'm sorry, your son has been dead for awhile."

"That's impossible. He was alive fifteen minutes ago," She snapped.

"Not according to his temperature."

Deb looked at Helen's face but kept working. Helen didn't answer. She just kept staring down at her boy and squeezing the resuscitator. Tater shoved her nose between the double swinging doors, walked over and sat below Barry's table. She had sniffed and probed and finally found her way to her friend.

The doctor exploded: "How'd that dog get in here? Deb, get it out of here! Deb?"

Deb never changed her rhythm, meanwhile pleading with the doctor silently with her eyes. She couldn't stop, not until Helen was ready.

"Helen, I sympathize with you, but you can't bring him back. Touch him.

Come on, there might be other wounded coming in and we're understaffed as it is."

Helen stopped resuscitation and took Barry's mouthpiece off. She rubbed some of the dirt blotches off his face. It was as if he slept like a toddler. She hadn't really cried yet, tears, but not a cry. She flung herself over her boy and wailed.

Tater pranced and whimpered at the sight. But a whimper was all she could do; the dog couldn't bark, a hunting accident several years earlier left the animal without voice. She nudged Barry's hand with her nose and waited for a response.

Deb Philbin left the table so Helen could be alone with her boy. Though many years older than Helen, they were best friends and she felt the loss. She wondered about her grandson who was also on the mountain.

The doctor affirmed to Deb, "Look, I believe I gave you an order. Get the damn dog out and get this place ready in ten minutes."

Dr. Tim Remington was new in Colebrook. He hated being there. Transferred from a larger urban hospital by the Federal Health Board, he resented the lack of respect nurses gave him. He had graduated from an Ivy League school as a surgeon; now here he was, stuck in a backwater village to replace doctors who defected from the local health alliance.

Helen pulled her son to an upright position and hugged him--rocked him like a baby. Deb watched, motionless. She turned to Tim and spoke deliberately, "She needs a little time."

"Don't use this tragedy as an excuse to undermine me again. I'm sick and tired of it. Get the dog out and clean up the place or I'll write you up for insubordination."

"You don't understand. They killed a mother's son!" Deb shouted. Then she couldn't stop her own tears, "*You* get the dog!"

Tim walked past Deb, pointing his finger in her face, "I'm writing you up!"

When the doctor reached for the animal's collar, Tater snapped at him with flared teeth and bit his outstretched hand. "Ahhhhh! That damn dog bit me. The sheriff will take care of this." Tim stomped toward the door. To Deb he repeated, "And I *am* still writing you up."

Deb set her jaw, "Kiss my ass, Doctor!"

Helen continued to rock her son, now singing a lullaby. Her worst fear had been realized: Now, she was thoroughly alone.

Tater watched and somehow knew. She'd seen death before in the hunt, partaken of it in feast. This was different. A friend who had been a daily part of her life for seven years lay cold as the groundhog had. And the soul who laughed and tossed sticks for her to chase, had gone elsewhere. Tater collapsed below the table with chin on forepaws, feeling an emptiness she couldn't understand.

Lush green rolled from hill to hill; all was cut to carpet level. The tree lines lacked the usual scruffy weeds that customarily line a golf course. Artificial rock formations rose above the grass here and there. On the far side of a pond, President Winifred and Chief of Staff Lucas Bennett were planning their final putts on bluegrass around the sixth hole.

Security personnel, all dressed in black overcoats with receivers plugged in one ear, encircled the area. They talked to one another through transmitters clipped to their lapels.

An Army Private chauffeured Secretary of Defense Kyle Paz to the green in a cart; they stopped at the edge of the green. The ball Lucas had putted cut to the right of the hole and passed beyond it ten feet. He turned to the intruders with contempt.

Kyle reported grimly of the Dixville incident to President Winifred and Chief of Staff Bennett.

A security person above the valley watched as Lucas slammed the golf cart twice with his club and hurled the putter into the pond. The President shook his head and paused in thought. A flock of sparrows fluttered about the leaves of a nearby tree and caught the security guard's attention; the guard looked to see what stirred them so.

Chapter 3

Seated in the first row at the funeral service, Helen caressed a photograph of Barry with the back of her hand. A flood of memories . . . his first day of school. She smiled; *He was so frightened--standing there at the bus stop with his little backpack on. And that blond-haired girl in his school play who had a crush on him; he was so bashful.* She scraped a tear from her cheek and pulled a tissue from her purse to wipe her nose. "I won't forget a thing," she whispered to herself.

"That's right," confirmed Max seated beside her. "We won't forget a damn thing." He referred to the Feds and his vow of revenge. The evidence he had found at the massacre site confirmed everything Butch had said: It *was* Army Regulars. Washington denied everything. Max concluded that if justice existed in this nation, it had to be taken.

More like brothers, Max and Barry had done a lot together: hiking, canoeing. Max helped Mr. Ronolou whenever he could. His relationship with Barry had been critical after Helen's divorce. Helen had asked him to help her by taking her son to sporting and Scouting events. Her intent had been to create a male presence for her child; a bond had formed. Max *wished* he had been with Barry that day at Dixville.

Medium height and stocky, Max had chocolate-brown hair and piercing dark eyes. He felt responsible for the Scout Troop attack because he had organized the smuggling ring used to bring medical supplies to the States from Quebec. He concluded the Feds automated ambush had been waiting for them. Max had grimly helped collect the scattered remains left at the Dixville Massacre. He was well beyond grieving; Max's mind whirled. He sucked his teeth and planned his next move.

Desperate measures to circumvent the Federally run health care system had come about after a decade of economic decay. Taxation due to The War on Terrorism and Federal regulations created the downturn. A year before, the Northeast Kingdom of Vermont had formed a community covenant to take care of local needs, bypassing Federal HMOs. Max's smuggling operation supplied the Northeast Kingdom as well as the newly formed Colebrook Covenant with medical supplies. The Dixville Massacre, as the media dubbed it, consolidated the hatred of rural Vermont and New Hampshire toward big government. Despite the cover-up by the White House, everyone in the region knew about the Massacre through illegal CB broadcasts near Todd Hill in Vermont.

Colebrook's First Congregational Church had the original straight-back pews installed at the building's dedication in 1802. Though refurbished many times, the structure still proclaimed the same principles elders envisioned at its inception. The same bell in the church's white steeple that rang to assemble the community for the War of 1812, the Civil War, World War I, and World War II, now rang sixty-four times--once for each child lost. The clanging echoed through the valley as people walked toward its source in silence.

At the request of aggrieved parents, local police, firefighters, friends, and neighbors blocked off all roads into the village to keep out reporters or politicians who wished to attend.

State Police came to reopen the town for government officials. On the outskirts, reporters from the major networks, with umbrellas and yellow rain slickers reminded the State Troopers of their First Amendment right to cover the event. But Colebrook citizens had drawn guns to ensure their privacy in mourning. Though the Federal government had outlawed private ownership of handguns and high-powered rifles years earlier, New Hampshire's people still lived by the Second Amendment--as envisioned by the founding fathers. State Troopers and reporters alike noticed the thickets on the surrounding hills: Grim-faced Colebrook men dressed in camouflage came into focus through the drizzle; they were scoping reporters and police with high-powered rifles. But to enforce Federal Law would have been a second bloodletting. The local residents didn't flinch.

Meanwhile inside the church, Mrs. Larson sat near the back with her three remaining children. Throughout the service, she repeatedly looked down the pew at a lone man seated near the aisle in a dark, Armani suit. Mrs. Larson was active in the PTA, a member of the Board of Trustees in the Congregational Church, and she supervised the Daisy Girl Scouts for her youngest. During the school year she worked part-time in Colebrook at the diner on Main Street. As a result, she knew everyone in town. This man did not belong here.

Near the end of the minister's eulogy, the stranger in the aisle seat got up and left the church. Mrs. Larson ordered her kids to stay put; but she raised her sizable frame and followed the man in the Armani suit outside.

"I can't believe it! I just can't believe it!" Bradley Conrad sputtered. "Damn it! I am Barry's father. You had no right telling your Colebrook cronies to keep me out. No right!"

Helen sat in the car with her ex-husband and blandly watched the road ahead. She accepted a lift home from the funeral with him, presuming she'd have to put up with his criticism. She was too numb to care. "This is some kind of cruel joke," Helen reflected aloud You're finally anxious to visit our son after the boy's death.

"What?" asked Bradley. "Stop ignoring me. You could at least be civil. I'm his father."

"You *were* his father; you stopped being his father the day you walked out and shacked up with that bimbo of yours--ah, what's-her-face."

Bradley pulled over at a convenience store. "I haven't had anything to eat since breakfast. You want anything?"

She said nothing.

He shook his head and climbed out of the car. Bradley knew there was no talking to her when she got like this. He left Helen to wallow in her bitterness as the car idled with the windshield wiper whisking.

Bradley Conrad worked as a Federal Agricultural Extension Agent for the Northeast Concern. He advised farmers and farm co-ops about crop trends and sale prices and gave talks on herbicides, pesticides, and soil composition. He still looked good: tall, dark hair and solidly built; the pudgy waist that accompanied most middle-aged men had passed over him. He was active in sports even while married: summer softball, skiing, and touch football on Sunday mornings while Helen and Barry went to church.

Helen resented Bradley leaving her. She had been the darling of most men in Colebrook at one time. But she thickened up after having Barry, which changed her into a chunky, middle-aged mom. Her facial beauty was still there: high cheekbones and thick, blond hair. Her narrow, dark brown eyes added an oriental enchantment. But the alluring contours that had formerly attracted men hid somewhere beneath thick thighs.

She regretted the body change; a once proud, self-assured woman changed into the ordinary. But as Barry grew up and transformed into a little person, she found her life centered on him, enjoying his happiness, preparing him

27

for his chance at life. With Barry dead, her life reeled out of focus. Bitter thoughts dominated her mind, leaving her alone in a world of suspicion.

Bradley returned with an ice cream cone. "What was all the ruckus in town about?" He started the car and continued on.

She looked at him squarely to say it, "A Federal Agent got stabbed in the back with a kitchen knife."

He turned quickly, "For real?"

Helen closed her eyes to narrow slits, "You should be grateful I kept you from getting into town."

Bradley shook his head, "I should have had Barry living with me, the way things are in this armpit of a place."

"This 'armpit' is my home. It was Barry's home. We were born here. Stop the car, I'm getting out. I don't want any favors from you." When he continued down the road, she yelled, "Stop the damn car!"

"Now, you don't mean that, Helen."

"'I don't mean that'? You mean to say I don't know what I'm saying?"

"Stop, Helen, I don't need this. Not after today." He paused awhile, but couldn't keep from saying it: "You've made it a point to put all the blame for us breaking up on me. It wasn't just me. You had *something* to do with it. That, and your bullheaded brother Max, trying to take my place as a father when I'm not around. I resented the hell out of that."

Helen stared at the side of his face, enraged. Bradley was fully aware of her temper and watched her warily out the corner of his eye as he drove--still licking his ice cream cone. But he glanced at the road at just the wrong moment: Helen took a roundhouse swat and drove the ice cream in his face, rubbing it into his pores and down his shirt. Bradley jerked and shouted as the car swerved to the opposite lane. Helen jammed her left foot on top of his, on the brake, skidding the vehicle to an abrupt stop in the middle of the road.

Leaping out, she slammed the car door and kicked it, then stomped off into the woods adjacent to her home. Shortly after entering the forest, Helen followed a worn trail through an open stand of hemlocks. Gray light from clouded skies peeked through the conifers. Droplets clung desperately to needle tips--only to be yanked loose by a gust of wind that stirred through the trees. An August wind, colder than usual, whispered sounds and carried fragrances of evergreen. Helen noticed none of it.

She stumbled upon a rustic campsite just off a trail: Rocks encircled a fire pit, a brush lean-to was off to the side. Its roof was an old plastic table cloth--her table cloth. Helen looked around the camp and found a box. She lifted the lid and discovered her kitchen knife, some silverware, matches, and a picture of Tater and her with Barry. Her eyes brimmed with tears as she studied it. It seemed like just yesterday they had taken that hike and set the camera to automatically photograph them in front of Cascade Falls. Helen looked through all the articles and smiled; she would have scolded Barry for playing with knives and taking her kitchen utensils. Now she sat in his lean-to and recalled what a solid young man he had become. She couldn't recall when he stopped asking for a bedtime kiss; she wished that nightly routine hadn't ended.

Helen followed the trail out of the woods to her lane that curved between large pine trees. She spotted Max's truck in her driveway. Her brother waited for her inside.

The White House (August 17)

The decor in the Oval Office was a seventeenth century motif, from the carpet to the ridged, Baroque furniture. Near the window, a Gothic birdcage of wrought iron and mahogany housed a peregrine falcon. Like its relative the hawk, its eyes zoomed in on unsuspecting prey: this time, a small bird in the forsythia, safe beyond the windowpane.

"You screwed up, Captain! It *was* Captain, wasn't it?" Chief of Staff Lucas Bennett pranced about in rage. Captain Thomas was their scapegoat for the Dixville incident--at least unofficially. "How could you let that gun cut loose like that--without anyone watching over it? What the hell happened?" President Clifford Winifred and Secretary of Defense Kyle Paz looked on as Chief of Staff Bennett performed the debriefing.

Lucas was medium height and lanky, rather good looking with dark, slicked back hair, dark eyes as well. A disappointment to women who looked on him longingly, the tiny tattoo on his left cheek denoted his lifestyle, and he was not the least ashamed of it. In fact, he had been described as arrogant; Lucas always had a look of contempt. He listened to other's ideas but Bennett's opinion usually had a dig within it, designed to poison the source of other's suggestions that vied for the President's favor. He was Chief of Staff, young, and he had the power to include or exclude anyone from the audience of the President.

Captain Thomas sat at attention; eyes fixed, head up and facing forward; his brown skin glistened with sweat. "The metal sensors were shutdown.

And for some reason no soldiers had been designated to watch over the unit, sir. Even without supervision, AutoMen used mass, heat, and motion as a qualifier for targeting."

"And who shutdown the metal sensor, Captain?" Bennett stared at the soldier from the side, only inches away from Thomas' face.

"I take full responsibility for anything that happens under my command, sir." Thomas' expression and tone never changed. And he did take responsibility; they stationed four AutoMen on the trails of upper New Hampshire and Vermont. Twice, smugglers got by them. As Thomas' commanding officers applied pressure, the technician had taken it upon himself to change the program on the AutoMen so the reprobates would be detected.

"That isn't what I asked, Captain! I asked who, Captain? Who?"

Thomas rotated to Bennett now, "I said I take full responsibility for my men, *Mr.* Bennett." It was a stare-down. Thomas didn't blink.

Lucas had contempt for the military. Even after fully integrating the armed services with women and ethnics, there was still that macho camaraderie among males who served. Bennett resented the gays' condition in military life, how they were excluded from off-base activities; the straight-male faction of the military still had their own exclusive cliques.

Secretary of Defense Kyle Paz stood near the door at the back of the room, finally unable to contain himself. He cleared his throat before speaking, "This isn't necessary, Mr. President. This is a debriefing, not an inquisition." General Paz, a brawny Latino with wavy hair, had made it to the top because of his political savvy--knowing whom not to rile. In this case, he had to speak up; Captain Thomas had been a victim of events.

It had been the President's idea to stop the contraband medical supplies smuggled from Quebec. Chief of Staff Bennett had approached Paz three months ago in a meeting, the Secretary recalled well:

"Use Army Regulars, the Rangers from the Capitol here. We want to keep things quiet. The National Guard can't be trusted to keep their mouths shut."

"I'll begin as soon as I get my orders," said the General.

"You have your orders."

"Nothing in writing?"

"You know what we need as an outcome. Make an example of someone." Lucas Bennett leaned closer to the General, "Draw some blood."

General Paz squinted as he stared back at the Chief of Staff, "I don't like this. It isn't procedure." The General knew what Lucas meant, but he didn't like having no orders to authorize his mission in the North Country. He had seen death before . . . and the idea of neutralizing scoundrels smuggling contraband from Quebec didn't bother him, but Kyle knew nothing about the people of the North Country. The tactical skills demonstrated by southerners in the Tobacco Wars a year earlier had surprised the White House; the Tobacco Boys, as they were called, inflicted tremendous casualties. In war, missions don't always work out the way they are planned.

"Politics contradicts proper procedure," Lucas explained. "You've come too far not to understand that, Kyle. You're a smart man. Don't worry, we don't plan on pissing anyone off before the election. If we succeed in settling the North Country problem, President Winifred gets the credit and you move up in the party. If it doesn't work out, you get the blame but you still move up in the party. I don't have to tell you how it works."

Now, when Paz's premonitions about the North Country directive had come true, he wasn't about to let an officer under him hang when the White House had initiated the mission.

Lucas broke the stare first, looking to Paz with contempt.

"You're right, General," said the President. Lucas backed off and looked around the room impatiently as President Winifred continued, "But it is a major screw-up and could have been damaging if there had been survivors." Winifred looked at the laptop monitor on his desk that displayed a list of names of Colebrook's Scouts; Butch and Thad Rousell weren't on the list. "Captain Thomas, you're responsible for any loose talk from your team. That action at Dixville was classified top secret and remains that way." He looked to everyone in the room, "Are there any questions?" Clifford then turned to Secretary of Defense Kyle Paz, "General?"

"I would just like to say one thing, sir," Thomas spoke up. He sniffed-- and blinked to hold back tears, "I've been a disappointment to you. I accept any action taken against me, sir." Captain Thomas firmed his jaw and resumed his military posture; the large, solidly built man stood statuesque.

"Don't worry about it, Captain. You're dismissed." Winifred reached for his computer, closed out the program, and opened the hand-held planner for the day's itinerary.

Captain Thomas saluted the inattentive President before walking out the door. General Paz followed him.

The President combed his fingers through his sun-bleached hair. "I have to talk to the press in twenty minutes, Luc." He looked up from the screen, "Are we set up?" Winifred looked presidential: tall and blond, broad-shouldered and slim at the hips. He had survived many scandals throughout his political career. By now, nothing could startle him.

"We're set." He waited a moment. "But what do you want me to do with Thomas?"

"You said there was no paperwork," Winifred answered. "He's a soldier. Soldiers do what they're told. We need to concern ourselves with civilians."

"You have a private interview now with CBS News," Bennett reminded the President.

"Oh, that's right. I see it here." Winifred smiled and closed the screen to his planner and strode over to his private office through an adjacent door.

Bennett smiled; he loved manipulating the news media. They favored their party anyway, but Bennett felt responsible for keeping them in their camp. He had introduced Nancy Atherton of CBS news to Clifford. It had been the longest extramarital affair the President had had. During a time of national turmoil, favorable news coverage could be hard to find.

Chapter 4

In the hall, General Paz caught Thomas and spoke in a low voice. "Captain, I want you to know, I'm with you on this. Everyone is at fault here."

"Yes, sir."

"Charles, don't 'Yes sir,' me. You've been through too much."

Captain Thomas looked away to a distant place. "They were all young boys. Gut shot, most of them. General Beaudock ordered me to leave a wounded one. A boy about the same age as my son." His eyes began seeping. "I have trouble sleeping. I'm sure the others on my team feel the same. No one talks about it, General. The President doesn't have to worry about any of us saying anything. It isn't something you brag about."

"This isn't over," said Paz. "I'll keep in touch."

The helicopter whirled and turned out of control, plunging downward toward certain death. Raindrops hit like darts on Billy's face through the broken cockpit's windshield. North winds bit to the bone and stirred him to consciousness. He yanked the controls of the helicopter upward. In his eleven-year-old fantasy, William Winifred could hardly feel his arm from the gunshot wound he received during his escape. The bullet numbed his left side all the way to his fingertips, but he could move it, if he willed. He continued through the storm-drenched cold, feeling nothing but the spectra of death chasing him. Then something flashed from the foothills below, *it had to be a Stinger missile,* Billy thought. He popped the decoy flares and cut right, narrowly averting the Sung vase on a stand next to the wall in the corridor. He gently landed the toy helicopter safely onto the red carpet before his father's private office.

William Winifred had never had an episode so close. That could have been the end of Government Operative 440, Billy Winifred--and the 1031-year-old Sung vase in the hallway. He pulled out the two-inch pilot from the toy helicopter and adjusted his helmet and arms. He checked the rotor; that was the weakness of this model.

33

The office door flung open and CBS Correspondent Nancy Atherton walked out as she chatted with the President. It was another private interview. She nearly stumbled over the boy's back as he crouched over his model. "Shit. What the--" She caught her balance with a hand on his back. "William, what are you doing?" Her face flushed.

"Checkin' my copter. See, they got to be serviced every thirty-six hours." It surprised William, too. His brown, innocent eyes gazed upward without allegation.

His father came to the door. "William, you need to play some other place. Lots of people come and go here." He turned to Nancy, "Are you all right, Ms. Atherton?"

"Oh yes. I'm fine." She skirted around the child, "Thank you for the interview, Mr. President. We'll have to finish it another time," she let the words dangle as she continued down the corridor.

The boy looked up at his father and lifted the helicopter to be admired.

The gesture startled the President from his view of Ms. Atherton leaving. "Oh, nice gadget, son." Winifred looked at his watch. "Oh!" *The news conference.*

Journalists packed the White House Press Room. They jotted down notes on pocket computers; some gave preliminary commentaries to viewers from where they stood in the crowd. Nearly a third of the Press Corps were young, pretty women. They played to the President's partiality to blondes. In the past, the color red attracted the attention of some presidents, now puffy blond heads dotted the room. Veteran reporters overlooked the President's obsession with blonds; Winifred represented their political ideology. The few repulsed by the display kept it to themselves--not wanting to be estranged by their own.

Nancy Atherton gave preliminary comments before a camera about "The Dixville Massacre," as the media had dubbed it. She wore a purple pantsuit with a strand of pearls hanging well into her unbuttoned shirt. Her blond hair fluffed out from her ears, precisely displaying looped earrings. Not a blemish could be found on Nancy, an appearance so crisp, so clean, so proper, few men approached her for a date. They considered her out of their league.

"Ladies and gentlemen, The President of the United States," stated a young woman from the podium. Taped commentaries ceased, silence swept the room. People talking among themselves stopped in mid-sentence and turned to listen as President Clifford Winifred pushed buttons on a pocket computer and scanned the teleprompter in front of him. He began to speak, but caught himself with a quick gasp for breath, then paused as though holding back tears. Everyone waited anxiously. "My fellow Americans, few tragedies cut so deeply to the soul as the loss of children. I can't pretend to feel the pain the Dixville families are going through at this moment. Those boys were American children and when their souls left this planet, some of us went with them. Excuse me." President Winifred turned away and wiped his eyes with a hanky and resumed his spot at the podium with resolve. "I promise you, as your President, I will find the perpetrators of this hideous act and bring them to justice. There is no place on earth those murderers can hide!" He hit the podium with his fist. "If they flee, there's no country far enough! If they fight, there is no army great enough! Let God be my witness to this oath!"

Journalists applauded and cheered the President; his words moved them. President Winifred's sincere address caused eyes to moisten. The tragedy extended well beyond New Hampshire and touched every parent in the country.

"As tragic as this massacre was, we must not let the children of Dixville die in vain. Our fractured nation has many serious wounds. The blood of those boys will bind us and renew our efforts to help the poor working class families they came from. And as a nation, we can reassert our efforts to rebuild America and console the Dixville families, renewing their faith in a government that protects them."

Applause erupted from the audience. Clifford waited. "There are many of you out there who want to help. You can. The White House will send investigative teams and troops to the region to catch these terrorists. Though this nation is financially strapped, we're asking for any support the American people can give to the families in crisis at Dixville. The American heart is an inexhaustible resource that has never failed us in times of tumult, during war, or in the times of economic hardships of today. We will endure the Dixville tragedy, more united as a nation, setting aside all our ethnic and religious differences to focus on a common cause. To the Dixville families: Our hearts go out to you in this time of grief."

Clifford paused and turned from the cameras to reporters in the audience. "I'll take questions now."

Every hand in the room went up, some reporters waving their arms to capture the attention of the President. Nancy Atherton casually raised her hand from the far left side of the room. "Ms. Atherton from CBS News," said the President.

"There were reports that a boy nearly survived the attack. Could you confirm or deny that?"

Clifford pulled out an electronic note pad from his coat pocket that had details of the incident. He studied it, "The accounts from Dixville varied. Smugglers still have a grip on the region, and the grief-stricken families at the scene were unable to give details because of the hysteria that followed. There was an incident reported about a boy who somehow survived the slaughter. Families at the scene said the boy's dog sniffed out the trail and found him at the ambush site. The child's mother was there and struggled to keep her son alive, but to no avail. The boy died on the emergency room table."

Reporters jumped from their seats, waving hands, calling out.

"Yes, Ms. Swanson of NBC News."

NBC journalist Kay Swanson, an African-American woman, scanned her notes before asking, "Did the boy say anything about what he saw?"

"All indicators point to smugglers. The Dixville Notch area has been active with groups moving drugs, weapons, and such. We had sent teams to the area, which made it more difficult for them. Evidently the smuggling ring wanted to send the Federal Government a message. Unfortunately, a Scout troop received it."

The flurry of waving hands and calls from the group returned. This time President Winifred recognized a Caucasian male. "Yes. Steve Morrison." The President recognized the redheaded reporter from Spectator News.

Though young, Steve Morrison had covered a number of assignments around the globe. His father had been a journalist--always on the road. Morrison followed those footsteps. Home to him had been the pocket computer he used to write. His few friends would often see him staring at the screen. The reports, with digital imaging, could be sent from bars, motel rooms or lobbies, anywhere he had phone access. When asked about his home Steve would recite motel rooms where he stayed. He had just returned from the Amur Valley, Russia. There, American troops aided the Russian government in containing a Jewish group vying for independence. Steve considered himself an objective journalist, and didn't placate the White House as many of his colleagues did. His coverage of the Amur revolt did not support the White House. Winifred choosing him was a surprise. The reporter quickly pulled the gum from his mouth before speaking, "Sir, evidently the accounts from the families at Dixville varied widely in content and cooperation. In fact, the town of Colebrook blockaded the roads of the village and, at gunpoint, prevented reporters and government officials from going in. What would explain this, Mr. President?"

President Winifred looked to the floor impatiently. He shook his head before speaking, "Have you no shame, Mr. Morrison," the President glared at him. "To stand there and imply that grief-stricken parents would hold back the truth . . . you have no business wearing that press badge and being in the same room with the rest of these fine people." He backed away from the mike with moistened eyes. "I'm sorry. This Press Conference is over." Clifford stormed through the side door of the Press Room.

Lucas Bennett, Chief of Staff, waited in the short hallway outside. "That was the best news conference I've ever seen you do, Cliff. You had them by the crotch. And that white guy, he must have defecated in his boxer shorts. We'll never see his moronic face in the news business again."

"I did chew that kid's ass out, didn't I?" The President smiled, the moistened eyes vanished. "I can see this incident as a turning point for this country, Luc. This tragic mishap could give the people something to rally behind."

As the President spoke, Bennett noticed Winifred's zipper had been left down. He pointed.

Winifred noticed his Chief of Staff's gesture. He looked around and discretely zipped up his pants. He whispered to Lucas, "Do you think anyone noticed?"

"Your suit jacket most likely covered it," consoled Lucas quietly. "*And you were behind the podium the entire time.*"

"Oh." Winifred thought about the incident as he ran fingers through his hair, then smiled and waved at approaching senators.

Colebrook, New Hampshire (September 2)

Weeds had started taking over the trail that crossed Mohawk Creek and cut through the pines to Helen's house. Just off the trail, Barry's lean-to now housed other creatures: a pair of chipmunks stored hickory nuts in one of its many caches at the base; field mice roamed through the shelter unencumbered; a fat, gray spider waited at the edge of her web, poised to crawl up and lunch on anything entangled in its snare.

At the trail's end, Helen's house was surrounded by thick pines and carpeted by a layer of dead pine needles. It hadn't changed. But the sun cut through the needle canopy at a lower angle. The greens of nature that were so vibrant a month earlier had dimmed to olive. A Wild Cucumber pod exploded and sprayed its seeds twenty feet away. Late summer weeds lost their flowers, holding burs in their absence. And a golden retriever did nothing but lay on the bed in Barry's room, dry and clean and away from it all.

Helen sat in a chair at the kitchen table and drank coffee--listened to the gossip of CB channel six. She hadn't gone to church since the funeral. Helen could not believe in a God who would allow such a horrible thing to happen to her boy. She got up from her chair when someone knocked at the door. The Rousell brothers. Helen opened the door and spoke glumly, "Hi boys. What can I do for you?"

"Well, ah." Helen's appearance astounded Butch. She looked like a zombie, sickly, with sunken eyes. "Thad and me just thought that Barry would have wanted someone to take Tater out every once in awhile."

"You two pretend to know what Barry would have wanted?"

"We was Barry's best friends."

Helen realized how she sounded. "Well, come in." She gestured at the kitchen table, inviting them to sit. "You two want cookies?" Both nodded. She searched through the bottom cupboard and found some old, stale ones still around from before Barry's death. In fact, the shelves and refrigerator were bare.

Helen had little use for food, living by herself. She drank coffee in the morning and alcohol of some sort at night. She waited out her time in the place; with no job she couldn't pay the mortgage. Electric bills kept piling up; she had been behind on them even before she had lost her job at the hospital. In the month since Barry's death she lost fifteen pounds. The anxiety and despair never went away. Seeing the radical changes in Barry's mom since Dixville, with the vacant eyes and drawn cheeks, made the Rousell boys uneasy--such a rapid transformation they had never witnessed.

"You okay, Ms. Conrad?" Butch asked softly.

In a resigned tone, "I'm all right." With a tired smile, "I'm all right," she repeated. "And thanks for asking." The two menacing little Rousells whom Helen always felt had had a negative influence on Barry now seemed angelic. Butch, usually loud and boastful, said please and thank you. Helen knew they had been through a lot, and wondered how the last boys of Pack 220 survived the horror of that day. Butch told the Dixville story to adults only a couple of times--and never spoke of it again. "How many cookies do you want, two or three? Barry usually had three for a snack."

"Three, please."

Helen placed the cookies on napkins and went back to the sink to draw two glasses of water. "I don't have milk, boys. I hope this will do." She sat down and sipped her coffee. A minute passed before anyone said anything. "So, how's school going?"

"Pretty good," answered Butch. "The teachers don't yell at me like they used to. Mrs. Harley knows about the Dixville Massacre. She tried to make me and my brother go see a shrink friend of hers but I told her, 'There's no way in hell me and Thad is going to see a damn shrink.' Oh, I'm sorry. I forgot we shouldn't swear."

"Go on."

"That's it. Well, that and there ain't no more Scoutin'. No one wants to start a new troop. Me and Thad ain't even official Scouts anymore. After the massacre, the Colebrook selectboard told the Daniel Webster Scout Council to take me and Thad off the roster--like we died up there or something." He rubbed his nose with the palm of his hand. "I might as well have, I'll probably have to start as a Wolf again," Butch whined. "I'll never be an Eagle at this rate." He looked up at Helen with questioning eyes. "Moms can be Akelas. Down at Lancaster there's one. And I saw one at the regional Pinewood Derby last year."

"Sorry, I can't help you. I've got problems of my own. Besides, I'm not a mom anymore." It hurt to say it--the fulfillment she had had as a mother, the beaming pride of having a good boy as a son. Helen recalled the time Uncle Max surprised Barry with a puppy. Only four years old at the time, Barry had groomed the pup, fed it; he put the animal in a box next to his bed that night. The two had become inseparable. Barry named it Tater; the puppy loved pushing potatoes across the floor with its nose. Though Helen had been perturbed at Max for springing the present on them, she soon realized the value of Barry having a companion. Tater walked Barry to the end of the lane each morning to catch the bus--and greeted her son as he got off the bus after school. Every day it was a race to see who would get to the house first. Tater always won.

"Ma'am," Butch whispered to Helen. "You okay, Ma'am? Ma'am?"

"Yes. Yes." After returning from her daze, Helen forgot what they had been talking about. "How you doing, Thad?" Thad looked out the window and didn't respond.

"He's doing fine but he don't talk," Butch spoke for him.

"Oh, I'm sorry. Do you mean, he doesn't, or can't, or what?"

"He just doesn't want to."

"Does he talk to you?"

"No, but I understand what he means. See, ever since the massacre he's got the ghost."

"He's got the ghost, huh." Helen had been around Butch enough to know he had a propensity to spin tall tales, turning the ordinary into something grander. But Thad, he had been a reserved boy before the tragedy. *This is probably why teachers want to get Thad psychological help,* she concluded.

Helen tried to get Thad's attention, "So Thad, will you talk to me?" He remained fixed on an object out the window. "Just say hi or something." He wouldn't respond. Helen put her hand on his; she realized she wasn't the only one suffering. After Barry's death, Thad needed a friend. The despondent dog upstairs needed a boy. "I'll get Tater."

Colebrook, New Hampshire (November 7)

Helen and her ex-husband Bradley sat and reminisced about the good times. The woodstove flickered through the screening. Helen couldn't recall him ever being so considerate. Tonight he listened; she had a lot pent up inside to talk about. Bradley shared the emptiness she felt from Barry's death. His appearance at her door confirmed his grief as a father.

Helen was grasping at any string of happiness. He had taken her out to dinner. Later, they sipped drinks at home. The passion escalated. She knew she might have regrets, but tonight she didn't care.

Tater pranced at the door, then scratched it. Helen pulled away from Bradley's embrace. "I've got to let her out before she scratches the door any worse. The problem with having this mute dog is that they have to scratch to tell you what they want." The dog was out most of the day with the Rousells and now wanted out again.

Bradley refilled her glass with Chardonnay.

"Tater stays out all night sometimes," she commented on her return. "I suspect she's with Butch and Thad during the day. I have no idea what she does at night."

"You don't have to keep the dog anymore. I'm sure I could find her a good home. I meet a lot of farmers. Tater would love it on a farm. A lot of people would love a dog that doesn't bark."

"Naaa. I've gotten attached to her. Besides, Barry loved that animal. I couldn't give her away."

"So, tell me more about this Wizard in the Vermont Covenant?" Bradley asked.

"Hardly anyone in our covenant has seen him. Feds have been trying to stop his CB radio broadcasts for over six months. The Wizard designed a communication link to connect the Vermont and New Hampshire Covenants." Her voice raised in excitement, "They're setting it up right now."

Helen reflected on what had first attracted her to Bradley. He still looked handsome: six-foot two with thick black hair, athletically built--a large, solid jaw his most defining feature. He made her feel protected. Talking to someone filled the lonely void tragedy had left behind.

Romance captured her and held her firmly in familiar arms. Helen couldn't remember Bradley this affectionate, she followed the route passion took her.

She slept breathing heavily, again reliving the Dixville scene in a struggle to give Barry life in the back of Max's truck. She wiped sticky blood on her dress and reached back to find her son's face, to breathe life into him again. The smell of raw gut permeated the air as she groped about the bed, searching. At last she realized where she was. It took a second to recall the night's events, then she noticed Bradley wasn't in bed any more. Car lights glowed beyond the trees. She slipped on her robe to investigate.

Though Helen knew the trail that went by Barry's lean-to, it took awhile for her eyes to adjust. She crept toward the light slowly. Late November air chilled her to the core; her sweat-soaked gown stiffened from the cold. She watched Bradley talk to the men in the white car. The rear license plate was intact; locals clipped the upper right corner of the plate. "You bastard!" she mumbled. Bradley was one of the Feds--the people responsible for the murder of her son.

Something moved in the brush near her. Tater sat a few feet away and watched the same scene with interest. Like the Rousell brothers, the dog had become a survivor, reverting to her roots with the wild. "Let's go, girl," said Helen. "We've seen enough." Helen went back to the house, changed into a clean gown and went back to bed.

Bradley skulked in five minutes later and dropped his pants before slipping under the sheets. Helen lay awake in bed for an hour until she was certain he was asleep.

Then she slipped out, donned hiking clothes and boots, and grabbed a flashlight. She and Tater hiked toward Max's deer camp at Van Dyck summit. Max had been working all day setting up the communication link between the covenants. After making several wrong turns, Helen finally followed the dog to Max's camp.

"The Feds know about The Wizard," blurted Helen as she burst into the room.

Max could hardly see who it was at first. Luckily he recognized the voice; he lowered his shotgun. "How'd they find out? Do they know I'm here at the camp, or what?"

"They just know The Wizard is in the area," said Helen, nearly crying. "I'm so sorry! I'm so sorry!"

"The Wizard left already." Max pulled a chair over, "Sit down. Now, collect your thoughts," he insisted. "Tell us exactly what happened."

Butch and Thad were also at the deer camp. They had come to meet The Wizard and help set up the communication system. Groggy, Butch crawled out of his sleeping bag on the opposite side of the shack. He rubbed his nose with the palm of his hand as he approached to listen.

Helen continued with her story, "Well, I spent the day with Bradley and mentioned The Wizard and that the Vermont and New Hampshire Covenants were setting up a communication link. This evening, I saw him talking to the Feds out on the main road."

For the Vermont Covenant, The Wizard had designed a closed communication system that used lasers. A modem fed a signal into a beam and used unidirectional nodules as receivers. The signal followed a cable from the receiver, and was spliced into a telephone line. E-mail went to an Internet service provider in Quebec and then returned to Island Pond, Vermont. If ever discovered, the Feds wouldn't be able to tell where the signal originated. They would have to search a six-mile radius, giving the Covenant time to leave.

"I never liked that bastard!" stated Max shaking his head. "Never did. Did you tell them anything about the communication link? What type or where we're mounting it?"

"No. I didn't know."

Max concluded, "They already know The Wizard is somewhere in Vermont." Consoling Helen he continued, "The Wizard left already; I don't think much harm has been done."

Max was still concerned, "But Bradley knows that I've done a lot of work with electronics; it's too much of a coincidence. The Feds will check me out. I'll try to send a message through the link to Vermont tomorrow, then go back to Colebrook and lay low for a while." Speaking to Butch, "You boys will have to take Helen back to her house. Send Thad back if you notice unusual traffic through the valley." Butch nodded.

"I'm so sorry!" Tears ran down Helen's face. "I'm so stupid."

Max held her by the shoulders. "Listen, little sister, you have to go back. You have to act like nothing happened--and if Bradley asks you anything, give him info that sounds good but is totally false. Then they won't know what to believe."

By now Thad had awakened and stumbled over to the group. He put his arms around Helen's neck; the hug from his small slender body surprised and comforted her.

"Don't worry, boss," Butch declared all-knowingly. "Me and Thad won't let nothing happen to your sister."

Helen had breakfast ready for Bradley when he walked into the kitchen. He put his arms around her waist as she flipped an egg over in the skillet. "I've got to give a talk to a co-op in St. Johnsbury this morning, but I'd like us to spend the rest of the day together." He nibbled her ear.

"I'd like that, too. I'll bake your favorite pie for dinner," said Helen as she glared coldly at the wall behind the stove. "Be sure to drink the fresh-squeezed orange juice on the table over there. It will cure what ails you." Helen had no intention of baking a pie that day; her orange juice would take care of that. It would make him violently sick in about an hour.

Chapter 5

Helen woke from her dream and sat up in bed. The pounding on the kitchen door at last awakened her; she rolled over and turned on her lamp to look at her watch. "Good Lord, it's one in the morning." She put on her slippers and robe, "This had better be good!"

Thad and Tater waited at the door, peering away from the house into darkness. He wiped his nose with his sleeve. A snap in the brush made him jerk back to that direction. Tater perked her ears and flared her teeth.

The porch light came on. "What are you doing here?"

Thad strained, trying to speak.

"Well, what is it?" She could see from the boy's panicked look, something was wrong. Tater continued staring out into blackness and took several steps toward the woods, ready to strike. "Is it Max?"

"Thad shook his head no."

"The Feds?"

He shook his head yes and opened the screen door. Grabbing her robe, he began tugging.

"Are they coming?"

He shook his head affirming it and drew her out the door.

"No. I have to get some things." Helen ran in and grabbed pants, shirt, and boots, then ran to Barry's room and snatched the picture of mother and son at Cascade Falls. She paused a moment--and found Thad tugging on her robe again. Seconds later, the two were out the back door with Tater in pursuit.

When they finally dared to stop and turn around, they could see flashlight beams darting about the house from their vantage point in the thick pines up the hill. Holding her bunched clothes under an arm, Helen watched the enemy ransack the only home she had ever known, in their search for her. Tater cocked her head, her eyes danced, following the flashlight beams below. In early December, snows had melted, but the bitter, damp air quickly chilled the motionless trio. Thad grasped Helen's hand and led her fumbling through the darkness. Tater paused for a moment to watch their home defiled by strangers, unable to protest.

The Rousell hideout was a large wooden teepee made of cedar logs with mounded dirt; moss and ferns covered the structure. An opening at the top allowed smoke to escape from a stacked-stone firebox inside. The rocks radiated warmth from an earlier burn; red coals remained. Thad gestured to Helen to sit on one of the mattresses as he went about feeding the coals with kindling stacked around the walls of the structure.

Helen sat shivering and hapless, hugging the only things she had left in the world. She watched the boy purposefully go about his chores. *There is no expression of fear in this child's face,* she concluded. She couldn't help but wonder what they went through at the Dixville Massacre. After Thad's mute effort to warn her at the house, she knew the tragedy had had a traumatic impact on him. He noticed her watching him and looked back.

"Whee te whee teeeeah," Butch's secret whistle pierced the air.

Thad responded with the same shrill pitch. Moments later Butch flipped up the tarp and paraded in. Tater bound through the door behind him, tail wagging. She had gone back to check on Butch after escorting the two to safety. She lapped Helen's face.

Helen dropped her clothes and held the dog away. "Please Tater, give me some space." To Tater, this was all an adventure.

"We kicked their ass, Thad," Butch boasted. "I flattened every tire on their cars with my Scout knife while they were up at the house." He looked over to Helen. "I see you rescued Barry's mom. That's rugged, Thad. Real rugged." He said to Helen, "Me and Thad take care of our own, you know," Butch noticed she was shivering; he went over to a trunk, opened it, and pulled out a jacket to put around her. "We won't let the Feds get ya. You're safe here. Only Thad, Barry, Tater, and me know about this place--and now you, of course. Not even Max knows about it."

Helen looked at the jacket and noticed it was Barry's. Butch saw her expression. "That's Barry's. He still has stuff here. We started this place in the spring. It sure came in handy. It sure did."

Helen didn't say a thing--just sat glumly and watched the fire regain life from the added twigs. It smoldered and popped--eventually, spewing out flames, adding new life to nearly dead embers. Ashen smoke strayed side to side, eventually wading to the peak and out the opening at the top of the hideout. A scent of burned cherry lingered from the smoke trail. She watched-

-and listened to Butch ramble.

"And we've got food. Thad, get Ms. Conrad some food."

"No, thanks, really."

"No," continued Butch. "We got plenty." Thad handed a pack of cookies to his brother; he opened it and handed them to Helen. "We got enough to hold out three weeks and that's not counting food we could get hunting. Tater's a tracker, you know. If you get lost in the woods we could find you with her. She's got a real good nose. The best nose on a dog I ever seen. The Feds are too stupid to use dogs. But if they did we have trip lines and snares all over the place; the snares would catch a dog."

Helen opened the pack and pulled a cookie out, smelling it before biting into it. "Do the snares catch Tater?"

"Caught her once, then she learned. Most dogs wouldn't learn like her. Tater's smarter than most dogs. We hooked up a harness on her; Barry, Thad, and me had her help us drag logs up here for the hideout. Oh, she's still your dog. We just exercise her. Barry would want that. Tater has taken a real liking to Thad though."

Tater raised her eyes at the mention of her name. She lay stretched out on her own padded bed next to the warm rocks that circled the fire, poised and waiting to absorb any heat that oozed between the gaps in the stone. The dog lay her head on the fluffy cushion with eyes open and recharged from the activity of the evening. Helen watched the animal and realized this was a frequent experience for Tater. It explained why the dog had stayed out all night since the Rousell brothers started borrowing her. "Doesn't your mother say anything about you boys running around all the time. I don't mean to seem ungrateful, but shouldn't you be home?"

"It's okay with Mom as long as we don't hurt anyone. That's what she says, 'As long as you don't hurt anyone'."

"Butch, does your mother know where you are, and some of the things you two do?"

"Mom drinks a little. And she goes to bed early if her boyfriend isn't staying over; if he is, they like it when we go out. Sometimes we stay here. Sometimes we stay at Max's deer camp. Thad and me are rugged. We're the last of Pack 220. We're not afraid of nothing. If Thad and me come across another robot gun and see the red lights come on, we know exactly what to do. We'd shoot out the sensors. It's got to have sensors to see the motion and heat. And we carry flares too. We can light 'em and throw 'em out as decoys. We're ready, Ms. Conrad. A Scout's always prepared." Thad shook his head, agreeing with his brother.

"There's nothing wrong with being afraid, but you boys need a normal life. You shouldn't be sitting around planning how to attack the Feds."

"We used to do a lot of stuff in Scoutin' but we're not members anymore. I can never be an Eagle Scout unless there's an Akela. So we're starting our own secret pack, Ghost Pack 220. We're rebuilding the troop. Gettin' more kids every day."

"So people join every day, huh?" Helen treated everything Butch said with suspicion. He had a way of talking as though all-knowing.

"Yep. Every day." Butch began telling her about Dixville Notch: how Mr. Ronolou had had him and Thad drop to the rear of the troop and help as his assistant; how Mr. Ronolou jumped in front of the bullets while he yanked them down behind a rock when the shooting started. "I was going to go get Barry but Mr. Ronolou wouldn't let me go. The Akela said I couldn't. A Scout always obeys the Akela, ya know. Mr. Ronolou got up and took twelve hits to draw the robot gun away for Thad and me so we could escape. That's rugged." Butch shook his head agreeing with himself. "When the Feds arrived in the copter and were checking out the scene, a Black guy looked right into our hiding spot, but for some reason he didn't tell on us. Then after they flew off, we jumped out of the dirt and started making a stretcher for Barry. They patched him up, ya know, but then left him there to die."

"I know." Helen knew Butch exaggerated about Mr. Ronolou taking twelve bullets, but she wanted to hear more.

"Thad was the last person Barry talked to." The glow of the fire flickered across the boy's face as he spun his tale--his narration compelling. "Barry told Thad he loved ya."

The phrase jerked tears from Helen's eyes. She winced and looked to Thad who nodded. "Butch Rousell, you'd better not be feeding me another cock-and-bull story!"

"No, Ma'am. Cross my heart and hope to die. Honest to God. Right, Thad?" Thad bobbed his head earnestly. "Anyway, that was the last time my brother said anything. I think he's got the ghost."

"The ghost?" Helen knew he was making things up now. They looked at Thad sitting across the fire.

"The ghost," Butch confirmed. "Like on the old *Star Trek* movie where Spock transferred his soul into Doctor McCoy. I think they're sharing the same body." Butch was careful not to word this part of the story as fact. He didn't want to offend.

"Well, how big is your Ghost Pack?" Helen jumped back to a less sensitive topic. Tater rested by the warm rocks surrounding the fire. The heat converted their damp, dreary surroundings into a cozy cocoon, forcing the cold to retreat out the very gaps it had entered. It was a camp-out, the dark cedar timbers replaced a black forest; the blazing fire leaped and snapped.

"You want to join?"

"What?" The boy's question startled Helen out of a daze.

"The Ghost Pack? Ya know, be a member?" asked Butch.

She shrugged, "What do I have to do?"

"You already did the first part. You heard the story about the massacre at Dixville Notch. Next, you have to cut your thumb." Helen cringed. Butch unloaded his jacket pockets looking for his pocketknife. A small, 22 revolver was among the items that came out.

"Is that thing real?" asked Helen.

"Oh, you bet. Borrowed it from my Uncle." He opened the knife and slipped the blade in the fire. "This kills all the germs, ya know."

Helen rolled her eyes at the dramatic presentation. She knew that if she went along with this thing, she'd have to give the cut a heavy dose of antiseptic. But her attention was drawn back to the gun. "Is that thing loaded?"

"A gun is no good unless it's loaded. You can't shoot an empty gun."

"Let me have it."

"I can't do that, it's my Uncle's."

Butch pulled the knife out of the flame and waved it through the air to cool it, then wiped the soot from the blade with a filthy hanky he pulled from his back pocket. Helen shook her head, *So much for cleanliness*, she thought. "Now Butch, don't you cut me much."

"Trust me. Just enough to bleed." He held her thumb and sliced her.

"You cut me deep!" She put it in her gown. "I trusted you!"

"It's got to make a scar."

"Now give me the gun!"

"I can't, it's my Uncle's.

"You have to. I'm your new Akela." The name Akela, means "a good leader," a word taken from the *Jungle Book*. The title is introduced in early Cub Scouts and carries through Boy Scouts. Respecting authority is a main facet of Scouting.

So Butch knew what that meant. He could officially become a Scout again--eventually an Eagle. He handed over the weapon. "There's sixteen of us in all. Every time I tell about the Dixville Massacre I get a new member to the

Ghost Pack."

Thad snuggled up on the mattress beside Tater, with an unzipped sleeping bag over both of them. Butch dropped thicker logs in the fire for the night and went to his mattress to turn in as well. "That's your place, where you are." Butch pointed to the remaining cushion where Helen sat.

Helen recognized Barry's sleeping bag at the head of the mattress. She reached for the bundle and unrolled it.

"When's our first meeting?" Butch inquired.

"Sometime soon. Someplace secret. I don't know." Helen lay on her side and watched the fire. Butch did the same. Tater and Thad slumbered; Tater twitched in a dreamscape chase for a rabbit.

Helen gazed hypnotically at the fire's dance. So much so soon: First she had lost her son, now the rest of her life was gone. How could she survive living out here? She wondered if any place existed for a single, middle-aged woman wanted by the law; she felt very alone.

Tater stirred from her sleep, walked over and lay on top of the sleeping bag next to Helen. She licked her hand. She patted the dog on the head. "What do we do, girl."

Butch heard the comment. "Don't worry Ms. Conrad. Me and Thad will always be here for ya."

Colebrook Covenant Meeting (Noon, November 11)

Mr. and Mrs. Philbin, a sixty-year-old couple, graciously allowed the Colebrook Covenant to use the basement of their one hundred eighty-year-old home for meetings. There were five members present: Mr. and Mrs. Philbin, Harv Madison Max Sessal, Vanessa Larson.

It was the oldest house in Colebrook; the original stone wall was around much of the basement. Years ago, the former owner had laid brick across a rear entrance, the remnants of a passageway once part of the underground railroad used to smuggle slaves to safety over a century ago. Now, a fluorescent light illuminated the drab surroundings. Organized clutter of stacked canning jars, boxes, and shelving lined two walls.

Scattered conversations vied for dominance.

Max yelled out, "Hold it. One at a time!"

Harv Madison, short, plump, with black bushy eyebrows, spoke out from the silence, "I say, go ahead with what we're doing. We can only supply Helen with an attorney." The Feds had launched the raid on Helen's house based on her revelations to Bradley; they thought The Wizard was in town, possibly set up in her home. No one in the Colebrook Covenant knew Helen had gone with the Rousells; they presumed she had been arrested for drugging her ex-husband with prescription medicine. Under present martial law, suspects could be detained for an undetermined length of time.

Max wasn't about to give up that easily. "Someone with experience might be able to get her back. I met three guys from the South the other day. They want to arrange a meeting with us. I believe this bunch was involved in the Tobacco War rebellion." Five years ago, the Federal Government had taxed tobacco farmers so heavily they began selling their crops on the black market. Federal agents began seizing farms. An organization called the Tobacco Boys formed. Like their ancestors of the Civil War era, they were superb fighters. Last year, the White House sent Army Regulars to Georgia and quelled the uprising. Massive casualties were incurred on both sides. "They wouldn't say how many there are in their group, but I got the impression the number is sizable. They might be the ones to get Helen back before she's moved out of the area. Since the Dixville Massacre, we've received money from all over the country--a little over two million dollars so far. We could easily back them." It was ironic: President Winifred's plea for contributions to the American people to help the families affected by the Dixville Massacre would be used to fight his administration.

Harv wanted to quell this talk of bloodshed. "I think you should meet them, but to step into a fight using these Tobacco Boys is crazy. I've been in the military. We don't want to get involved with a militia. We don't know who these guys are or what they believe. We certainly don't want anymore deaths."

"Unless it's a Fed," Mrs. Larson cut in. "Were any of your kids murdered?" The huge woman was adamant. Excluding Harv Madison, everyone in the room had lost a loved one in the Dixville Massacre: Mrs. Larson, a son; the Philbins, a grandson; Max, his nephew Barry.

"Well, no."

"Then shut up," she snapped.

Max intervened, "So what do you suggest, Vanessa?"

"I want to be there when you meet them," she responded soundly.

Colebrook, New Hampshire (November 12)

Subject: Bean Town

Date: Sunday, 12 Nov. 2023 9:13:054
From: Hman <blue_jay@quebec.net>
To: Xman <sparrow@quebec.net>
Cc:
Attachments:
A most elated howdy to you all. Got your note, goat. Communication is
critical. I'm the man with the plan and have control of the bowl. Was there
ever any question? I don't think so, joe.

I heard that the hawk came and kicked the Xman out of the house. Not to worry, Murry. Take your time slime. They took the Xman to the Bean Patch. I just know these things. I'm in the know, you know.

It snowed like a banshee in heat last night. All roads closed. No problem, I drive the optic highway. Get out of my face, ace! Move over, rover! I'm coming through with all RAMs running. Beep! Beep!

Using Max's laptop computer, Helen responded to the maniac communication person in the Vermont Covenant, code named Hman. She was at Max's deer camp with Butch and Thad, Tater curled up by the wood stove. It was direct E-mail, but they still couldn't be explicit; the System Operator running the Web site could read any letter if she chose. Helen pushed back from the table, "Butch, you and Thad jump on your skis and get a message to the Philbins. Tell them I'm safe at Max's camp and that the Vermont link is up and running. Tell them that according to information across the river, Max is in custody and has been taken to Boston already."

Just after the Colebrook Covenant meeting yesterday, Max had been picked up on Main Street by four federal agents. The Feds believed Max was The Wizard. Under the temporary martial law, citizens could be detained without due process. Max had been one of many the government suspected who had been incarcerated.

The boys slipped their gear on and started out. Butch turned and gave Helen a Scout salute before going--Thad as well. Helen forced a smile and saluted in response, but she had other things on her mind.

As a fugitive, she had come to stay at Max's deer camp. The Rousell hideout was virtually concealed, plants had covered it even before the big snow, but it was small and dreary inside. At least the deer camp had windows. And, before Max had been taken, she relieved her brother at the communication site so he could spend some time at home. Helen learned that Butch and Thad spent a lot of time at the deer camp. They were the ones who turned on Max's computer and checked the E-mail when he didn't return. It had occurred to Helen that the Rousells might be skipping school; now, she was sure of it.

During these days in hiding, Helen had plenty of time to ponder her situation. Turning to the window, she looked across the span toward Sugar Hill. Puffy snow coated everything, accumulating up to eight inches on narrow tree limbs. It was a windless storm where large flakes floated down and set quietly in place. She had watched it through the night; it gave her time to reflect. Helen had considered turning herself in; so far she had only been responsible for distributing prescription drugs and doping her ex-husband's drink. Bitterness convinced her not to. The Feds were responsible for the death of her son, and Bradley was a part of that group. Up to this point, she had not been involved with the Covenant.

Helen pulled the picture of Barry out of her shirt pocket and stared at it. She spoke aloud to herself, "This is a town where people stop their cars to let you cross the street. My biggest gripe used to be cleaning up after the dog." Tater's eyes rolled up and her tail flopped once, knowing Helen spoke of her. She reached over and patted the animal's head. "I don't know what to do now. I guess I don't see much of a future for me, Tater."

She thought about Max. "He was so sure of himself. 'There are still things worth fighting for,' he would say if he were here." Lifting the picture of Barry again, she gazed at it and smiled. Tears formed and rolled down her cheeks; she could taste the saltiness as one crossed over her lip.

Helen had been an avid reader. She particularly appreciated poetry. A single verse from a poem she had read in high school haunted her: *Crush my dreams and I'll awaken.* Though her life had been ordinary, her son Barry had been exceptional. A child who had been a total joy to be with was taken from her by a heartless administration concerned only with preserving itself. At the time, she hadn't known what the verse to the poem meant. "Max is right," Helen spouted to herself, "there are things worth fighting for." She *had* awakened.

Chapter 6

"What do you know about the Dixville incident?" asked Paz. The Secretary of Defense sat across from Steve Morrison of Spectator News in a restaurant located near the outskirts of Washington D.C. General Paz positioned himself so he could view the rest of the establishment, particularly the entrance. Waitresses and busboys rushed from table to table, scurrying to keep up with the noon rush. A myriad of conversations riddled the room as the two studied each other's faces for clues.

Steve chewed his gum anxiously, he wasn't sure how to proceed. Kyle had phoned him, extending an invitation for drinks. The Secretary of Defense hadn't clarified his intentions. Another oddity: from the background noise, Steve could tell the General had made his call from a pay phone. Steve knew Kyle had a reason for inviting him there. It wasn't social; such a thing doesn't exist in Washington D.C.

The General was probing, "What do you know about the Dixville Massacre?"

"I only know what I've heard through the media," replied Steve, smiling at his own joke. When Kyle failed to react, Steve continued seriously, "I listen in on the CB broadcasts out of the North Country. Some nights I can pick it up. They tell a different story than the President."

"What's coming out of the North Country is true."

The reporter stopped gnawing his gum, "What?"

"You heard me." Kyle confirmed.

"Why am I here, General?" Steve knew this new information source was a big break for him, but he couldn't understand why Paz would divulge such information. The General could be indicted.

Paz had trouble telling him. He looked away as he spoke, "We are on the brink of a reelection year and--"

"The Massacre? What really happened, General?"

"What would you say if I told you that the Dixville Massacre was a tragic mistake, and that some of us in the military would like to set the record straight before the North Country starts their own revolt."

"Whose mistake?"

"As commander of the armed services, mine." The General finally turned and looked squarely at Steve. "I could live with the version of events the media tells, but I'm not about to see more civilians sacrificed up there to cover-up what happened. It has to stop. Intelligence has it that some of the Tobacco Boys have found their way up there and have built up a militia of over one hundred men. We increased the number of battalions in the North Country, but it seems like every other day one of our troops is shot in the tri-state region. We believe it's them. They're the only ones with the skills to evade us like that. Their cause has widespread support by the locals--and for good reason. There's a lot of pissed-off civilians since the Dixville thing. This is nothing like the Tobacco uprising that began with taxes. These people lost their sons, nephews, and grandsons. This has stirred up a bunch of folks and turned into a regional fight. I don't want to see this country torn apart because of my screw-up. Revenge can be a powerful motivator, especially when a bunch of kids were--well, accidentally murdered." Steve was stunned. He couldn't believe he was the only one hearing this. He looked around to see who else was in the room. Kyle went on, "What killed those kids was a MAN, a Multi-sensory Automated Neutralizer, designed to take down ground movement. The troops call it AutoMan. They weren't designed to take out targets below a certain weight. Tanks and full-grown people with weapons, yes. Not kids and wildlife."

"I've never heard of such a thing. Why did you choose me to tell this to?"

"I believe Spectator News will follow-up on this story. If this thing in the Northeast is going to end, it has to come out in the open." The General began collecting his things to leave. "I have another meeting."

"I'd like to find out as many details as possible before I publish." Morrison chewed excitedly now. He was the only reporter with a source like this. *The story of the decade, and mine.* "Winifred has a good relationship with the media. If this is going to be a pissing match between the President and me, I want a full bladder. Where can I find out more."

General Kyle Paz dropped a ten on the table to cover the drinks and tip. "At the Dixville Massacre site you can see the physical evidence. Hopefully, if they know you're coming, you won't get shot."

"Hopefully! What do you mean by that?"

"They hate reporters up there." With his hat tucked under his arm, Paz weaved between tables and chairs on his way to the exit.

After Paz had left, Steve pulled his computer out of his pocket and turned off dictation mode. He had it all digitally. He thought about how he could get into the Dixville area without the locals knowing he was a reporter. He spoke to himself aloud, "'Hopefully I won't get shot' . . . Shit!"

The Philbin's sugarhouse near Colebrook (December 6)

They hid in darker places of the night and spoke in whispers of sedition: of killing and injustice, of fairness--desperate people seeking retribution. Vanessa Larson slurped and stared into her cup of coffee. Helen paced across the floor, stopping occasionally to watch a sound she heard. Harvey Madison stared at the door of the shack reciting articles of tolerance to himself. Beyond the door, three dark figures walked on crunchy snow in the shadows of the pines. They stopped at the edge of the clearing and waited for a cloud to pass in front of the moon.

Mrs. Larson answered the door of the sugarhouse. Three men dressed in white camouflage walked in and bunched up on the left side, kicking snow off their boots. The tallest man named Tumult had a wiry look about him, hunched and slightly bow-legged, the posture of a toughened rodeo cowboy. He stopped and stared at the three locals with disdain; they were not what he had expected.

Tumult had always had a dark side, but what the Tobacc tax had done to his mother and father gave him an excuse to kill. He was a racist. He was a Nazi. And he despised anyone who defied him.

Snake, also with raven hair, shared the same physical characteristics but with black, plastic glasses. He removed his glasses and cleaned off fog using the tail of his flannel shirt that extended below the white jacket. His expression was less hardened than Tumult. Snake was not only leader of one of the three militia forces, he was also the technician for his group. He made it his job to keep up with technology for all three militias. Snake and Tumult were brothers. And in his mild-mannered way, Snake was the only one who could reason with Tumult. This talent didn't make Snake less dangerous, he simply understood the power of manipulation. Like Tumult, Snake was cunning, but he didn't share the extreme ideology.

Austere, the maple-sugaring shack consisted of open timbers on walls and ceilings. Sixteen-penny nails driven into studs held web-covered sapping tools. Thousands of feet of plastic tubing hung in coils from the walls. A propane lantern hung from a coat hanger and cast tilted shadows of varied shapes with its yellow glow. The latent sugaring shack still housed an overbearing evaporator that filled a third of the place. Dry heat from the woodstove below the evaporating vats drew out the bitter scents from green, cherry logs that were corded beside the firebox.

The three Southerners looked about the room at Mrs. Larson, Helen, and the short plump Harvey Madison. "Holy Jesus," Tumult finally said. He broke his stare, looked down and sighed, "This is it? This is your so-called Covenant. I walked all this way for this? Piss!" He started putting his gloves on again.

"Hold it," whispered the third Southerner. "We gotta hear 'em out," he whispered. "We can't just go. They could offer shelter and supplies." Chaos was the youngest of the three. His chiseled, gladiator build tapered to narrow hips. Removing his coat, beneath his shirt he exposed bulging biceps with cords of muscles that rippled with each move. His dark hair was cut short, giving him a cleaner, military look. He didn't appear threatening at all, nodding and smiling when he entered. Unlike the other two, Chaos joined the cause in the Carolinas out of principle: The Tobacco Tax had destroyed their family farm. The three Covenant leaders noticed the difference: He was willing to talk. Chaos turned to them, "Where's Max?"

"The Feds got him," Mrs. Larson spoke up. "We're here in his place. You got a problem with that?"

"It's just that we expected Max," replied Chaos.

"Is this all ya got?" asked Snake. His brother Tumult waited to hear the reply.

Vanessa retaliated, "I got news for you dipsticks: Looks are deceiving. I've killed a Fed in my day." The comment sounded ridiculous coming from the obese woman. Tumult smirked at the imagery her claim concocted.

Helen didn't blink, maintaining her stalwart pose. "According to Max, you said we share the same cause."

"Well, now, did I say that? 'Great liars are also great magicians,'" Tumult quoted Hitler as he turned and left.

Chaos and Snake hesitated to go. A nagging question held Snake back, "How do you communicate without getting caught?"

"You haven't paid for that one, partner," said Vanessa coldly. "I'm sure it's inferior to anything you've got."

Snake flipped her the bird and followed Tumult out the door.

Chaos spoke softly to the three Covenant members, "Let me talk to them.

I'll be right back." He grabbed his coat and hat.

Away from the shack, the two Southerners mumbled between themselves. Tumult pulled out a small case of filterless, home-rolled cigarettes and lit up; his cradled hands blocked the wind. He enjoyed the cigarette, squinting with each suck, holding the smoke in and pushing it out his nose and mouth.

Chaos caught up with the two at the edge of the tree line. Tumult wanted nothing to do with the ragtag locals, but Chaos saw their value in supplies and refuge. "If you don't have the support of the people, you have no base; we need a haven."

"I don't deal with weenies and dykes, but if you think you can get something from them, you're welcome. They might be good for something other than defecating, copulating, and procreating." Tumult turned and crunched off through the snow.

Snake held back. "Just find out how they're talkin' to the Vermont Covenant. We've got boys scattered everywhere in these parts with no secure way of talkin' to 'em." Chaos nodded as Snake turned and followed Tumult.

"They're talking out there." Helen peeked through the window like a conniving child. She considered the Southerners the answer to Colebrook's struggle and the return of her brother Max; they were the ones with the skill and resolve to follow through with a fight. Chaos seemed polite, a southern gentleman of sorts. He was cute, better groomed than the others, with dark brown eyes capped by long lashes.

Harvey's voice was filled with disdain: "We're better off without that crew. They have no loyalty to anything."

Helen pulled back from the window; she paused for a moment: "The third one's coming back." She went over to open the door. "Did your friends agree?" she asked, closing the door behind him.

"First of all, they're not my friends. They're associates. And Tumult thought it would be a good idea if I spoke with you myself. Do you mind?" Chaos gestured to sit down. Helen shook her head yes as he took off his coat and draped it over a nail near the door. He sat down at the table across from Harvey. They looked at each other warily.

"Coffee?" asked Vanessa. Her question broke the men's gaze.

He nodded yes. "I'm Chaos. I'm more of the tactician. I also train the recruits in fighting and survival skills. My politics are light-years away from the others, but I respect them for their ability to fight and elude the Feds. You might view them as redneck lowlifes," he smiled, "but they're a force to reckoned with." Mrs. Larson handed him the coffee. "Thank you, Ma'am.

You're very charmin'.'" Chaos handed out compliments easily; he smiled at the sizable woman before sipping. Then he paused to reflect before speaking, "There aren't as many of us now, but we're growing in numbers. It's like the philosopher Dryden said long ago: 'Courage comes from hearts and not from numbers grows.' We do share a common cause: freedom from oppressive government." He sipped again. "This coffee is absolutely delicious, ma'am. You're so gracious." He sipped again. "At the end of the Tobacco Wars they had us cornered in Georgia's Oke bayou. We took out two Feds for every one they got of ours, and they had topnotch equipment. Tumult came up with the notion of usin' reed shafts as snorkels and crawlin' through swamps on our bellies to the river, and eventually out of there. Twenty-six of us got out that way." His story held the listeners spellbound. He smiled, "We had leaches all over us." Helen and Vanessa cringed. Chaos laughed. He put a hand on Mrs. Larson's knuckles, "I would show you the markings from it, but that would be inappropriate in the presence of ladies."

Harvey enjoyed the tale. It might have been true; they had gotten out of their predicament somehow. But he could see the man's magic had less to do with 'tactics' and more to do with charm. The Southerner didn't appear to be a bigot like the other two, but the strong southern drawl seemed to contradict racial and ethnic enlightenment.

They talked of the future throughout the evening: of Colebrook, of the country--their fate if the Feds chose to advance into the perimeter in force. One thing was agreed: Winter was not a good time to force the soldiers out of Colebrook. Chaos would arrange to keep his portion of the rebels in a more isolated region northeast of Dixville Notch. In exchange for protection, the Colebrook Covenant would feed and outfit them. The Covenant had a sizable amount of cash tucked away; donations to Dixville families were still pouring in from around the country. Though not stipulated exactly, from the quantity of supplies he asked for, Helen got the impression his force alone numbered well beyond two hundred. He wouldn't say.

"And my brother Max. We need to get him out of a compound in Boston." Helen's tone shifted to a regrettable pitch.

Chaos' eyes narrowed as he considered a delicate response to Helen, "There are casualties in war, Ma'am. If we take a force down there to the city with all those roads and open space, the Feds could swoop right in. Other than the fact that he's your brother, Ma'am, there's no reason to risk it, certainly no tactical reason. It wouldn't help the cause."

"It wouldn't help the cause?" The steely comment incensed Helen. "He's the leader of the Colebrook Covenant. Without my brother, your rebels won't get so much as a tea bag from us--and that won't help *your* so-called cause."

"We're not suggesting an attack," Harvey negotiated. "A small group could get in and easily stay under cover in Inner Boston. Police and Federal Agents leave the gangs alone. The gangs are better armed than the Feds."

"And my lily white face would fit right in, right?"

"There's also a tactical reason," Helen vied. "The motor-guns. They're a weapon that uses gasoline as a propellant. For them, anything can be melted down into balls and used as shot. If you acquired the motor-guns, you would have superior weapons and unlimited ammunition. There's your reason-- that, and our backing."

Motor-guns were jerrybuilt contraptions that looked like a weed-whacker with a broached barrel for cooling. A local machinist in Boston had developed the device. It could pop out eighteen rounds a second. Though hodgepodge and heavy, it was the most devastating weapon in the city. Few police officers had seen one that wasn't burping out lead balls in their direction.

Chaos looked at Helen and considered the advantage of equipping his rebels with motor-guns. "'Everyone is the architect of his own fortune'," the Southerner quoted. "In March. We go in March."

Chapter 7

Dixville Notch, New Hampshire (December 10)

Chickadees chased the two boys up the trail in an effort to land on their caps where sunflower seeds had been placed. The black-capped little birds were so comfortable with them, they would eat kernels out of their hands, or in this case, chase them for the snacks the Rousells placed atop their hats. Butch and Thad had led a number of people to the massacre site. This time it was different: Using a phony international press ID, Spectator News reporter Steve Morrison convinced the boys he was a Quebec journalist. The reporter from Washington felt his anonymity was safe in a region where few people were able to afford television reception because of the communication tax-- and he was dealing with kids. Though the Rousells were skeptical, the stranger offered them a sizable amount of money.

Steve had rented a car in Quebec and drove in from the north. He found Butch and Thad alone on a side street and convinced them he was a foreign journalist, and that foreign reporters would present the truth. The prospect of notoriety appealed to Butch.

The narrow, snow-packed trail to the massacre site had become a common snowmobile route for those paying homage to the boys who died there. Butch and Thad had skis strapped to their backpacks for the trip down. They passed through a desolate world of snow-laden trees with humps where boulders rose and pushed the evergreens apart, at times, allowing sunshine to peek through between the treetops. Butch and Thad drove the tips of their ski poles into the packed snow and steadily plodded up the steep trail.

Morrison continually slipped, often clawing on all fours or using trees along the trail to pull himself. He endured the still cold of the forest trail, but on the edge of the massacre zone, the wind whipped up snow from the clearing and tossed it in their faces. Covering his ears with his gloved hands, he tucked his face into the top of his coat.

At the Massacre site, Steve pulled a digital camera from his coat pocket and began clicking shots. It looked desolate, as though there had never been life there. He noticed bullet holes through the tree beside him, then other such holes in trees nearby. "What the hell did this?" He looked at a gaping hole through a sixteen-inch tree trunk; a tree sparrow had since nestled in the cavity to escape the elements. The Spectator reporter stepped around to the back of the tree and found dried bloodstains. "They shot right through the tree and killed them," he mumbled to himself. He clicked several pictures of the phenomenon.

"You said you weren't an American Reporter," Butch declared sternly. He noticed a Spectator News identification tag on the camera. "What's with the camera?" The two onlookers stood side by side feeling double-crossed, Thad, the silent adjunct. "So, that ID you showed me was fake."

"Look Buddy--" said Steve.

"It's Butch."

Steve reached in his breast pocket and pulled out his wallet. He held out four twenties to Butch. "You got your money." The money flapped about in the breeze as the two boys scalded the stranger with their gaze.

"Well, if you don't want it, fine." A shot echoed through the valley below, several miles out. "What was that?"

"A Remington 306." Butch stated flatly. "It has a muzzle velocity of 2000 feet per second. You're one dead Fed." The money continued flapping in the wind as the Rousell brothers began untying the skis from their backs, preparing for the downward plunge.

"Boys, I'm not like the other Journalists," Steve claimed. "I'm trying to find out the truth about Dixville."

Thad tugged on his brother's arm and pointed to the Boston Bruins tiepin exposed through the reporter's open coat. Butch turned to his brother and nodded. "You from Boston?"

"I grew up just outside Boston," Steve was lying again. He didn't know what the boy's fascination was with Boston but he played along. Steve Morrison had no place he called home.

Through the communication system at Max's deer camp, the Rousells sent notes to The Wizard regularly. He had told the boys Boston was his home; the Rousells had developed an affinity for the city. They had heard about the expedition in March and planned on going. Butch didn't trust the reporter but admitted the connection, "The Wizard is from Boston, too. He can do just about anything. He's in the Vermont Covenant, ya know. But me and my brother have to know the truth about you before we can tell you anything."

Steve squatted in front of the boys. Reaching into his pocket, he pulled out a pack of gum and offered them a stick. Each boy pulled off a mitten and cautiously accepted a piece. Steve unwrapped one for himself. He could no longer dismiss the boys and simply get a story and go. "I'm here because I believe the White House has blamed this massacre on the smugglers, and smugglers didn't do it. I believe the *Feds* lied to hide something else." Steve was careful to use their terms. He pointed to trees at the edge of the clearing, "Now, I'm sure. Smugglers don't have weapons that could do that. Now, do you want to help me get the bad guys, or do I have to do it by myself?" No response. Steve shrugged, "The Wizard . . . can you tell me anything about him? The Feds have him in Boston."

"You got that wrong. They got the wrong guy." Butch decided to tell him; the money was good. And if the reporter was lying about his desire to 'find out the truth,' things would be no different than before. He walked up to the reporter. "Give me the money and follow." Steve handed Butch the cash and entered the clearing with the boys. "It's okay to come out in the open as long as you're with me or Thad. Everyone around these parts knows us. But there's a guy around with a Ruger semi-auto that would just as soon pop you in the face as look at you." He turned to his brother with a smirk, then walked over to a brush pile in the center of the clearing where the AutoMan had sat.

Boulders and stumps held a foot and a half of snow mounded above open ground. A pile of flowers were blanketed with a dusting of fluff; they had been laid there within the last couple of days. Butch pointed to the larger brush pile. "That's where the RoboGun sat, in that brush pile there. It shot tank-killer bullets that could go through anything. The bullets were made of depleted uranium, encased in a hardened, Teflon-coated, titanium case." Butch made it his business to know about weapons and ammunition. He listened to Max and others talk.

"RoboGun? How do you know all this?" Steve's mind raced with questions. General Paz had told him about the military's AutoMan, the same type of weapon the boy spoke of.

"We're members of the Ghost Pack 220. Only members of the Ghost Pack know what really happened up here."

The reporter became impatient with Butch. "Well, are you kids going to tell me?"

They shook their heads no. "Only the members know the real story," replied Butch.

"You speaking for your brother too?" asked Steve.

"My brother doesn't talk since the massacre but I know what he means." Both boys stood side by side, unified in their response.

It occurred to Steve that the Rousells needed more from him than just the money. "How do I join, boys?"

Butch lifted the side of Thad's hat and whispered in his ear. Thad shook his head yes. "We was held back at the end of the Pack to help as assistants to Mr. Ronolou; he was old and we could help him 'cause we're rugged. A Scout in the middle of the Pack noticed the red lights of the sensors. Then all hell broke loose. The Akela took three bullets in the chest but yanked my brother and me down behind that rock over there before the bullet spray widened."

Steve looked in astonishment as the lad recited the folklore. He thought no one had lived through the attack, and now, here he was in the presence of the only two survivors. It meant an exclusive interview for him. Steve found the story difficult to swallow at first, but as the tale progressed, with the intricate details and names--the fact that Butch described the AutoMan--the impact was overwhelming.

"Me and Thad popped out of the dirt over there, loaded up our friend Barry and hauled ass down the hill. Thad's the fastest Cub in the Pack, you know." Steve shivered in the blistering wind that now blew freely on open ground; he listened in awe to a finely honed tale of bravery, loyalty--and death.

Washington, D.C. (December 19)

"Ladies and Gentlemen, the President of the United States."

"Only once in history has the life of this Union of States been so imperiled that the Federal Government found it befitting to thwart those threats by force. In the mid-1800s, our forefathers fought against the injustice of slavery, to preserve this nation we call the United States.

Last week, in the outback of New Hampshire, armed hooligans killed thirty-two National Guards in a bloody shoot-out. The next day, terrorists from the Northeast Kingdom of Vermont attacked and killed twenty-seven more. Again, there comes a time in our existence as a nation to defend our laws, our union.

As President of the United States, I took an oath to uphold the law. I am bound to preserve this union of states, and I will do so vigorously. I will do so forthrightly, with all the militias and regular military at my disposal. The tragedy at Dixville must not linger. The tiny town of Colebrook and the surrounding region are held captive by thugs. I intend to free those citizens in the Northeast and destroy the gangs gripping the region."

Journalists in the Press Room stood and applauded instinctively. Chief of Staff Lucas Bennett, Vice President Margaret Sorenson, and Secretary of Defense Kyle Paz stood directly behind Winifred and clapped conservatively. An unenthusiastic exception was Steve Morrison of Spectator News; he stood complacently and stared. Nancy Atherton sat in her usual pose and applauded accordingly.

"Martial Law has been enacted during the last two years of this administration. I will be extending Martial Law and asking for a vote of support from the House and Senate to suspend the writ of habeas corpus, so the Armed Forces can move quickly in this matter. The military may detain suspects without due process for the safety of the public." The President cleared his throat and looked away from the teleprompter to his audience. "This act has the support of the American people. No region of the country should be exempt from taxation or regulations at the expense of another."

The room erupted again, with reporters raising their hands for questions. "Yes. Ms. Atherton."

"Mr. President, what started the shooting in Colebrook?"

Clifford glanced down at his pocket computer on the podium, "A Guard attempted to question two boys about a package they were carrying. One of the boys stabbed the Guard with a knife. The local militia up there are apparently using children as couriers. When the Guards tried to capture the two for questioning, shooting erupted. The crime syndicate in Colebrook took no prisoners. They call themselves the Covenant and they're well armed and well organized. One more thing: In subsequent fighting, a well-trained, tactical squad inflicted many casualties in a raid on an armament cache in Lancaster, New Hampshire. Raids by this group forced the Guard out of the region."

Nancy Atherton raised her hand again, requesting, "Follow-up, please," as other reporters jiggled around her like fleas.

"Ms. Atherton."

"When will you regain control, and how many casualties are we willing to take in the process?"

"We aren't willing to take any casualties, Ms. Atherton. But we will minimize deaths by using overwhelming force. What the Guard didn't have in the North Country was heavy armaments. When we go back, it will be in full force with air support."

"Here, Mr. President. Here. Mr. President. Mr. President." A cacophony of voices resounded throughout the room.

"Ms. Kristen Mallory from TBS News."

Kristen shook her head and swayed her blond hair out of her eyes. She briefly glanced at Steve Morrison before she spoke. "Why did the Colebrook smugglers use depleted uranium bullets--more commonly called tank-killers--against Pack 220 in the Dixville Massacre, but not one bullet of this type was used against the Guard in New Hampshire or in Vermont?" She turned to Morrison with a satisfied slither on her lips.

Winifred looked down at the pocket top screen searching for an answer. He could feel his neck warm and suspected his face was reddening. "Well, you must be referring to the baseless accusations in the Spectator News." He punched buttons on his computer as though scanning for notes. "We are uncertain that the bullets you're talking about were used by the smugglers at Dixville--"

"Oh yes," shouted Ms. Mallory. "I have one right here from the massacre site." She lifted a small wooden box and opened it. A bullet sat tucked inside the lead-lined container. She used a pair of tweezers to lift the bullet up for all to see. "How would a group of backwoods smugglers get hold of such a sophisticated piece of technology?"

"It is very likely that New Hampshire smugglers had some sophisticated weaponry at Dixville," stated the President. "Guards come home on leave; one or more could have worked in requisition. With all the weapons caches throughout this country, armaments could have been stolen by people from within--small amounts, of course," Clifford tilted his hand toward the reporter who displayed the bullet, "the reason for the limited production of such projectiles." Winifred scratched his nose and looked directly at the inquiring reporter. "I'm not sure what you're implying. Are you suggesting, Ms. Mallory, that the United States Military, under the command of the President of the United States, set up and murdered those boys at Dixville? And if so, for what reason?"

Ms. Mallory stammered, "Well, ah, perhaps it was a mistake--"

"Absolutely, Ms. Mallory, and you made it," Winifred continued. "Journalists have a duty to dig out and report the facts--not to opinionize and then present it as fact."

"I was at the site--" Steve Morrison blurted.

"This concludes the news conference," said the President, stepping up to the mike, "since there seems to be no further substantive questions." The President and Cabinet members walked from the Press Room, leaving journalists waving hands and yelling unsolicited questions.

Clifford Winifred spoke freely to Paz in the corridor off the Press Room. "What the hell prompted that Spectator reporter to go up there in the first place? He could have been shot. And his accusations only encouraged the Covenant to react."

"I have no idea, sir. Morrison is different from other reporters," the General concluded. Paz always told the President what he wanted to hear, meanwhile, he had successfully planted the seed of truth.

"Let me in!" Clifford could hear his Vice President's booming voice beyond the Oval Office door. "No, I did not have an appointment," Margaret Sorenson opened the door, forcing her way by Chief of Staff Bennett. "Get out of my way."

Bennett followed, "Sir, she didn't have an appointment."

"That's okay, Luc," he said. Then he spoke to Sorenson, "I'm sure this is important if you feel you have to intrude."

"We need to speak alone," Sorenson insisted. Bennett closed the door but stayed inside. "Without him," voiced the Vice President as she rolled her eyes back toward the Chief of Staff.

Winifred nodded to Bennett. Bennett shut the door firmly as he left the room.

"I hate that sneaky pervert," Sorenson declared resolutely. She had always wanted to say that. The Vice President was fifty-nine years old with dark hair streaked by gray strands. She displayed a firm and sometimes charming personality; but this wasn't one of those times. She had served as governor in the state of California for only two terms before Clifford Winifred requested her as his running mate. He chose her because she was female, which appealed to the progressives, and because she was repulsively conservative, pandering to another constituency. As an African-American, she helped capture the urban vote. But California's fifty-four electoral votes were her most appealing quality. This assured Winifred's election in a very close, three-way race. In his Inaugural speech, the President vowed to use the talents of the Vice President as an active partner to ease the burden of his office. After three years, that promise had yet to be realized. She walked up and stood behind one of two, seventh century rosewood chairs bound in aged leather and studded with hand-forged nails. She clutched the top of a chair, imbedding her nails into the leather. "Are we alone?" she asked.

The peregrine falcon peered at her from behind its wrought-iron bars. Like its relatives in the hawk family, the bird's intense vision focused in on one's eyes, searching for fear. Sorenson never liked the creature and couldn't understand why anyone could appreciate such an aloof animal that projected contempt with every glance. She felt President Winifred surrounded himself with scheming personalities--individuals as well as animals.

"What's that supposed to mean?" President Winifred replied.

"Is this conversation being recorded?"

"I record nothing in this office. You'll just have to take my word on it, Ms. Sorenson. This couldn't have been addressed at a Cabinet meeting?"

"No. It couldn't." She circled the chair and sat down, pausing to look at the front of the desk before turning up to confront the President. "I need to know what you're doing in the North Country. What's your intelligence?"

"Ms. Sorenson, our only contact up there was made ill by his ex-wife-- And where do you get off needing to know anything? Just get to the point. I've got too much to do, to be sitting here listening to this."

"I know about Dixville. And I know about AutoMan. This crusade you're on in the Northeast has to stop. The troops are needed in the Amur Valley. The Russian problem you got us involved in hasn't gone away."

"Is this a threat?"

Sorenson got up and walked to the double doors in back and turned for a final word, "Steve Morrison will have company slinging accusations your way. The rest of the media can't ignore the Vice President's claim as well. I think it would start a congressional investigation before the elections. That wouldn't be good." Margaret Sorenson knew Winifred would do anything to stay in office.

Secretary of Defense Kyle Paz waited for her just down the hall from the Oval Office. Nearly at attention with his hat tucked under his arm, he waited for the result of her meeting.

The narrow corridors of the White House were common places for staff to chat, sometimes jest, but often there were prearranged meetings among supposed passersby. The halls were a good place to speak of private things, a place without ears. Kyle strategically positioned himself in a blind spot where surveillance cameras couldn't record their meeting. If staff passed by, the conversation would shift to small talk.

As soon as Vice President Sorenson was close enough Kyle asked, "Did you record it?"

"Yes, but he didn't say anything," Sorenson replied. "He looked stressed. I'm certain he'll pull the troops out of the North Country. They need some downtime up there until we can sort things out."

"As I said, I couldn't allow this to go on. I appreciate your intervention, ma'am, and I'll keep you briefed--discreetly, of course." The General abruptly walked in the opposite direction, nodding to staffers approaching him in the hall.

Chapter 8

"Why do you want to use a laser sight on a rifle to communicate?" asked Helen. "Doesn't it bother you to have someone aiming at you with a rifle when they want to send a message?" Chaos had asked Helen to send a note to The Wizard requesting the schematic diagram of their laser device. The Southerner was preparing line-of-sight communications for their trip to Boston in March. He intended to use the laser sights on their rifles as a carrier beam. Helen glanced over to the Rousells with a stern look because they had led the Mountain Boys to Max's deer camp.

Chaos had learned about their laser communication system from the eleven new recruits Snake sent from Vermont's Northeast Kingdom. He thought the system could be used in battlefield communication. Until now, they had used high frequency whistles to stay in constant contact, but the range was limited.

Chaos had brought six men with him on his visit to Max's deer camp. All of them were armed with a rifle or autopistol. A heavy fellow, their technician, drew a schematic drawing of the device he thought would work, but he wanted a copy of The Wizard's plan.

Butch and Thad sat on the bunk in Max's tiny communication shack. It was standing room only. The weaponry of the soldiers mesmerized them. Three of the rebels had M-30 Strafers, complete with laser sight. Two others had longer barreled sniper rifles made in Israel: The Masada.

The Masada had three scopes: a day scope, a night scope, and a heat scope that were used to find their targets. A laser directed the projectile to the ruby-red hot point. Limbs unfolded from the barrel and butt to anchor the weapon securely. Two buttons controlled stepping motors for final adjustments. A small, on-board computer with a digital readout embedded in the stock, calibrated wind speed, barometric pressure, temperature, and trajectory; from this data, the computer made minute adjustments to the aim. The rifle wasn't designed to be held and fired, but could be. Its firing pin was triggered electronically by push button. Butch and Thad studied every detail of it--amazed by the size of the bullets on the belts looped over their shoulders.

Butch and Thad had often visited the Mountain Boys' campsites. Butch told his story of the Dixville Massacre to anyone who would listen, gaining new converts with every telling. In return, the Mountain Boys accepted them as one of theirs. They taught the boys their ultrasonic whistle signals and even gave them the mouth reeds and ear receivers to hear it with. The Mountain Boys whistled simple commands and used Morse Code for more complicated instructions. The Rousells used the whistles to send Tater commands; animals could hear the high pitch tone without a receiver.

Chaos had made a seven-mile trip on skis from Crystal Mountain to make the request. "It's simple, and we already have the laser sights on our rifles. You see, friendly fire is our worst enemy in our style of fightin'. Our boys overwhelm a point on the enemy's perimeter and raise hell from within, splitting up into teams and overpowering separate pockets of resistance. The enemy winds up shooting at themselves in the confusion. We need to know exactly where our boys are. The whistles are fine for close communication but we need something secure to send messages longer distances. I don't know why your people held this laser info so close to the chest. It's a closed system. Even if the Feds knew about it, they couldn't intercept it."

Chaos noticed the cable slithering from the back of the portable computer that led to the bottom of a closed window. He shook his head and smiled, "You folks are so clever. Shootin' a beam all the way to Island Pond. That's amazin'. That Wizard's quite a guy. I'm eager to meet him. He should be working for NASA or something."

"There you go. It's sent." Helen couldn't tell him very much about the laser system. She wasn't sure whether to trust them. The scene was intimidating, six formidable looking men dressed in white camouflage gear; they all stared down on her. Chaos seemed pleasant enough; Helen wanted to believe him. But she knew that Tumult, the man in charge of everything, was a racist, a chauvinist, and a jerk.

"Our technician thought the laser device could carry voice signals," Chaos continued. "We have enough components for say--six senders. A receiver node could be made of woven copper strands and used as a hat. I'd like to hear The Wizard's opinion on that."

The Rousell boys listened intently. They were caught up in the intrigue--Helen was more leery. She suspected Chaos had well over a hundred men, but she wanted to know. "If we somehow got the components in Boston, how many communication systems are we talking about?"

"About eighty for starters."

Helen looked down and nodded, "Will that number cover most of the Mountain Boys?" It was a cat and mouse game between Helen and Chaos.

Chaos squinted and thought before speaking. A smirk formed across his lips: "That would give one laser communicator to each attack pack in my group."

She looked out the window and pondered. She had no idea how large an attack pack was.

Helen's house (March 12)

Helen returned to her house after the Mountain Boys drove the Feds out of the North Country. It felt good to be surrounded by familiar antiquities--if only for a short while; she packed in preparation for their trip to Boston. Helen represented the Vermont and New Hampshire Covenants on the excursion. She was also in charge of the $980,000 brought to purchase supplies and weaponry.

With Max gone, Helen had ended up as Colebrook's Covenant leader. She hadn't sought the position, but the local Covenant, composed of Mrs. Larson, Harvey Madison, and Mr. and Mrs. Philbin, had chosen her. Vanessa Larson wanted the position but no one trusted her; Vanessa's passion for vengeance blurred her judgment. Helen had accepted the position, and in doing so, made a decision to get involved in the struggle. She just hadn't envisioned being in charge of it.

"Spectator News was the only major news organization to run your version of the Dixville Massacre," Steve Morrison stated flatly from Helen's porch. "We broke the story first."

"I appreciate the notion that you didn't let the facts ruin a perfectly good story. Look, I've got other things to do right now." Helen began closing the door. Steve stuck his boot in the crack. In answer, a 22-caliber barrel nosed through the crack of the door at his face. "I would appreciate it if you got your foot out of my door, buster!"

"You wouldn't shoot me, would you?"

"Do you want to find out?" Only a sliver of Helen's face could be seen and the deadly black hole of the barrel showed through the gap. "This is only a twenty-two, but it has Rhinos in it and it'll poke a hole in your face you'll really notice!"

"Hold it! Hold it! Your dog brought me here. See? The Rousell boys had me follow your dog here. Really." Steve didn't think she would shoot but he pulled his foot out of the door anyway. He had interviewed enough people in his career and instinctively knew when someone was serious--chewing his gum more vigorously now.

Helen widened the door and saw her dog Tater standing in fresh snow. The fluffy stuff lightly coated her back and head. "So, my dog finally came home." Then Helen got to thinking, "What boys?"

"Butch and his brother."

"Butch! Take off your gloves." He did, and exposed an ugly scar on his right thumb. Stitch marks remained from when he had had it taken care of by a doctor. "I hope he cut you deep."

"Deep enough to require stitches. Can I come in?"

She widened the door and dropped back into the kitchen. Tater bounded onto the porch and through the door. "Butch said he was just going to prick me to draw blood. That little prick pricked me all right."

Helen looked down at her watch. "You have five minutes and then you leave." Tater pranced in circles on her rug near the door and pawed at it before laying down. Small snowballs stuck to the longer hairs of her underbelly and legs. The golden retriever grunted as she hit the floor, planting her chin on her paws. Tater's eyes darted from Steve to Helen in an alert response to their curt discussion. "I have no idea what you want," she said.

Butch had told Steve Helen was the Akela, the leader of Ghost Pack 220. Steve thought this meant she headed Colebrook's rebel movement. But the reporter wondered when he found her alone at home. It never occurred to him that Butch was referring to his Scout leader, though in Butch's mind the commander of Ghost Pack 220 was of formidable stature.

Helen didn't look like a hardened leader. With the anxiety from Barry's death and her self-destructive fast, she had slimmed to the delicate weight of her younger years--displayed quite effectively through her thin, gray T-shirt and faded jeans.

Steve noticed. He also noticed the camping gear stacked in the room just off the kitchen. "You going somewhere?"

"What do you want?" She ignored the question.

"I want to know everything. The details. Everything. I want to talk to all the leaders of the Ghost Pack, the Mountain Boys, the Covenants; I want to be where the action is."

"To sell news stories."

"I don't deny that. This is my job."

"What about other journalists? What do they do?"

"I'm not them. I don't get into politics. I am completely unbiased."

Helen lowered her head and shook it. "I can't believe it, I almost fell for that line. Get out of my house!"

"Look, I'm not leaving here without a story." Steve Morrison sat down with a smug glint in his eyes and stared back at her. His gaze turned to astonishment when Helen lifted the revolver and blasted it by his head. The impact of the muzzle blast jolted him off his chair onto the floor. With wide eyes, Steve shook his head; he nearly choked on his gum. After regaining his voice, "Why'd you do that?"

The deafening boom of the small-caliber gun startled Helen, too. The blast inside the room contained the sound. In a jittery voice now, "If you don't get out of my kitchen, I'll shoot you where you sit!" Helen pointed the gun at the reporter. She knew she had to get rid of him before the Mountain Boys came to pick her up.

Steve went to the door. "You didn't have to get violent, lady! I'm trying to help you."

"I thought you were neutral."

"Fine, lady!"

Steve stepped onto the porch. As he tried to turn in retreat, two Glock 24 autopistols jabbed him on both sides of his neck like bookends. The men pinched the muzzles to his throat and pinned the reporter against the doorframe. One of the guys looked for a sign from the large, bearded man with a furrowed brow seated on a snowmobile parked in front of the place: Wolfenstein.

One of the original Tobacco Boys, Wolfenstein had fought with Tumult, Snake, and Chaos in the Carolinas. He had been at the forefront, second in command in Chaos' triad. Unlike Chaos, Wolf, as some called him, was quiet, mumbling out orders that were followed without question. He made no excuses, nor did he accept excuses from subordinates. Wolfenstein was noted for his intolerance. Most rebels thought of him as mean.

"You're early," Helen said, surprised to see him.

Wolf didn't reply, just continued his examination of his captive. He uttered simply, "We heard a shot."

"It was nothing. He was just leaving."

"Do you always shoot at your guests?" Wolf yelled from his snowmobile.

"He's a reporter," Helen replied.

"That explains it." Wolfenstein nodded to the soldiers to grab the reporter. Rebels escorted him off the porch with gun barrels still pressed to Steve's neck. "We'll take care of it from here, Ma'am."

"What do you mean?" Helen wanted clarification.

"Ma'am, he knows too much."

"You're going to kill him? He doesn't know anything about what we're doing."

"He can see the packed snow machines and sleds. He knows we're on the move." Wolfenstein turned his back to her and calmly watched his rebels tie up the reporter.

"Let's see what Chaos says," Helen contested.

"Yes, ma'am."

Helen looked back at the row of armed men mounted on snow machines.

Chaos zipped toward them from the back of the caravan. He pulled up to the porch, only to find himself rushed by Helen pleading for the life of the reporter. Chaos looked at Wolfenstein as Helen talked to him. Wolfenstein shrugged.

"Hold it. Hold it." Chaos raised his hands. "Please." He looked to Helen, "Wolf wouldn't hurt anyone." Chaos got off his snowmobile and headed toward Steve Morrison.

On hearing the comment, Helen turned to look at Wolfenstein, the man now standing by his vehicle, wiping snow of gauges. Wolfenstein towered to six foot, four; topped with massive shoulders and a burly face, hair ran down his neck and into his coat. He held a Glock autopistol with a thirty-three round clip extending out the handle; an M-30 Strafer rifle was strapped over his shoulder. "You have got to be kidding," she muttered to herself. For a reason she couldn't define, Helen trusted Chaos to do the right thing.

"Spectator News was the first to break the Dixville story. I'm on your side," Steve pleaded with the Southerner. "Jesus! They're not really going to kill me, are they? I'm just a journalist."

"I can't let you go," said Chaos.

"I want to go with you. Think of me as insurance, a way to document what really happens. Otherwise the public only hears the White House spin on things."

Chaos loved seeing Steve squirm. Rebels hated the press, reporters always twisted the truth to fit their political persuasion. "A patrol saw you with the Rousell boys on Dixville Mountain a while back. Did those boys cut you?"

The reporter forced a smile, "They got me good." He pulled off a glove and showed him.

Chaos hadn't planned on hurting Steve, but he wanted to scare him enough to discourage the reporter from giving Spectator News information detrimental to their cause, if given the opportunity. Chaos didn't trust the reporter to keep his oath made to the Ghost Pack. "Thomas Paine said: 'Reputation is what men think of us; character is what God knows of us.' I realize honor and integrity may be new concepts to you boys in the media, but you're bound by the Ghost Pack Oath. If you betray us, there will be no place on the earth you can hide. You will do exactly as Wolfenstein says; you'll be with his attack pack. If you're seen making radio or phone contacts without clearing it with him, Wolf will decide what to do with you. Is that understood?"

"I understand."

"Then, welcome to the Mountain Boys." Two men with scarred thumbs shook hands as puffy snowflakes fell about them. The vague outline of Dixville Notch posed an ominous reminder of their fragile alliance.

Chaos walked back to the skidoos and ordered two men to take the reporter in the house to check him for radio devices and equip him with a white parka and proper footwear. "We got to get out of here while we still have the cover of snow blocking Hawkeye."

Hawkeye was the name the Mountain Boys had given to a spy satellite positioned over the region. An unscheduled launch at Cape Kennedy in December caused Snake to believe the Feds launched it just for them. He claimed he hadn't seen that satellite up there before. So Chaos took no chances; they waited until cloud cover to travel. Even nighttime wasn't good enough. They speculated that the satellite might be equipped with thermoscopes that could spot clusters of people moving on the ground by tracing body heat.

Butch and Thad emerged on skis from their trail through the hemlocks. Tater bounced off the porch to greet them. With tail wagging, she pushed her head into a flurry of patting hands. Chaos came over to greet the Rousells.

"I got E-mail yesterday from The Wizard," Butch reported to Chaos. "He's on his way to Boston and said he would try to work on a phone link and send me a note while he's there. He said he'll meet you at Union Wharf on the 17th."

"And I don't know what he looks like," Chaos responded.

"He'll know you." The Mountain Boys were out of their element in Boston; the inner city was nearly all African-American.

Chaos just smiled. Butch had begged him to go with them a week earlier.

He knew the boy was being coy. Butch had met The Wizard; yet he never disclosed details about him. The Rousells maintained their allegiance to Helen, despite their awe of the armed fighters.

Two rebels carried Helen's gear out and packed it on a sled. She found a spot to sit on top and tightened up her white parka in preparation for the trip. Butch, Thad, and Tater approached her.

"Any orders for us while you're gone?" Butch asked.

"Yes. Don't talk to any more reporters, Butch. You almost got the guy killed. And don't go around cutting people. Keep that knife in your pocket."

Helen waited for some kind of finality. "What is it?" The boys gave a Scout salute. Helen hesitated but finally did a halfhearted salute of her own. After an awkward pause, Thad gave Helen a hug. She instinctively returned the squeeze, absorbing the sensation of little arms looped about her neck-- the small, vulnerable frame of a child. A swarm of memories returned--of Barry--of sunny days. She wiped a tear from her eye with her mitten. "We gotta go while the snow flies." She sniffed and avoided looking up at them as the boys walked off. "Hey," she called after them, "you boys take care of one another. And take care of Tater for me," Tater still sat resolutely beside her sled. The golden retriever looked up at Helen with a trusting lap-dog grin. Helen shook her head no, "Sorry girl. You have to stay."

Helen patted Tater on the head. She had warmed up to the animal since the Dixville ordeal. Tater reminded her of Barry; the dog and boy had been inseparable. But taking the dog to Boston wouldn't be right. And Thad, needed the companionship more than she did.

Butch led Tater off and waited by Max's truck. They waved good-bye as the procession of snowmobiles with sleds took off down the trail. Two or three people rode on each rig. Chaos was in the middle of the pack and gave the boys a thumbs up and winked as he roared by. Butch and Thad returned the signal. Other soldiers did the same, the boys returning the sign as each passed. Helen responded with a wave and a restrained smile as the caravan trailed off through puffy flakes and disappeared into the forest.

Butch and Thad watched the sound until it diminished into the distance. They looked at one another, then down at Tater. Thad nodded to Butch.

Butch understood, "Right, Thad. They ain't seen the end of us." He pulled an electronic notepad out of his pocket and turned it on. A note appeared: *Union Wharf, Boston.* "Nope, they ain't seen the end of us."

Chapter 9

Chaos' company traveled in groups of about fifty each, on different routes toward the coast of Maine. Point teams with cash in-hand forged ahead to secure trucks and vans for transport in Portland. The groups communicated only with the laser transmitters, devices the technician had managed to rig on riflescopes. Point troopers for each company would laser information back to the headgear of someone in each group, but the communicator only worked if there was direct line-of-sight. Maine's flatlands made it difficult to get enough elevation to scope-in the receiver and speak to them. Snowmachines blazed a trail as the rest of the expedition used cross-country skis.

They weren't the redneck dolts Helen thought them to be. Many of them were from the North Country. They ranged in age from seventeen to thirty. A surprising number were from the Midwest. She recognized three young men from Colebrook. They greeted her by name. When they spoke to Helen, or even Steve, they used Ma'am or Sir. They were a disciplined lot who appeared to be in good condition, skiing thirty miles the first day proved that.

Point teams prepared camp and collected firewood; cloud cover allowed them to have a fire that night. When Helen's group arrived in the valley, a warm yellow glow seeped through the trees ahead. A spot had been cleared in the snow for Helen's tent. One of the young men detached a tent and flung it into the air where it instantly uncoiled into a five-man tent, her quarters for the night. Steve Morrison had to bunk up with four rebels; he was expected to endure the austere conditions the fighting men did.

After dinner, everyone sat around the many campfires and chatted or listened to CB radio skip. Most listened to channel 6, The Wizard's station. Tonight, their guest host was 606 from South Carolina, a prerecorded broadcast.

Steve Morrison sat beside Helen at a fire. The reporter still brooded over the incident at Helen's house. "This must be the most idiotic thing I've ever done in my career--what's left of a career--if I survive this. Hell, we could be jumped by Army Rangers right now and shot." Helen gave him a perturbed glance. "What?" Steve didn't understand. "I know you people lost a lot in the Dixville Massacre, but going up against the government is pointless. You must realize you can't win."

"I guess it doesn't matter anymore. When my son's life was taken, so was mine." Helen turned and looked squarely at the reporter, "Have you ever loved someone so deeply? No parent should ever outlive their child."

"Well, I don't know--"

"No. You don't know. If you knew, you wouldn't be sitting here whining. What happens to me doesn't matter. The Feds did more than murdered sixty-four kids; they crushed our dreams. They took our children. They violated our homes." Helen shook her head, "And we're pissed. We are *so* pissed! There's your story, reporter. Write it down." Helen reached into her coat pocket and pulled out a electronic notepad, "Here. Use this."

Steve took it from her and began scribbling down the words, then stopped. He looked up like a scolded puppy. "I don't need to write it down. I'll remember."

The exchange between Helen and Steve had stilled other conversations around them. Only distant mumbling could be heard at other fire circles. Eventually, Steve struck up conversation again by asking rebels around the fire where they were from. One young man said he was from North Carolina, another, Georgia. Crucible was the youngest of the original Tobacco Boys who survived the Tobacco Wars. Still freckle faced at 20 years old, in a southern drawl, Crucible declared his home was Colebrook.

"How's that?" Morrison questioned because the southern accent was obvious.

"It's like the boss says," the rebel quoted Chaos, "you know you're home when you're willing to fight for it." The lad looked at Helen, "Right here's our home, Ma'am. We're here for *you*." Other rebels at the fire circle nodded in agreement.

Chaos entered the group and poured a steaming cup of tea from a metal pot poised at the edge of the fire. He looked around cautiously; lively discussion was absent here. He brought the tea to Helen. "Hi. I thought you might appreciate some warm, mint tea. Keep your gloves on, it's a little hot." He sat down beside her. "This time of day is nice. If there's cloud cover, we sit around the fire and shoot the bull. Someone usually has a comment about Crucible over there. With those freckles, it looks like he stood behind the wrong cow."

"Thank you." She smiled. The steamy cup radiated between her hands as she huddled to the glow of the campfire; damp March air swiped her back. The rebels' confirmation of their devotion to the Covenant's cause had suddenly bolstered her spirit. To that point, she had felt alone, many miles from home.

Most of the Tobacco Boys had come to the North Country after hearing The Wizard's broadcasts about families left shattered from the Massacre. Helen had met Chaos only twice before this. He charmed everyone. Helen also felt the allure: His good looks weren't the only attraction; he was mysterious in his own way, never really talking about himself. His philosophical quotes showed he was a thinker, possibly well educated--not like Tumult and Snake, the white trash that led the other factions. Chaos seemed kind.

The incident at her house that morning disturbed her; she had never seen the warrior side of this group. Helen realized the Tobacco Bunch were responsible for hundreds of casualties in their own uprising and wondered if they would have ordered the reporter killed or if it was all an act.

"This is as good a time as any to ask," said Helen. "How will you get Max out?"

"Well," an awkward hesitation ensued, "Ah...I could show you."

Helen glanced at Steve.

Steve blurted, "I don't think it's likely I'll sneak off to a pay phone out here and warn anyone." Steve looked past the Southerner's charm; he hadn't forgotten about the incident that morning.

"I'm sorry, you're absolutely right. It's not likely you would tell anyone of the plan, but it is possible. The fact is, only five others and myself in this expedition know where we're going and what we're there for. What the soldiers don't know they can't tell. It's not that they're traitors to the cause, it's just that the Feds have been known to use chemicals to jog memories. At least that happened to us in the Tobacco Wars."

"Can the Federal Government drug prisoners like that?" the reporter questioned.

"Mr. Morrison, you haven't had the pleasure of meeting Tumult, my overseer. Unlike myself, he is compelled to quote Adolph Hitler. His response to you would be: 'You stand there with your law. I stand here with my sword. We shall see who prevails.'"

The reporter quipped back, "But Hitler didn't prevail."

"I disagree with Tumult's ideology. But, sir, that fanatical little Nazi got beaten by the sword."

Chaos turned and led Helen to his tent on the edge of the encampment. Inside, he pulled a pocket computer from a front pack beneath his coat and laid the unit near a larger unrolled view screen. The vinyl-like monitor glowed when receiving the signal, displaying what appeared on the small PC. He brought up a map of the compound in Boston where the Feds held Max.

Helen preempted the Southerner's briefing, "I want to get something straight: We're getting Max, right?"

"Correct. Attack packs will take you and Max out of the city immediately. Another group will remain behind as a distraction."

"One other thing bothers me," Helen continued. "This seems to be a large group of well-trained fighters here. Why so many?"

"E-mail from The Wizard said that there were a number of large gangs in Boston. If they are united under one leader as they were awhile back, this endeavor might be in jeopardy. Our mission is twofold: One, to gain custody of Colebrook's Covenant Leader; and two, to purchase as many armaments as we can carry back. If we run into a problem, I want enough forces to deal with it."

"One of Colebrook's Covenant Leaders? You make my brother sound like a military objective."

"He is a military objective, Ma'am. Honest leadership is a treasure in these times. Getting him out of Boston and back to the North Country is our first priority." Chaos turned his attention back to the view screen and began explaining the map.

Helen watched distantly and rubbed her hands on the sides of her snowsuit. She felt a streak of uncertainty race through her--the very thought of attacking a Federal compound. "Excuse me. How many guards are there at this compound?"

"It's a small compound. About thirty to forty in all, with perimeter guards armed with Colt pistols."

"How can we be sure this is going to succeed?"

"We can't be sure it's going to succeed." Chaos waited for Helen to absorb this possibility. "It's natural to have last-minute shakes. I assure you, Ma'am, we plan to go in cleanly and come out cleanly. We're not looking to shoot guards just doing their jobs. If there's a mishap though, we will have the forces to secure an exit out of the area. The other team leaders and myself have learned a lot from The Wizard about the city. Our connection with him there is crucial." Helen nodded her head and looked at the map on screen.

"The plan is simple." Chaos continued. "Two of our boys go in as Max's attorneys. They'll be placed in a private room for a conference. Our men will overpower the guard at the door and tie him up inside the room. They'll signal us at the window so we know where they are, we'll get them out of there with a tether stretched to another building. They'll be on the ground at the secured end of the tether ten seconds after the window is taken out. Perimeter guards will be held at bay with cover fire."

"It sounds easy."

"You need to understand, Ma'am, that the Federal Government is a huge bumbling bureaucracy, manned by very complacent, pencil pushers. That's why this country is the way it is."

"I'm sorry," said Helen. "I guess I am getting the last-minute jitters. This whole trip to Boston isn't what I thought it would be. I expected a small crack team would quietly go in and come back out--something more sophisticated."

"That's why you're fortunate to have me." Chaos grinned. "You're just having honeymoon jitters. Once the strike team penetrates the compound and executes the plan, you'll wonder how we ever pulled it off."

Helen and Chaos stood awkwardly as they gazed down at the screen that lit up their faces with its chill-blue glow. "If that's it, I guess I'll turn in." She started to go but wondered, "Do you have family in the Carolinas?"

Chaos directed her to a bundle to sit. He found himself a spot on an ammo box. Chaos started with his life as a boy on his father's tobacco farm: He spoke about his brothers and the shenanigans they got into, the Sunday afternoon church socials, the volleyball and softball games. It was a reflection of gentler days when his family lived in the same house; the three brothers conspired together in mischief--and sometimes fought. "The Tobacco Tax broke my Momma and Pappy. The Feds kept saying 'grow corn, grow cotton.' It's not that simple when everything on the farm is geared for growing one crop. It's quite an investment to re-equip a whole farm, especially when there's no money to do it with. Like many others in the Carolinas, we sold some of our tobacco on the black market to help feed ourselves. When the Feds came and confiscated the farm, it broke my folks' hearts. It killed my Pappy; he stopped working altogether--died a year later." Chaos stopped a moment before saying it, "Shot himself, actually. From that point on, my brothers and I went from raising tobacco, to raising hell."

She hesitated to ask, "And your brothers?"

"Well, let's just say they're doing their part for the cause." Chaos couldn't tell her Tumult and Snake were his brothers. Everyone concealed their identity using nicknames; relatives were never spoken of.

Helen winced. She found solace by sharing hardships. A veiled force tugged tears from the edge of her eyes. It made her reflect on her own plight. Her question had been answered: Why these Southerners were here to help them. They shared the same heartache, the same enemy.

"Ma'am, we didn't get to the North Country by accident. We came out of the Oke Swamp in Georgia and heard about the Scout Massacre through The Wizard's CB skip. Feds used those AutoMen against us in our fight; we knew what it was like in Dixville. Nothing human could have been that merciless. I convinced Tumult we belonged here. Besides, being around you people helped us forget about our problems. I know about your loss, Ma'am. And I feel it is particularly difficult for the mothers of those boys. Their bond is much closer." He quoted a portion of a poem he had written:

"There is a place in mothers' memories
where ageless children say kind words,
when aspirations pause
and life alone enjoyed."

She wiped her eyes and smiled in relief. The words sent chills through her. His verse described her condition exactly; the difficult trials of parenting had faded. Brighter scenes remained. "I guess I owe you an apology. I thought you guys were a bunch of disgruntled rednecks. But how did you link up with someone like Tumult, and where do you guys get these names?"

"Everybody has a--well, call it a soldier's name, so the Feds can't trace us to our folks back home. As for my name, it kinda came about because of the combat tactics I use. My real name is Virgil. Please call me Chaos. Say what you want about Tumult, but you want him on your side. Granted, he's a Nazi and a racist, but in a fight he's exactly as his name predicts. He started the Tobacco Wars. They were called the Tobacco Boys back then." Chaos smiled reminiscing. "My brothers brought me into the group the day I graduated from the Citadel."

"I've heard of that," said Helen.

"What you heard about it was gracious, I'm sure. Everything I learned there about tactics and strategy was worthless after doing maneuvers with the Tobacco Boys. They started out as a paintball league, you know." Helen nodded. "Oh, yeah," continued Chaos, "they fight in packs of twelve to penetrate enemy lines, then they shoot 'em up from the inside. The Feds wind up shooting their own guys with friendly fire while the Tobacco Boys know exactly where their troops are because of our communication systems. Communication is critical with that type of helter-skelter combat. Tumult's paintball league developed that fighting style and with it, we've pushed back Guard battalions ten times our size in the Tobacco Wars, inflicting tremendous casualties."

"Your group doesn't seem to be racist like the others."

"Oh, I'm not one of them. Tumult's part of the triad shares the Klan's mind-set. Snake is more reasonable. One thing's for sure, Ma'am: You want these SOBs killing their people and not our people. When the smoke clears and fair government is restored, they can go back to their paintball tournaments and the keg parties that follow."

"I know you're sincere but I have trouble sharing your optimism."

"Despair makes optimists of us all. I have no other course."

Helen felt a sense of security with Chaos. She was attracted to his brown eyes and sincere disposition--and of course, his charm. The incident at the house had bothered her earlier, the fact that he might be a wanton killer beneath the Southern chivalry. But that had been laid to rest tonight. He was compelling in a quiet way; she understood why he had the trust and loyalty of his young rebels.

Toward the end of their visit they kissed, but like the Southern gentlemen he was, it went no further. His powerful arms wrapped around her, made her feel secure. Even though the threat of an Army reprisal was always there, she had a protector, Chaos: the philosopher, the poet, the warrior.

Tumult's Attack Packs in Old Boston (the evening of March 15)

Four rebels held a captured gang member down and outstretched his palms as Demig drove a 20-penny spike through the Black man's flesh into a sheet of three-quarter-inch plywood.

"Ahhhhh! I can't tell you what I don't know. Please! Please! I can't help you. The gang leaders were Sable, Pumice, and Tar. I told you that." The gang member turned the other way as Demig held the nail to the pad of the other hand and solidly swatted the spike with the hammer through flesh and bone into the wood below. "Ahhhhh!" The victim's face beaded with sweat. His mind raced to understand why the southerners tortured him--"Sable's place is on Washington Avenue. I told you that."

Tumult's Mountain Boys had occupied a rundown housing project in the heart of Boston. Dark, sooted buildings exposed the structures' jagged features: broken windows, fallen sections of brick, crude textures of masonry. Gads of CB antennas pointed to hope across the skyline.

Spiked to the plywood and looking up at a water-stained ceiling, the Black man regretted pulling a gun on one of the rebels. Now, dull light from a propane lantern illuminated the walls with a beige glow. The people before the lamp performed their macabre drama on the shadowy wall, where black-hearted antagonists acted out a ghastly scene. He watched the prone silhouette on the wall and wondered if it was really him.

"You told us that before," said Demig. He walked over to Tumult who instructed a recruit, and waited for a break in conversation, "Sir, I don't think he knows rat shit."

Tumult ignored Demig and continued instruction. A few minutes later, the recruit returned to his pack, leaving Demig and Tumult alone: "Well," said Tumult, "finish him off by nailing down his feet." He thought a bit. "And put one through his face. Sink the head of the nail right to the cheekbone. I can't stand a man that whines." Tumult turned about, ready to check out another attack team.

"But, sir. He doesn't know."

Tumult nodded his head and paused. "That's not the point." He explained in a quiet, polite manner, "See, we're establishing relations with the indigenous people here. When the gangs see us on their turf, I want them cowering in corners, not taking potshots at us from windows and doorways. That spiked up afro will send a message to all the monkeys out there, and in turn, we'll have fewer casualties. When I'm finished, they'll be giving us all their motor-guns."

"I see."

"Well, that's the problem, Demig. You don't see."

"Sir?"

"How long have you been with me?"

"Three years."

"I would think by now you would know you don't question the chief's orders."

"Sorry, sir."

"Demig, you're a valuable fighter. In fact, you're like a little brother to me, but don't question my judgment again or your ass will be nailed to a board, too."

"Yes, sir." And Demig knew he meant it; he knew what Tumult was capable of.

Tumult's technician, Glitch, stood out of hearing as Demig finished his conversation. Unlike most of the men in all three units of the Triad, Glitch was pushing sixty years of age. Though not officially a commander, technicians were respected and gave orders because of their vital importance to the group. They stayed out of firefights, going into risky situations only to fix tactical gadgetry. Glitch was lean, and a heavy smoker. Deep wrinkles streaked his face and neck, particularly his forehead when he squinted or smiled. He had previously worked outdoors as a power-line repairman. Glitch was an amiable man and beyond those years of having to prove himself to anyone. "Excuse me, sir," he said to Tumult who turned to face him. "I'm getting a jamming signal to the northwest, bearing 315 degrees. The signature matches our equipment."

Tumult put his hands on Glitch's shoulders, squinting his eyes as a snake-lipped smile formed, "Chaos is on his way. Is it so close that we can't listen to local radio?"

"We can get local stations."

"Glitch, let's you and I go in and roll ourselves a smoke and listen to what the media says is happening. Then I'll make my guess at what that sly son-of-a-bitch is up to." They walked to the back room, Tumult's arm over the older man's shoulder as though they were old pals.

Chaos' triad was to rendezvous in Lexington. The local sheriff had become suspicious of the group of young men around town and had done a photo ID check through Fednet; Helen and Chaos' faces had been matched. The Mountain Boys fled Lexington but the Feds had been alerted, closing in on them by ground and air. Chaos' had left an attack pack of Virginians as a decoy. As the Virginians headed east, the larger force of rebels had gone west to catch Highway 90 to Boston.

With their frequency jammer signal, the Virginian attack pack had lured the Army east to the Walden Pond area. They had taken the side roads mostly, eventually pulling their gear, and walking through wetlands and timber stands. Army Regulars surrounded them. Three rebel snipers outside the encirclement, armed with Masadas, had shot nine Army Regulars from three hundred and eighty meters out. Government soldiers who saw their buddies beside them slump dead, fired more vigorously at the larger group before them; the Army recruits had no idea snipers had shot them from behind. A nine man attack pack broke through the perimeter and had begun eating away at both sides of the circle, all the while, snipers in the distant hills really did the dirty deed. By the end of the skirmish, 31 Regulars lay dead, only three of the Virginians had been taken captive, and two rebels had made it past Army Regulars and headed to Boston.

As Tumult and Glitch walked to the back room to listen to the Government version of events at Walden Pond, Demig stood reluctantly considering the gruesome task of nailing up the African-American's feet. Feeling a bit squeamish on returning, he stuffed the Black man's mouth with a used hanky and set out spiking the feet into the board. Finally, he drove a spike through the cheek bone as two more men stopped the victim's head from bobbing. The boy-faced rebels subduing the victim kept checking each other's expressions for some reaction of protest.

Chapter 10

Helen and Chaos' company found a place to sleep the next night in a large abandoned church tucked among rundown townhouses. Narrow streets laced the area. Beside the church's double doors, the engraved *A.D. 1887* announced the building's permanence despite the decay around it. The chapel's gray stone construction, now colored black from years of pollution, was stacked four stories high and spanned nearly a quarter block. It still served as a refuge for those in need. Inside, laminated arches spanned the sixty-foot ceiling--the stale aroma of old. Ornate carvings of Angels watched from above, as did a house sparrow, nestled in a grassy pocket on the ceiling. The broken panel at the top of a leaded glass window was the sparrow's only escape.

Four model planes, wingspans each stretching eight feet, loaded with explosives had been brought from the trucks and hung on the walls. All were named after inconsequential birds: a smaller aircraft called the Starling, a black-capped plane called Chickadee, the bicolor gray and white Junco, and then the Sparrow. The technology came from Snake's element of the Triad in Vermont. They flew the models visually using infrared transmitters.

At 5:00 a.m. the next morning Helen attended a meeting with Chaos and his attack pack leaders. She listened to him lay out a tentative plan: The first day, they would purchase electronic parts for laser senders and receivers to maintain secure communications in the city; then locate for purchase motor-guns from a cooperative gang; and rescue Max from the Federal Building the second day and go.

It was an ambitious first day but they didn't know if the Feds knew they were actually in Boston, or realized the sheer size of their expedition--about three hundred in Chaos' group alone. Chaos wanted to complete his business and get out quickly, knowing that the Feds would eventually decipher their coded radio signals. For all they knew, the Feds could be preparing to blockade the city.

Helen rode the streets of the Back Bay section of Boston in a semi-truck filled with three attack packs. The New Hampshire Covenant maintained control of the money through Helen. Wolfenstein was in charge of tactical decisions.

Wolf rode in the cab with Helen. Any conversation Helen initiated with the man ended in "yep," or "nope," or other short responses. Helen thought it might have been because she was the only woman on an excursion of all men, but Wolfenstein was that way with everyone.

The driver of the rig, Crucible, was sociable. The awkward, freckled-faced young man was more inclined to talk about himself and the events at hand, foregoing the quiet, macho routine Helen saw in the pack leaders. "This is the first time I've ever been in a big city. I'd hate to get lost here," stated Crucible.

"It's not so bad once you learn a few of the major arteries." Helen navigated the group using a detailed, city map on a pocket computer. Every street was marked.

Crucible chattered about the Tobacco War, his home in South Carolina; a friendly, gullible young man, he hadn't stopped talking since Helen had initiated the conversation. Helen asked him if he really might settle in Colebrook.

"I found my home," Crucible replied soundly. "My home is the Pack. And of course, the Pack is stationed in Colebrook. We share a common cause."

Wolfenstein pulled his gaze from the passing buildings and looked across the cab at the young man.

Crucible clarified his statement. "Well, it is." Wolf turned his gaze back to the window.

One thing was for sure: Wolfenstein was no dolt. He watched everything. When they passed a metal fabrication shop, he stopped and took Helen inside and purchased 2' x 8' sheets of plate steel to line the inside of the truck. Helen paid while Wolfenstein directed a welder to cut anchor holes in the iron for mounting. In forty minutes they were off again, heading to an electronic wholesale house The Wizard had indicated.

Problems arose on their return to the church. The Wizard's directions seemed to take them out of their way; from the map, Helen could see a much shorter way back to the church. She convinced Wolfenstein to take the shorter route through the heart of town.

The ambush happened on Washington Avenue, southwest of Old Boston. Members of Tar's gang saw white guys in the truck cruising the strip and phoned ahead with cellulars. A motor-gun pummeled the driver's side blowing apart Crucible instantly. Wolfenstein took a hit to the forearm and dropped to the floor, pulling Helen down with him. Wolf pushed the brake pedal by hand; the truck skidded to a stop.

Steam oozed out of the front of the truck. The mist hissed, and meandered upward from an apparently lifeless hulk. Six lanky gang members dressed in spandex with turned up baseball hats approached the rig cautiously. An alien silence reigned, but not for long. The gang members flinched as they heard the accordion door roll open at the back of the truck. They all aimed that direction while glancing skittishly at the cab windows. The man with the motor-gun in the gang revved the Husqvarna two-cycle engine and grinned.

At a dead run, three Mountain Boys leaped like gazelles out the back of the truck and shot in mid-air, taking out two and wounding two more before even setting foot on pavement. They continued sprinting for cover behind vehicles fifteen meters down the street. Four more Mountain Boys followed, but this time they dropped straight down and shot from behind the rear wheels of the truck. As the man with the motor-gun tried to follow the sprinters down the street, a myriad of bullets from the second team of gunners vented him, leaving him dead where he stood. At least one motor-gun was now in their possession. One gang member escaped up an alley. It all happened in two seconds--choreographed death as an art form.

Wolfenstein whistled for someone to come to the cab. A young, long-legged rebel named Bird Dog opened the door. "What's the status?" asked Wolf.

"One of them went up an alley."

"Get 'em, Bird Dog."

Bird Dog flipped a lever ejecting the 33-round clip from the bottom of his Glock 24 and shoved a fresh one in the handle as he rounded the front of the truck in an accelerating sprint down the alley. Helen began crawling out the door of the cab. Wolf grabbed her belt and kept her in. "You keep your ass on the floor."

"What!"

"*I* handle the skirmishes." Wolf moaned as he crawled over her, oblivious to the blood streaming down his arm. "If you have a problem with that, take it up with the boss when we get back."

Wolf looked around Helen at Crucible and saw the slumped body over the steering wheel with multiple holes through his face and head. Wolf's face muscles went limp. He sighed, "Get into Crucible's side pack there and pull out the red disk case." Helen timidly unzipped and dug through the side pack, eventually finding the red case and handing it to the pack leader. Wolfenstein then pulled out a sterilized wrap from his side pack and bound his arm, tying it with his teeth and remaining hand. "Much obliged," he mumbled as he walked to the back of the truck. He left Helen alone in the cab with the bloody corpse.

Still in shock, Helen reached up to feel Crucible's carotid for any sign of life. After actually looking at the young man's head, she realized how stupid it was to check for a pulse; his head was nearly fragmented by motor-gun balls. She slumped back to the floor, "Oh, God," she muttered, wondering about the significance of the memory disk.

Bird Dog sprinted down the alley. As legman of an attack pack, his job was to sprint ahead of the group to capture and hold a tactical position, or to run down strays like this. Legmen were lean and in good aerobic condition.

Bird Dog spotted a blood trail halfway down the alley and stopped abruptly at a dumpster. He held his breath a second and listened--and heard a voice.

A black face popped out from the edge of the doorway with a cellular in one hand. He spotted Bird Dog and shot four rounds in his direction, pinging the dumpster with each round.

Bird Dog stuck his gun out shooting five rounds back, followed by gunning-to-the-source, the technique of walking toward the target using constant gun fire to keep them at bay--shooting at any head or hand poking out of cover. Bird Dog chipped away at the brick's edge en route, finally closing in and shooting the victim with three rounds at point-blank range. Black Rhino bullets shredded on impact, tearing large portions of bone from the victim's skull. Blood and human tissue plastered the cove where the gang member lay.

The African-American sat slumped in the entrance clutching a Mexican version of a Beretta in one hand and a cellular phone in the other. A balky voice squawked from the telephone. Bird Dog picked it up. "Hello."

"Who the hell is this?" an authoritative voice asked from the other end.

"This is Bird Dog, sir. Who is this?"

"What kind of stupid name is that?"

"Ah, well--"

"Did you kill my boy?"

"I'm sorry, I had to, sir. I was taking fire and my orders were to stop his escape."

"What gang are you?"

Bird Dog paused a second and looked at the scar on his right thumb. "Ghost Pack 220, sir."

"You son-of-a-bitch! You're outa town. You wait right there, I'm going to come over and shoot your ass myself." The line went dead.

In the main chapel of the church, Helen and Wolf sat to the side; others went about their own business. The hum of varied noises squelched private conversations. "I'm so sorry this happened," Helen said as she bound up Wolf's arm; she had no idea changing the route would cause such a catastrophe. The motor-gun ball had gone in just below Wolf's elbow and came out near his wrist.

Wolfenstein held his arm suspended in mid-air; he hadn't flinched through the cleaning or wrap-up but now his pain showed. Speckles of sprayed blood from balls whipping into Crucibles' head spattered Wolfenstein's face and beard. "They just started shootin'," he said.

Helen sighed with a crack in her voice as she spoke, " . . . and that poor boy."

"Name was Crucible."

"What?"

"We called him Crucible because he went into the fire and came out unscathed. He was right beside me when we escaped the Feds by goin' through the Oke swamps. Some of them got alligatored or just plain lost from the group, but Crucible stayed right by me. Did exactly as I told him. He was a good fighter, Ma'am. You could always trust Crucible to hold up his end. He wouldn't back off for nothin'. It wasn't right that those Afros just shot him like that. I'm pissed off. I'm sorry, I usually don't talk that way in front of a lady but he was a good boy. He shouldn't have been gunned down like that. Is that the way these Afros fight down here, just haul off and shoot somebody for just driving down the street? They don't know us from Adam."

"Well, I don't--"

"I mean, even if they were out to hijack the truck, they didn't have to shoot the driver. You think they just shot him 'cause he was a white boy? There were other trucks on that road."

"Probably not. Maybe it was the out-of-state plates."

"He must have had six holes in his head before you could even blink. I'm not pleased about this. Not pleased at all."

Helen gave up trying to join his soliloquy conversation. He hadn't heard her. This was the most she had ever heard Wolfenstein speak. Helen saw the sentimental side of the gruff, bearded man, but the vengeful rhetoric that followed, frightened her. She attempted to change topics. "How did you get this scar?" Helen referred to the one on his thumb pad she found while cleaning him up.

Wolfenstein looked at her strangely. "We get cuts all the time, ma'am."

Chaos walked by, "Wolf, I need to talk to you a minute." The two of them walked to the back of the chapel, and ascended a flight of stairs to the second level, and stood at the top of the landing. "I'd like to find out why you came back a different route from the electronics supply outlet. The route through Old Boston was out of your way, you know. You had no trouble getting there."

Wolf blinked several times. The blood loss, along with the walk upstairs, made him woozy. He hesitated, and looked down on Chaos saying, "I'm sorry, sir. I screwed up."

"I'm not lookin' to place blame, Wolf."

Wolf's tone became harsh. "I'm not lookin' to place blame either, sir. It's my responsibility."

"I understand. Enough said," Chaos nodded. Many people across the country considered the rebel forces from the North Country, terrorists. 'Integrity has no need of rules,' Albert Camus had said. Like Chaos, Wolfenstein fought for what was right. Chaos never questioned that; it's just that Wolf was unable to express himself.

Chaos turned and went down the steps he had come up. He suspected that Helen had something to do with the decision; she had the map of the city. But ultimately, Wolf was in charge; and he knew procedure. At the top of the narrow staircase, dimly lit by a small octagon window above, Wolfenstein paused in the glow of variegated blues from the leaded glass. The typical stagnant smells of a closed up building filled it all--muffled voices drifted up from the chapel. Wolf hung his head in regret.

Helen had had no idea that each soldier prepared their own letters home in the event of their death. She found a memory disk inside a red carrying case on a table in the chapel and thought it might have been the one that belonged to Crucible. She put it in a pocket computer and viewed it:

Dear Ambrosia,

I am Randall Colby, you might remember me from high school. If you receive this note it means I've passed away. My pack leader told us to prepare a letter to our loved ones; you came to mind.

I'm not sending this to you to make you feel guilty or to imply that you thought you were better than others. To the contrary: You're a special soul that radiates goodness beyond your physical beauty. This letter is to let you know who I am and what I've done, and that I wasn't the geek in high school everyone thought I was. You are now the protector of my secrets and the keeper of my most cherished thoughts.

I was one of the few to survive the Tobacco Wars, escaping with men like Wolfenstein, Six Pack, and Henchman. Now, we're over 1,000 strong and growing. We're defending the families of the Dixville Massacre. We share a kindred spirit here. Commander Chaos says we struggle for freedom.

Please remember me.

Randall

Helen felt responsible for what had happened--knowing it could have been prevented if she hadn't taken them through the center of town when they returned. Then to peer into the soul of the earnest young man she had talked to just hours before . . . .

"That's a man's personal property. Nobody looks at that but their loved ones!" stated a rebel coldly.

"I'm sorry. I didn't know."

"You just don't start snooping into things that don't concern you!"

"I'm sorry." Cold stares pierced through Helen as she got up and stood in judgment. "I had no idea."

"Hold it, guys," Chaos intervened, "get back where you belong." The group shuffled off.

"Well, aren't you going to say something?" asked Helen.

"You're right, you didn't know about our letters home. And you didn't know that taking a detour would cause things to end up the way they did this morning. No one knew. The Wizard didn't explain why he gave us directions to go the long way to the electronics warehouse." He put an arm on her shoulder. "One thing's for sure: Mistakes are costly in this game. And it is a game we need to play well."

Chaos' comment helped Helen realize how simply changing routes could lead to such dire consequences. To that point, she hadn't felt responsible for what had happened this morning. She would think things through more carefully from now on.

Later that morning Steve Morrison approached Helen as she treated another soldier, "Helen, I need to talk to you a minute."

She turned. "Oh," her tone dropped an octave as she saw who it was. "What do you want?"

"What went on over there? And what the hell happened this morning? I'm here to help you guys get the truth out."

"I wouldn't know about your article. I don't read tabloid journalism," Helen said coolly. She shifted to a more pleasant tone as she addressed the young soldier. "What's your name again?"

"Van Gogh, ma'am." He smiled. "I got called that 'cause I'm a leg-man. If they tell me to go, I go." His smile broadened.

The grin was contagious. Helen returned the smile, "My name's Helen."

"Everyone knows who you are, Ma'am."

"Thank you, that's sweet. Would you see me tomorrow so I can change the bandage?"

Van Gogh nodded and grinned as he left to rejoin his attack pack.

"You're real sweet on these guys," Steve commented sarcastically.

Helen clenched her teeth, "Now what do you want?"

"I'm a prisoner here. They tell me when to sit, when I can go to the bathroom; I'm under guard at all times. Oh crap, here comes my shadow," Morrison whined in a murmur as Wolf's group broke up. A young rebel walked over to them.

"Ma'am, is this man bothering you?" asked the man.

Morrison hung his head as Helen responded, "No, I'm fine, Sunny Boy. We're just having a private chat." The rebel walked off to another part of the church and sat down, still observing his assignment from a distance.

"Jesus, what is it with these names? Bubba or Jeffro, won't do? Everybody's a nickname around here. These hillbillies are going to get us killed. I just came along as a reporter. I don't want to get in the line of fire when the Feds crash in the door. Have you seen the Dixville site? Trees were blasted in half. Boulders were chipped away like plaster. As rugged as these guys think they are, they haven't a chance against that kind of automated technology." Seeing her face, Steve suddenly realized what he had said by mentioning Dixville.

Helen jammed the bloodied wraps in plastic bags and savagely tossed them in a trashcan below the table. She slowly wiped the table down with a strong bleach solution. "No, I haven't been to the site."

Steve's comment loosened stark images of that day. She continued fussing with supplies. Steve noticed Helen's mood shift. "I'm sorry. I just want to do my job that's all. Could you see if Chaos would let me have my camera back? Those guys can censor everything I send out. In fact, they can E-mail it to my editor. I don't have a problem with that. I could at least write about the North Country, we're not there anymore. I wouldn't blow your cover here. Keep in mind, if it wasn't for our break in the Dixville story, the Feds would probably have attacked the North Country by now."

Helen relented, "I'll say something to him, but no promises."

"Thanks. And one more thing. Got any gum?"

Two other packs returned that afternoon. One had cased the JFK Federal Building off New Sudbury Street and taken digital photos of it. Using spotting scopes, they had located Max on the fifth floor. The intelligence encouraged Chaos: Security was lax at the Federal Building and short-manned. He concluded the easiest way to manage the escape was the most direct approach: Infiltrate the Federal Building and cut communications. Then get Max get the hell out of Boston during the rush of the St. Patrick's Day parade. They would disassemble the motor-gun they had captured and make duplicates of it when they returned to the North Country.

A third group searched the city for Tumult. They knew he was here because they found his calling card, an African-American spiked to a sheet of plywood, dead. Chaos decided to continue with the plan without a rendezvous with Tumult.

Chaos met Helen that evening in a room on the second level of the church; it had served as the priest's residence at one time. Though starkly furnished and filled with musty traces from neglect, a single oil lamp created a romantic glow. It was quiet in this part of the city. The blocks surrounding the church were crisscrossed with narrow streets bordered by rundown townhouses.

Helen and Chaos had been attracted to one another since their first meeting in the sugarhouse. Chaos was good looking all right, his soft brown eyes his most defining feature. And he was solid, without a stitch of fat. He was capable of charming the pants off a woman, literally.

But the foreplay was more verbal than physical, with the Southerner asking about her personal life, the food she liked, what clothes she liked to wear. Until then, Helen hadn't thought of herself as a catch; the image of a chunky mom was still engraved in her psyche. Chaos made her feel beautiful again.

More than that, in the midst of a decimated city, his quiet persuasion engendered a feeling of security. The tender romance that ensued helped her forget the tragic loss of her son, if only for a moment.

"You're not going to stay through the might?" Helen asked as Chaos got out of bed and began dressing.

"I have to sleep with the men. It's good for morale. It's hard to explain. I don't want to put myself at a higher level or anything. I'm the commander, yes, but if I'm not with them, I'm not one of them." Seated in a straight-back chair, he began buckling up his shoes.

She accepted his explanation but found it awkward bringing up the next subject. "I spoke with the reporter today. Did you know their news agency was the first to publicize the Dixville Massacre as it really happened? That's what postponed the Feds immediate invasion of New Hampshire and Vermont."

"'Postpone is the operative word, too." The Southerner caught himself. "I'm sorry. I didn't mean to be rude. It's been a long day."

"Morrison said we could check his pictures and report before sending it out. He wants his camera back."

"I don't have a problem with that as long as one of our men is with him at all times. He can stick with Wolfenstein's group. But you let him know that tagging along with an attack pack can be dangerous."

Washington, D.C. (The evening of March 16)

What had been the East Room of the White House was now the Arabian Room. The influential politicians of Washington showed up at the reception and passed through a replica of Babylon's Ishtar Gate--the entrance to the temple of Bel built by Nebuchadnezzar in 575 B.C.. The hand-hewn trim made by American forefathers had been removed, replaced by graven images of the bull of Adad and the dragon of Marduk. The beasts were scattered symmetrically across the tiled wall. Security personnel, dressed as sheiks, stood indignantly at the entrance. Beyond studded doors made of Lebanon Cedar, were crowds of cordial people smiling deceptively.

The White House had been remodeled during Harry S. Truman's administration--also a time when they shored up the original sandstone walls and added one hundred and thirty-two rooms to the existing sixty-two. The total cost by the end of 1952: $5,761,000.

That wasn't uncommon. Other administrations added pools or spas or jogging tracks. Jacqueline Bouvier Kennedy completely refurbished the interior in the early 1960s, followed by a permanent art collection assembled in 1964 by Lyndon B. Johnson.

But the executive quarters had to be brought up to the times, representing the Global Village the U.S. had become a part of. Lyndon's collection of American art had been taken down. The Early American furnishings collected by Jacqueline Kennedy had been replaced by 18th century furniture from France or Germany or the Orient--always authentic. Every room had a national theme.

"Look at that bitch," muttered Chief of Staff Lucas Bennett to President Winifred. "She's working everyone. You were wondering where she got her info about Dixville, well there you go." They looked across the breadth of the tiled room to see Vice President Sorenson and Secretary of Defense Kyle Paz chatting with drinks in hand. The two smiled and nodded to one another. "He's the one who told her. He's gotta be."

"Sorenson has access to a lot of confidential information, if she only knows where to look. We can't trust her. And I wouldn't sell Paz short. *He* might be working *her*." President Winifred scooped some black, Iranian caviar with a cracker and held it just inside the cage for the falcon to snatch. "Kyle's too much of a political animal to go taking off on his own. He was in charge of the Dixville operation. We only told him to stop the smuggling. He knows he could be hung out to dry with the rest of us. You're making too much of this, Luc." The President sipped his sherry as he smiled and nodded at Senator Chavaza of California passing by. Both the President and Lucas Bennett looked again across the room at Kyle and Vice President Sorenson who now looked back at them. The two parties forced smiles and raised glasses to one another in a distant toast.

"I don't think there's a damn thing they can do. We're talking impeachment here," Sorenson vented absolutely. "Of course, my ass is in the same sling." She paused thinking, "What do you see as a next step?"

General Paz cleared his throat before speaking, "I think we need to act rather than react. There's a number of scenarios that could be played out: All this could be delayed and Winifred could get reelected. Or, due to some negative press, you could lose the election. In which case, the party in power would most likely call for an inquiry and indictments. And seeing how I was in charge of the Dixville operation, I would take the fall as well, I suppose, justifiably so," Kyle added regrettably.

"Don't you find it a little suspicious," Lucas continued as he rubbed the tattoo on his cheek, "that Kyle has been unable to squash the backwoods rebellion in the North Country, or even put a stop to the CB broadcasts coming out of there. Jesus, CB broadcasts! We're dealing with a bunch of woodchucks! There's been unrest other places, and we've pinpointed the leaders and brought them in. I think you need to consider getting rid of him. If you replaced him there's nothing he could do about it."

"I'll need to think about it," said the President. "What bothers me is that he has no motive to jump ship, and everything to lose. He'd be all but admitting involvement in Dixville. I don't understand that. Even Sorenson would be implicated." He turned his gaze from the other side of the room back to his Chief of Staff. "Well, she *could* be implicated. Just her knowing and not doing anything smells of cover-up."

"Lucas looks somewhat distressed over there," Sorenson placed her empty glass on the tray of a passing sheik. He stopped and offered her a second. She shook her head, "No, thank you." He moved on. "Doesn't that queer little man ever unwind?" Sorenson observed of Lucas Bennett. "I'd love to set him up somehow so Winifred had to replace him."

"That would be tough to do," said Paz. He's always thinking. We'd be smart to make our move before they make theirs."

Sorenson looked at the Secretary of Defense and slithered her lips to a smile as she strolled to mingle with First Lady Patricia Winifred's group in another part of the Arabian Room. She knew enough not to ask; she didn't want to know what Kyle was going to do.

Lucas Bennett received a micro disk from an aide and promptly pulled out a pocket computer from his breast pocket to load it in. He grinned as he read the note. "This is interesting. It's a letter to a sweetheart from one of the Tobacco Boys. Evidently, they write their own eulogy." Lucas jumped windows on his computer and beeped a message to the aide who had delivered the disk, to return.

The aide had just left the Arabian Room and had nearly passed through what had been the Green Room, now the Greek Buffet Hall. He heard the beep from the computer in his jacket, opened it to read the message, and returned to Bennett.

"How did they come by this?" Lucas asked the aide.

"The young lady it is addressed to in South Carolina received the letter and called us. Then she transferred the file online. She said she 'felt it was her duty to let us know.'"

"Thank you," Lucas replied. The aide turned on his heel and left.

Lucas handed the computer to the President, "This is interesting, Cliff. This says they're a thousand strong and growing--and they're down in Boston."

Winifred studied it for a moment, but became distracted nervously, brushing his fingers through his hair. Seconds earlier, he had glanced to the side of the room to find Nancy Atherton watching him. She was a bystander in a group engaged in their own conversation. Dressed in a tissue thin, pink and purple dress, Nancy shot a seductively long stare across the room at Clifford. The overacted display pulled a smile out of him.

"Mr. President?"

"Oh. Yes, Lucas. Let's go to the Map Room. This could be the break we need."

"You want Kyle to meet us there, of course?" Lucas watched the President's face for a response, testing him.

"I think not. We'll hold off on Paz's reaction on this one."

They went through the same door as the aide had, crossing through the Greek Hall, eventually down narrow stairs that led to the Map Room.

The room hadn't adopted the international flavor as other chambers in the White House--basic, but modernized. In Franklin Roosevelt's day, leaders plotted war strategies using color-coded pins on a large world map stretched across the wall. Now the room was totally electronic with a giant screen replacing the maps. A small portable computer controlled the larger display.

President Winifred closed the door behind him, all the while looking at the computer note on his pocket PC they had intercepted. "I don't quite understand this note, Luc. 'Now, we are over a thousand strong and growing.' How did this rebel die? There's nothing going on in the North Country right now. But there were some Mountain Boys killed above Boston, and rumors of some in Boston. But a thousand? How could they hide a thousand white guys in that city?"

"I'll get some FBI agents to try and trace the source of the letter through the Internet service provider. The rebel might have written it long before. The sheriff in Lexington also reported a number of large trucks pulling out of his town. Whether the trucks were full of men or equipment or empty was uncertain. We should assume they were armed rebels. I would presume they're in Boston to either get cash or get one of their Covenant leaders out; the convict's name is Max Sessal. We thought he was The Wizard. But now we know he's not." Lucas turned to the map and zoomed up New England, typing in numbers on the portable computer. "Assuming the rebels were divided evenly, there might be about three hundred in Vermont and three hundred across the river." He typed the numbers in on the large map on the wall as he spoke.

"And now three hundred in Boston," Clifford Winifred finished the theory for him. "The question is, Why so many to get one man out, unless your assumption was wrong and that the man in custody in Boston is The Wizard?"

"One of the compound officials overstepped his bounds and used a drug to loosen Sessal up. Ah, the official was reprimanded for it of course. Somewhat. You know what I mean." A smirk at the corners of his mouth formed as Lucas typed.

"That leaves a lot of unanswered questions, Luc. I think they're looking to get weapons or ammo in Boston. Check with the military on this and find me someone who dealt with this bunch before; we need to know their tactics. The last thing we need are the casualties we had in the Tobacco War. That little run-in above Boston with only one vanload was costly as it was. We'll take out their group using overwhelming force."

"What about Kyle?"

"Yes. Get him immediately. We need to keep the Tobacco bunch there in Boston."

Chapter 11

The last foreign encounter that had taken place in mainland America was the War of 1812. The British invaded Washington and burned the White House. From that point, all other threats to the American way of life came from within. At the turn of the 21st century little wars raged throughout the world. A nuclear flare-up occurred between India and Pakistan. The combined populations of the two countries dropped from 1.5 billion people to nearly half that.

And then the Israeli conflict. Just before dusk on April 9, 2011, three short-range, nuclear missiles were launched from Lebanon at the cities of Haifa, Nazerat, and a military base in a valley near Afula, biblically referred to as Armageddon. The Israeli anti-missile system hadn't had time to react quickly enough, the missiles obliterated their targets. Israel retaliated by launching an array of warheads from submarines in the Mediterranean and the Red Sea. Nuclear blasts flashed cities in Syria, Lebanon, Libya, Jordan, Iraq, and Iran within the hour. So came the reputation of the long-range sniper rifle: the Masada. The Israeli policy of appeasement vanished. Terrorists bent on the destruction of the Jewish people were identified and targeted for extinction by the legendary weapon that fired silently from miles away. Israelis developed special bullets with propellant and tail fins and a sensor tip that followed a laser to its target.

Colonel Francis Greely, 20th Special Forces Group (Airborne) had been at most global conflicts concerning U.S. interests, advising, heading covert operations, arming rebels to topple tyrants in Third World countries. He stood resolute before President Winifred and Chief of Staff Lucas Bennett twelve hours after their discussion at the White House reception the night before. He was a much older man than they had envisioned; wrinkled skin and gray, thinning hair, he was thin to the point his back and shoulders hunched. Greely did not look like typical soldier stuff. But he had served in countless global conflicts throughout his career.

President Winifred asked Greely why Paz had resisted ordering an attack on the rebels in Boston. "General Paz didn't order his soldiers into Boston because it would have been a bloodbath for our troops, worse than a replay on the Tobacco Wars," the Colonel explained.

Lucas objected, "But we've got the technology and the manpower."

The Colonel corrected him, "We have the technology."

A gap in conversation widened as the President and Chief of Staff looked at one another. This man wasn't what they had expected: a curt, opinionated, son-of-a-bitch, he didn't even look military.

"You were in command of the Okefenokee campaign, correct?" Winifred asked.

"Correct, sir, and that's how Paz and I know this isn't a band of hillbillies with shotguns. They are well disciplined and dedicated to a cause. The Media blew things out of proportion down South. They are not a bunch of redneck racists. Oh, you have individuals with their own opinion on things, but overall, they think of themselves as freedom fighters. That's the worst kind of enemy you can go up against. They had a number of things going for them in the Carolinas: They had the support of the people in the region and an erratic, unorthodox fighting style, which accounted for the high kill ratio they inflicted on us. And they had advanced weaponry. Most of all, they have topnotch fighting men."

"We have elite troops, Colonel," Lucas' tone changed to a more defensive pitch. "Our military is the best in the world. We protect our vital interests on every continent."

"They're the best in conventional fighting," asserted Colonel Greely. "And you're absolutely right, they're all over the world fighting terrorism. Not here. See, when the Tobacco Boys break the line and when they're shooting it out with our troops only meters away, they have the upper hand. They are not afraid to get close and personal. They don't panic under fire. Our troops haven't seen man-to-man combat in so many decades, kids nowadays freak out in close ground fighting. The Tobacco Boys thrive on that. They're also equipped with the Israeli Masadas, the most advanced sniper rifle designed to date. It has an extensive range and with the right bullet, can penetrate light armor. In the Carolinas they used 'em to shoot out our vision blocks and sensor ports on our Abrams tanks. They literally blinded us. When a trooper opened a hatch to see, Tobacco Boys launched a bullet inside the thing. Do you know what a loose bullet does inside a tank?"

"Well, not real--" The President was at a loss for words.

"It bounces around inside until it goes through enough bone and flesh to stop it--if it doesn't detonate a cannon shell first."

"We need to refocus here," said Lucas Bennett. "You're here to tell us what you know about their tactics and what can be done. They are beatable; you proved that in Georgia."

"I didn't. If you count the numbers, they killed a lot more of us than we did of them. Of course it wasn't reported that way. When it was all said and done, it was the swamp that killed a lot of the rebels. As for tactics, I would never engage them in a city. No commander would want house-to-house fighting with that bunch."

The President cut in, "If we locate their headquarters, we could use an optic-guided missile or even conventional artillery to take out their nest cleanly."

"That smart weaponry is only as smart as the people using it. Keep in mind, they're not afraid to take casualties."

Lucas became sarcastic, "So what you're saying is that the most powerful military force in the world can't take on a few hundred rebels. I get the impression you like these guys."

"You don't understand the importance of knowing the enemy. And yes, if I could choose a group of soldiers to serve under me, it would be the Tobacco Boys. Unfortunately they're the enemy. I'm not saying we can't beat them. I'm saying it will cost us casualties. One thing that helped us in Georgia was that we split them off from the citizens who supported them. They have to eat. They have to sleep. When they're out of their element they become easier to locate--as I suppose they are in Boston now." The separation of the Mountain Boys from their base made Greely reconsider.

"Would you be interested in heading this thing up?" the President asked.

The Colonel had anticipated the question: "If I can do it my way. That would mean bring in my own divisions with the most modern equipment. For example: I want the team of Seals now stationed in the Amur region of Russia. I need them today. They've had experience with snipers and house-to-house fighting. But if there's too many civilians getting hurt, I'm the one that calls it quits. Then we would just have to wait for them to leave the city."

"Those terms are fine," said President Winifred.

Greely looked the President straight in the eye. "I've got to ask just one question first, sir. I don't mean any disrespect by it. Did our troops have anything to do with the Dixville incident?"

"No, they didn't. It is a ridiculous notion prompted by Spectator News. It's purely political. I had nothing to do with Dixville, and quite frankly, I'm surprised you would ask something like that."

"I had to ask, sir. Morale is low with the communications blackout on the military. Keeping the troops in the dark only spurs rumors."

"Rumors is the operative word, Colonel."

The Colonel accepted the assignment and was given full reign over the troops and equipment used. He wanted to start immediately while the Tobacco Boys were still severed from the North Country.

Boston (1:00 p.m. on March 17)

From Chaos' vantagepoint, atop the sixty-two-story John Hancock Tower, tiny streets were cluttered with insect-like vehicles. They crowded and honked, anxious to pass through Columbus Avenue before the strip shut down for the annual St. Patrick's Day Parade. The gold dome of the State House gleamed like a Christmas ornament behind Boston Common. Other historical sights of Old Boston were also in view: the Park Street Church and Granary Burial Ground just beyond the Common and a distant pinnacle of the Bunker Hill Monument across the Charles River, three miles off. The Old State House peeked between the skyscrapers of downtown.

Huge military transport planes circled the sky above the city like predatory birds, holding their flight patterns for a turn to land at Logan International Airport across the Harbor. A Navy ZF-4 Pursuit plane roared over the Hancock Tower at a low altitude. "They know we're here," shouted Chaos. "Don't uncover those guns," he directed Wolfenstein. "For all they know we're up here to see the parade."

Chaos moved his command center in the early morning hours to an empty warehouse off Boston Harbor just as a precaution.

John Hancock's rooftop was an excellent communications point from which they sighted in a Masada's laser to a receiver node at their warehouse. They also had a line-of-sight to communicate with attack packs stationed around the JFK Building where the Feds kept Max and three Virginians.

Chaos noticed the stark Bunker Hill monument across the Charles River and wondered . . . . He went to the edge of the building and uncovered part of a Masada and focused the 100x scope on the viewing nest at the top of the monument. Two of Tumult's Mountain Boys looked back at him through Masada scopes of their own. Looking through the scope, Chaos waved. They waved back. If they had had one of the copper woven hats and amplifier he could have sent them a message.

"What is it?" asked Helen--with Steve Morrison listening intently.

"Tumult had spotters behind the church at Bunker Hill all this time. He knew where we were. They must use the location to receive and send visual signals."

"I thought you guys were on the same team. If he knew where you were," Helen questioned, "why didn't he contact you?"

"Like I said, we have a philosophical difference. You'll get to ask him yourself. Der Dutchman's pack spotted Tumult heading our way with an attack pack. You know, as much as we disagree, we both know we're going to have to work together to get out of this. Those aren't passenger planes. The Feds are moving in troops." He pointed to the sky. "We have to get Max and get out of here when this mob leaves the parade, *before* the Feds blockade the city. We could hold them off in the city all right but we don't have provisions."

"I'd like to understand the dynamics of this place," Chaos pondered allowed. "Excluding the gangs, of course, we haven't had ill will from the people here."

"How do you view yourselves as rebels?" Steve Morrison cut into the conversation.

"Is this for your own curiosity or some kind of interview?"

"You could call it an interview."

"How do I know you'll get it right? I have trouble understanding how you media boys prostitute yourselves day after day by supporting the failed policies of the White House. Rural, hardworking people are being punished."

"First of all, I can't help but get it right; you're sending it out for me. Just edit anything you don't like and feed it through the phone line."

"You just don't get it, do you," the Southerner countered. "We struggle for freedom. This nation that is all over the globe fighting terrorism, protecting the freedom of other people around the world, while communities at home aren't allowed to help themselves. Granted, with all of us, it's personal. In some way, we've suffered loss of property, livelihood," and nodding to Helen beside him, "some lost loved ones. But it's the principle of it. It's bad government, and America wasn't this way years ago." Chaos pointed his finger to the streets below. "The urban people might control the votes to keep these fools in power, but we can control the countryside. Without the land, they cannot eat."

A voice came from behind them, "You always gave a good speech, little brother."

Helen whirled around to see Tumult, looking her over lecherously.

He smiled at her reaction. "She looks surprised. I'll bet he didn't tell you we were brothers," said Tumult.

"No."

"It's not something he's proud of," Tumult continued. "My little brother thinks I'm a psycho, but when things get tough, I wind up saving his ass. Ain't that right?" Tumult looked to Chaos.

"I sent you a message about coming here for Max," Chaos said quickly, obviously irritated. "And I don't appreciate this cat and mouse game you've been playing in Boston. You're screwing up the mission by hitting on the gangs. Look, they're flying in Regular Army." He pointed across the harbor to the airport. "For all we know there's even ships loaded with more troops and supplies on the way."

Morrison discreetly scribbled notes on a pocket computer as they spoke; Tumult notice. "Who's the nerd? A historical recorder? You think you're making history here or something, little brother?" Tumult walked deliberately between Helen and Chaos to the tripod Masada with a blanket draped over it.

"I'm a reporter for Spectator News," Steve announced.

Tumult looked through the scope at the Bunker Hill Monument, ignoring his soldiers' waves. "He doin' a story on you? You running for President, little brother?" Tumult chuckled.

"They're sending in a censored story," said Steve.

"And who the hell asked you," Tumult answered the reporter not taking his eyes off the scope. He loosened the lock on the weapon as he watched the protest gathering at the front of The Old State House a mile and a half away.

Local residents had gathered in the square at the very point the Boston Massacre had taken place centuries before. This time they took advantage of the St. Patrick's Day press coverage to protest against the lack of protection from the gangs, the cutbacks in health care, and the reduction of social security. The leader of the rally recited party demagoguery about fascists and fairness. Further down Columbus Avenue gays, lesbians, and representatives from a Native American group stood in formation and held their banners for the St. Patrick's Day Parade.

"'A hundred fools do not make one wise man,'" said Tumult quoting Adolf Hitler. He refocused on the protest gathering at the Old State House.

"So, little brother, is this what you're down here for, to fight for the freedom of freaks and afros. And hell, I can't tell what *that* is," he discreetly punched a timer on the number pad of the Masada as he spoke, "a girl, or a boy, or one of those animals they surgically change for the county fair."

"They have the right to say what they think," stated Chaos.

Tumult turned away from the scope, "Well, I'm getting sick and tired of the whining." He logged in three consecutive shots and pressed ENTER.

"Your own men have trouble accepting the Nazi theme you've embraced. But listen, we have to work together if we're going to get out of here."

"Piss!" Tumult re-covered the Masada, stood up, and glanced at his watch. "When you say work together, you mean do it your way. You sent me the goddamn message about coming here before we could even talk about it. We're supposed to be a triad, little brother. That's three groups that function as one. You haul your ass off and do stuff on your own. I started this goddamn thing to begin with. How do you think you got through college? Huh?"

"Well--"

"I sent the goddamn money to Mom. She sent it to the Citadel. Those weren't scholarships, you stupid shit."

Helen and Steve looked at one another, stunned. The conversation caught Wolfenstein and his pack's attention. Tumult continued, "I was raising hell with the Feds and raising money for you while you were screwing around with the girls in college. I get sick and tired of having to explain myself to you. You try and make me out as some wacko Nazi around my own men. I don't appreciate that. You need to worry about your own people. I had to pick two of your Virginian men out of a building last night. And taking care of them were two boys." He points his finger at Helen, "They said this bitch is in charge of everything. Piss! I'm getting sick and tired of covering your ass." He glanced down at his watch.

"Boys?" The statement surprised Chaos.

"Boys. You got that right. They had a dog with 'em. And one of the Virginians had the shit shot out of his leg. We might have to cut the thing off."

"You're not cutting that leg off because I'm going over there," Helen vowed to Tumult. She was aghast; Helen couldn't imagine how Butch and Thad could have made it to Boston. So far away. She wanted to help the wounded Virginian, yes; but primarily, Helen wanted to get the Rousell brothers away from Tumult.

"Who runs this outfit, little brother? Those boys right about her being in charge? Are you so penie-tied by a woman that she's calling the shots?"

Chaos' patience was at its limit. He wanted to work with Tumult and get through this ordeal, but he'd put up with the humiliation long enough. The 'little' brother, along with other demeaning comments in front of his men grated on him. But Chaos didn't want to let his ego get in the way of a compromise with his brother. As diabolical as Tumult was, he always prevailed, landing on his feet despite insurmountable odds. Chaos respected that part of his brother. He always had. There were times growing up when he watched his older brothers get away with outrageous antics. Chaos watched and kept his mouth shut--always the good boy. Tumult had maligned him back then as well. Things hadn't changed. "There's no working with you, is there?"

"Sure there is. I'm leaving the city now before the Feds block us in. Pack up your stuff and let's go," Tumult ordered.

Chaos glanced over at Helen before speaking, "We can leave in a few hours."

"That's too late," said Tumult. "I can't believe you're going to put your part of the Triad at risk for one man. Especially, when you really came down for the motor-guns."

"We can't." Chaos replied in a submissive tone, "Is it all right if an attack pack and medic go over and picks up the boys and the wounded Virginians?"

"Oh, certainly." Tumult looked at his watch again. "I think you know where we're at." He waved to his men across the city at the Bunker Hill Monument and walked over to Wolfenstein's group to pick up a Masada wrapped in a blanket. Tumult unraveled it and looked at the circuit board taped to the stock, with a small condenser mike attached to it. "So this is how you communicate now. You beam over to someone's little beanie and speak." He pointed a red beam at the hat of one of Wolf's men and spoke into the device. "Hello there." The soldier jerked from the overpowering reception at such close range. "Can you hear me?" asked Tumult. The soldier nodded yes. Tumult walked over to the man and took his hat and receiver. "I appreciate the fact that you share your technology with the other triads, little brother." He rewrapped the weapon and hat in the blanket, "One word of advice on this escape plan of yours: Create a diversion that will keep the Feds occupied." He walked to the door, looking at his watch one last time. His attack pack had gone before him. "Are you boys coming with us or what?" Tumult walked down the stairway.

Chaos pointed to Der Dutchman's pack as a signal to go. They scurried about collecting their gear. He moved close to Helen, speaking softly, "I don't want you to go. I'll send a medic to stabilize him 'til they get him to the wharf. And they can bring back the Rousells."

"Would you rather lose one of your men? You really don't have medics. Believe me, Chaos, after what I've been through this past year, nothing can hurt me."

"But Helen, it would hurt me if something happened to you."

She grabbed her two backpacks and followed the others, looking back before entering the stairway. Their eyes met as she disappeared through the doorway.

Chaos turned the opposite way and scanned the skyline toward the JFK building. He wondered if he was making the right decision staying in Boston to get Max; Tumult's instincts were always right.

Suddenly, "Pooh, pooh, pooh," came three silenced shots from the Masada pointed toward the Old State House.

Mountain Boys attacked the Masada's tripod from all directions. The first one there tackled the weapon. "Holy shit!" said Bird Dog. "How the hell did that happen?"

Chaos pulled up binoculars to scour the city below. A faint flurry of gunfire came from the rally in front of the Old State House.

City Police began firing into the crowd. The protesters dispersed in terror. A semicircle of officers remained--two of them lay dead within the ranks, with four dead civilians sprawled and bleeding on cobblestone. A sizable chunk of stone had been split from a rock marking the first Boston Massacre.

(Two hours later)

Prudential and Hancock Towers gleamed and swayed, stretching far above natural heights--discrediting Babel's folly and affirming human capability. Made of glass and steel, they flexed in heavy winds--several feet at times--as a sparrow fluttered to and fro toward a crevice in the Old South Church below. Chaos watched the small bird's struggle. A Navy, ZF-4 Pursuit plane streaked past at subsound; the jet's roar chased the craft a quarter mile behind it.

The ZF-4 went well beyond the Hancock tower to pitch and roll for a return sweep of the building. This time the craft took a lower path and launched an AT-2 Shredder missile, then launched a second Shredder seconds later as the ZF-4 veered off target. Copilot Bronsen guided the missiles in through fiber-optic cable the size of fishing filament. Through her virtual-reality visor, she flew on the tip of the Shredder--accuracy on such a weapon could not be understated. The first missile blasted a gaping hole in the glass observatory two floors down, taking out a stairwell in the building. Racing through the first hole, the second missile entered the interior of the building and detonated at the elevator hub. Smoke billowed out the stairwell leading to the roof as Mountain Boys came out from behind the smokestack.

"Get out the Masadas. If they make that mistake again, we'll nail them," Chaos talked tough, but he wondered why the jet had shot missiles below the apex of the building and didn't strafe the rooftop. "How is it down there?" he asked one of the men who emerged from the smoke.

"The north side got hammered. The stairway and main shafts are collapsed. There doesn't seem to be any fire though. Just smoke."

Pooh! Pooh! Pooh! One of Wolfenstein's bunch fired on Army Regulars running into the base of their building.

Splat. A bullet caught a rebel in the head making him slump to a heap on the roof's tarmac top. The bullet continued through, hitting Step-n-Time in the thigh. "Damn!" he dropped to the roof and immediately yanked a wrap from his side pack and bound it. Everyone dropped to the rooftop. Rebels on that side of Hancock Tower peeked over the two-foot knee-wall through their Masada scopes or binoculars.

Steve Morrison was crouched beside the Mountain Boy hit with the bullet. Speckles of blood dotted the reporter's face and neck. He sat below the lip of the wall looking dumbfounded.

Splat. Another rebel got hit squarely in the binoculars on the other side of Morrison. The young Vermonter fell with his splintered face on Morrison's lap. "Oh God!" the reporter exclaimed.

"I see him. I see him, sir," yelled a rebel. "He's 97 degrees southeast. About a kilometer out."

Wolf looked down at his map below the lip of the building, "On top of the New England Life Building."

Chaos yelled across the tower, "Hold it, Wolf. You have to assume there's snipers on every side."

"Jet coming, sir!" The Mountain Boys with Masadas set their weapons at an estimated lead-speed of 300 to 400 mph, at a trajectory of one kilometer. As the jet approached, eleven riflemen rose, propped their weapons on top of the wall and fired. Four of Wolfenstein's pack rose at the same time, sighted in on the New England Life Building, and fired on the sniper.

Splat! Splat! Two more Mountain Boys' heads popped open like melons. But two of the bullets from Wolf's pack smacked the face of the Army sniper. Blood spattered up into the facemask of the trooper.

Smoke seeped from the ZF-4's engine. Instead of banking and firing a shot, the craft tilted in the direction of Logan International Airport.

Wolf got a good look at the sniper through his scope, "They're wearing thermo-suits, sir," he reported to Chaos. Thermo-gear looked like a camouflaged, space suit with a twenty-foot vacuum hose extending out the end to a vent fan. It sucked air through the gear to cool its occupant. The thermo-gear prevented heat signature to appear through an infrared scope, making a sniper difficult to spot.

Splat! A third rebel received a bullet through his shoulder that went through his chest cavity and out the opposite side. Chaos saw the hit and realized the shot had come from the direction of the Prudential Tower. Splat! Another Mountain Boy downed, caught through the thick of the neck.

"Everyone, to the west rim!" Chaos yelled. The Prudential Tower was the only building tall enough to allow snipers to shoot effectively into the top. Mountain Boys huddled against the west wall for cover. Syntax got shot in the hand on his run to the other side, leaving a trail of blood from where he was hit.

Wolfenstein grabbed the paralyzed Steve Morrison by the scalp en route and pulled the reporter to his feet, tugging him to the other side of the building by his hair. Steve hit the knee-wall hard with his shoulders and back. "Thanks, Wolf," said Steve after recovering. Wolfenstein looked back at him as he flipped levers on his rifle and shook his head in dismay at the dazed reporter.

Mountain Boys detached the scopes of the Masadas and individually popped up and scanned the Prudential for targets. Upon locating one, they reattached the scope behind the wall and came up for a shot. "Got one, three meters left of the north corner." The scene looked like a shooting gallery arcade from the Prudential's viewpoint, with Mountain Boys popping their heads up and down at various places across the west side of the John Hancock Tower's roof. "Got number two, midsection and back in." Legmen like Bird Dog popped up with binoculars to spot targets; they retreated below the lip to yell out coordinates, "Target, seven meters north of the corner, on the edge." Three Mountain Boys with Masadas popped up for the target, calling out the kill simultaneously: "Third target down, seven meters north of the corner, on the edge."

As the Mountain Boys systematically spotted and shot Army Regulars, another ZF-4 swooped in from the other side of the Hancock and leveled another AT-2 Shredder missile at the third level down, taking out the other stairway. The smoke buildup below forced more Mountain Boys out of the building.

Chaos crawled over to confer with Wolfenstein. "What do you think their strategy is with the missiles, Wolf?"

"I can tell you that a group of Regulars ran into the base of the building. Our boys below the blowout points can keep them from coming up the stairwells but I don't know if we can get down to support them--or get off the building at all."

"My thinking too, by surgically striking only the top floors, there isn't much damage done to the building. The Feds must think most of us are here," Chaos speculated, "and by knocking out the stairs and elevator shaft they think they've got us trapped."

"And they're right," Wolf replied. "But we still have over 200 guys scattered around in the city. All we have to do is get enough open space to laser a message to them. If we didn't have to fend off snipers from the Prudential Buil--" He noticed a small speck in the sky. From the speed and proportions of the craft, they recognized one of their model planes.

Chaos and Wolfenstein turned to one another recalling the model planes they had brought with them. It was the Starling, a brown and black-colored plane with the name Starling Striker painted on its wings. The craft flew a fraction of the speed of ZF-4s, but as it passed near the Hancock Tower, the Mountain Boys held their fire and watched Starling buzz by, zigzagging through air currents.

Down on the street, half a mile away, one Mountain Boy aimed his infrared gun at the model plane as another rebel held binoculars to the technician's eyes. The man's tongue lashed vigorously about his open mouth as he moved the levers side to side, controlling the fragile but deadly craft as it fought the currents 790 feet up.

Federal soldiers saw it coming. The Starling jerked side to side, finally floating through a broken panel of glass to the Prudential Tower's innards. "Whooooom!" Flames from the blast blew out three glass wall panels from their mounts. Another panel, nearly intact, plunged in a free fall toward the street. A looter carrying a TV looked up to see the glass literally pass before his eyes and shatter into tiny fragments that exploded on contact with the pavement. Particles shredded the man's pants and lacerated his legs. He felt lucky until he looked for the TV he had held; it lay broken on the pavement with the bloodied stubs of his arms on each side of it.

Mountain Boys continued firing as Federal Troops withdrew from the Prudential Tower. The rebels fired shots at glass panels surrounding the hole so winds could feed the flames.

Chaos smiled at his troops' expertise and crawled back to the northeast side of the building with Henchman's attack pack. They signaled the communications node near the JFK building.

Shots were still fired by Federal troops, but they were from lower elevations on surrounding buildings and from further away. Though outnumbered, the Mountain Boys had regained the edge of higher "ground." The rebels could now look downward at Army snipers on three sides.

Steve Morrison pulled a digital camera out of his coat pocket and zoomed in on the Prudential Tower. Smoke and flames billowed out of the hole just below the top floors. Dead Army Regulars were scattered randomly near roof lips and walls, they lay draped over their weapons. The Mountain Boys had their heads over the kneewall on the west side still scoping the tower. Shooting from the Prudential had stopped; other rooftops on the west side of the Hancock Tower couldn't harbor Federal snipers.

The reporter noticed a Federal soldier lying face down on the rooftop of the Prudential Tower. The soldier's head rose and appeared to be scoping in on their location. Steve pulled away from the camera's eyepiece and looked at the others along his side of the building to see if they had seen. No one appeared to be startled. Steve looked again through his camera to see if he was imagining things, and saw a flash from the muzzle of the Federal Trooper. "Look out!" He leaped over to Wolfenstein and pulled him down from the wall as the bullet popped the scope of the Masada he had been looking through.

The tackle peeved Wolf at first. Then he noticed the scope shattered on his rifle. Other rebels saw the flash and returned fire. The Fed rolled behind a wall and scurried to the security of lower levels in the blazing Prudential Tower.

Wolfenstein had never felt comfortable saying thank you, but this time he came right out with it: "Much obliged." Wolf had overheard Morrison begging different rebels for gum the past two days. He pulled out a pack from his shirt pocket and handed it to the reporter.

"Thank you," Steve responded pensively. Behind the cover of the two-foot knee wall, Morrison thought as he unwrapped a stick and put it in his mouth. He surprised himself. He had never felt a part of any group. Hell, he really didn't like them; they were so stoic and self-righteous. Yet, somehow, through their struggle to survive, he had developed a kinship. Their fate was now his fate. The reporter tried to steady his camera on the neighboring tower again but found his shaking hands made it impossible. As he worked on his rifle, Wolf glanced up and noticed Steve's distress.

Steve turned and slouched down with his back against the wall and watched: Syntax helped Chaos set up a Masada for a communications link to attack packs at the JFK Building, passing his commander the headset that plugged into the circuit board with his one remaining hand, Syntax's other hand had nearly been shot off by a sniper round. Step-n-Time, leg bound and bloodied, peeked over the lip of the south wall for hidden snipers, then lowered his head to the rooftop to bring color back to his pale face. Step's buddy lay lifeless beside him, his side pack open, the red disk case removed--a dead man's reflective words to a world that had only spoken harshly to him. The reporter lifted his camera and began taking pictures of the people committed to this struggle for freedom.

Chapter 12

The attack packs from the JFK Building had rescued Max and the Virginians but they encountered trouble getting through the Fed's sixteen-block perimeter surrounding the Hancock Tower. The infantry wasn't the problem, Mountain Boys picked them off with Masadas. It was the Abrams tanks. The tanks had line-of-sight to each other, so just scrambling radio communications wasn't enough. Then too, none of the tanks could be downed. New adapters shielded the vision ports from snipers. One problem became clear: Without taking at least one tank out of action, it was unlikely they would get through the perimeter.

Chaos signaled the packs on the ground to head back to the docks and plan their exit out of the city; it was hard to justify a rescue for so few. Getting by the Abrams tanks would cost so many casualties. The Mountain Boys on the Tower were now on their own. This didn't mean they were giving up; it only meant they would have to find their own way. The two attack packs below the blasted floor, kept the Army Regulars from coming up, but Chaos had to devise a way to get by the level with the blown-out stairway and elevator hub.

As far as they knew, the Mountain Boys had cleared Federal snipers off the tops of buildings to the north. Chaos donned a harness, clipped a repelling loop behind him at the waist and slipped a cord through it. "Wolf, when I get below, just have the others clip on and follow. By the time we get down to the base of the building the darkness will help us."

The little figure bounced off the top of the Hancock Tower and ran down the glass. Maroon and purple blends reflected his image as the sun set to the west. After dropping four stories, Chaos jumped away from the glass wall and pulled a Glock from his belt. He shattered the glass with autopistol fire as he swung into a room.

"Would you look at that son-of-a-bitch go! Ignoring the fact that my little brother is a bleeding heart, he has balls the size of the Goodyear Blimp. Son-of-a-bitch! He *is* good, running down the side of the building like that." Tumult lowered his binoculars and nudged Glitch. "You gettin' all this?"

Glitch nodded his head adding, "What can we do for 'em over there, boss?"

"Nothing. I won't help 'em. Besides, we lost our window of escape just going over there and warning 'em. I'm getting sick and tired of covering my little brother's ass when he screws up. We're taken on sniper fire as it is, being this close to the airport."

Tumult's communication hub at the Bunker Hill Monument loomed two hundred and twenty-one feet atop a hill overlooking Boston. The 6,700-ton granite obelisk represented heroism and glory. Now, with a panning view across the Charles River to the south, Logan International Airport to the east, and remaining suburbs of the north and west, the mystic pinnacle with its small viewing ports dotting the surface, lived up to its mystique. Tumult could view all parts of the city and signal down to his rebels positioned between the monument and the Charles River. Less virtuous revolutionaries now held the site, but they were every bit as dangerous.

"A message, sir." A young rebel held the earphone to his head. "They say, they're coming off the top and will try and break through the tank line within the hour." The rebel waited for a response from Tumult to recite a message back to the attack packs on the tower.

"Tell them, good luck." Tumult paused a second. "Yeah. And tell them to be sure and kick up that kill ratio. Yeah."

A sniper bullet passed through the crowded bird's nest at the top of the Bunker Monument. One Mountain Boy received the bullet through the side of the face, before it proceeded on to hit a standing man just below the chest, finally striking a third rebel through the arm before it continued through the opening out the other side of the Monument.

"Piss! You boys can't spot that guy?" Tumult was livid. Flesh and blood spattered all over the place. The bullet had missed Tumult by inches.

"The light's not good, sir, and they're in thermo-suits," one rebel responded.

Tumult started yelling. "Then get your ass out there with an attack pack and get behind those guys! Start setting some fires! Wind's blowing this way! Go burn those sons-a-bitches out!"

Three rebels ran down the spiral staircase to the base. "Those son-a-bitches will need those thermo-suits after we're done with them," said Tumult after the three young men raced out of sight.

"When we goin'?" asked Glitch.

"We're goin' to head out real late tonight, but before we do, we're going to set as many fires as possible to keep the Feds busy. It would be nice if my little brother and his group took off at the same time. They'd have trouble chasing us if we took off in all directions."

"Not all directions," Glitch looked off at the Atlantic.

In a small room at the base of the monument, Helen worked desperately on the Virginian's leg. His friend assisted her by handing her instruments and dabbing her forehead to capture sweat droplets forming. She heard about the attacks on the Hancock Tower and found her mind wandering off to conversations among Tumult's Mountain Boys in the other room.

Tater lay on the floor below the wounded man's bed, lending moral support with her sympathetic gaze. The animal could smell the traces of death--the blood and flesh of open wounds, the antiseptic used in surgery--the same odors that surrounded her during Barry's demise. She got up and trotted out the partially closed door to the main room of the Obelisk to join Butch and Thad where the bulk of Tumult's rebels waited.

Butch, Thad, and Tater had gotten to Boston by hiding on a seafood truck. Because Colebrook was at the end of the route in their delivery, it had been a straight trip to Boston's docks. The boys and dog simply climbed aboard while the driver was inside the Colebrook diner; they hid behind empty boxes. But the Rousells were in Boston two days before the time that The Wizard was to meet Chaos at Union Wharf. They had heard the Virginians shooting it out with a gang. After they teamed up, it had been Tater with her keen senses that helped them evade the hoodlums of Boston. Then they had found Tumult's rebels.

Helen hadn't had the chance to fully express her outrage with the boys; she was frantically trying to save the Virginian's leg. She had assisted in operations before but found that actually doing the cutting was totally different. The motor-gun shot had shredded the leg, five balls in all. Helen was concerned with leaving the young man without use of his leg. The knee was in terrible condition. She tried to reconnect muscle, but without additional blood to replace blood lost, Helen finally wrapped it up and injected him with a heavy dose of antibiotics. "Hope this works out. I'm not a surgeon, but I got out all the shot and tried to line some things up in there. It's important you keep it still for awhile."

"Thanks, ma'am." The wounded rebel was conscious through the operation. All Helen had for anesthesia was a local.

"I need to slow down in my old age, anyway," the rebel was still sweaty from his fever. The antibiotics would help, but not right away. "You'd best get back while you can. You know, ma'am, if you weren't with us, you could probably just walk out of here. They're not looking for someone like you at the check points."

"You're sweet," she held his hand. "But I *am* with you."

Mountain Boys began gearing up in the main room. Helen overheard their comments about the Hancock Tower and went to the main room. "What about the Mountain Boys in the Hancock Tower?" she couldn't help but ask.

"Commander Chaos went runnin' down the side of the tower, pushed off, shot a hole through the glass and swung in. Slicker than shit."

"Is he all right?" Helen followed up.

"I guess so. We received a message from them sayin' the rest of them would follow and leave the tower shortly."

Helen added, "They'll appreciate any help you give them."

"We're not going there. We're supposed to set fires on the north and east side behind the snipers. The winds should drive it to them. The boss' idea," the rebel said, reluctant to lay claim to the notion.

The Virginian cut in, "There's nothing but apartments and townhouses there. People's homes. There might still be folks in some of them."

"Just following orders. We can't locate them the way they shoot from the hollows of the buildings, especially in this light. They're wearing thermo stuff."

As attack packs talked at the base of the monument, Butch and Thad slipped up the stairs, Tater chasing them. At the top, Butch told Tumult how Tater had spotted gang members in the streets ahead of them, allowing them to maneuver through Old Boston without getting captured. "Me and Thad have been staying with the Mountain Boys all winter. We know the whistles and stuff. But if you don't want Thad and me to help spot that sniper, the Virginian can do it with Tater. He's worked with her, too. He'll tell ya."

Tumult turned to Glitch with a grin on his face, "We're not going anywhere, are we Glitch?" The rebel leader liked the notion of two gutsy kids and a dog, leading an attack pack and doing something grown men failed to do. It was downright inspirational.

"Well, Chief," Glitch took a final draw from his cigarette and tossed it out the window, "if that dog could spot 'em, it would save burning up all these homes and pissin' a bunch of people off."

"Yes," Tumult agreed. "All right, you two just get the hell out before I change my mind. You got an hour. And take the Virginian with you to head the pack."

After the Rousells left, Tumult thought aloud, "I'm impressed with those little sons-a-bitches."

"Heard say," Glitch added, "those boys were at Dixville." He glanced down at his bandaged-up thumb as he said it.

"Do tell!" Tumult nodded his head and scrunched his lips, "Tough little bastards."

"We got the go-ahead from Tumult to find the sniper with our dog," Butch loudly announced to all. "Tumult said the Virginian is supposed to head it up and we're to down them surgically. No fires."

"Just how're you going to do that, squirt?" asked one of Tumult's rebels.

Butch pointed to Tater. "Dogs hear and smell one hundred times better than people. She'll freeze when she spots something. Me and Thad will go to handle her."

Six rebels looked at the golden retriever, now laying with her chin on her paws. One of them commented, "I hope the hell you know what you're doing. That dog don't look like no Rin Tin Tin." Tater rolled her eyes toward them with a pouty gaze.

Chaos received the signal: The Wizard had sent falsified E-mail to the JFK Building and ordered the Feds to transfer Max and the Virginians to another facility in Boston. The Wizard and some of his friends had rescued the captives without a shot. The group now planned to neutralize a tank at Arlington Street in forty minutes. Chaos didn't ask for details. The Boston natives rigged a gas tanker truck with a flare so it would blow up on impact with the Abrams 111 tank on Arlington.

Sensors in the tank picked up the truck advancing. The crew inside thought nothing of a truck coming down the street until it kept picking up speed. Then they noticed the burning flare taped to its roof. They didn't understand the significance, but knew something was up. They spun the turret around.

It was too late. The truck with the trailer and all its gallons of fuel smacked into the tank lunging both forward on impact. Though the Boston man driving had jumped out just before the hit, the blast threw him back. Flames set fire to his clothing. He remained on the ground rolling over and over to get it out. Eventually he simply removed his pants and shirt. Grateful to be alive, the man staggered off the road to lay in the cool grass of Boston's Public Garden.

The Abrams 111 took off down Beacon Street trying to escape the inferno. The tanker had plunged into the turret of the Abrams tank. The tank's gun speared through the cab and into the tank of fuel behind. Its tank of fuel had folded like an accordion and clung to the Abrams in a death-grip. The resulting blast and flames were sucking the oxygen from within the Abrams. Fire engulfed the entire street and spread west as the damaged tank fled. Spilled, flaming gas followed the vehicle two blocks before the tank overheated. Its own fuel joined the illumination. A neighboring tank emerged from a side street and sat motionless, watching its kind wither in flames.

Just after the Wizard's attack on the tank, Chaos' tractor-trailer whirled out of Arlington Street onto Beacon--swiping through the flaming rubble. They slowed down passing Boston's Public Garden where Max and one of the Boston men stood with their hands extended. Without stopping, rebels on the back of the truck locked forearms and yanked Max and his friend in. Abrams cannon fire took off the edge of a building as they turned the corner. They whipped by the Shaw/54th Regiment Memorial--through Old Boston--on toward the warehouse on Union Wharf. The Wizard would meet them at the dock later.

In their madcap race, the vehicle swerved side to side, leaning on corners, jolting the buggy around obstacles that littered the streets.

Helen had packed and was waiting outside the memorial between the small buildings. She had kept the picture of Barry in her shirt pocket; it was something to help her remember the good times. After finding out too late that Butch and Thad had gone with the attack pack, Helen waited for them, but she was anxious to return to Chaos' triad at the wharf. Being around Tumult made Helen uneasy. She shook her head, mumbling to herself, *who would think they were brothers.*

Attack packs geared up inside the monument; they wanted to leave before the Army decided to encircle Bunker Hill with tanks. The radio frequency jammers did a masterful job of delaying tanks from moving forward. Not having rapid communication threw the Feds into a tizzy, bumping their communication technology back two hundred years. Orders had to go by carrier and rebel snipers were scattered everywhere to assassinate the messengers.

"That laser communication shit could give our boys an edge on gettin' around," Tumult remarked as he joined Helen outside for a chat. They were alone. "Why do you think my little brother didn't share that technology with me?" He put his arm against the wall behind her and leaned in closer.

Helen didn't like his intrusion, "It was The Wizard's doing. He designed the thing. I don't think there's any big scheme or anything. Your brother just asked The Wizard if such a thing was possible and when we arrived in Boston they got the parts and made them. Don't be paranoid."

Warm spring breezes drifted up from Boston Harbor to create a mist that crawled and clung to lower altitudes below the monument. Once dense enough, it would creep its way upward to the base of the obelisk. Within that fog, a vapor ebbed and flowed, picking at human remains for any morsels of life it might have missed.

Tumult saw the backdrop as romantic. He leered over her with a lap-dog gaze expecting some kind of response. Helen assumed it was his way to intimidate, but she wasn't about to give in to the fear: "I don't know what the point is of all this posturing," she looked at his arm propped against the wall, "I'm already interested in someone else."

"There's something my little brother didn't fill you in on: Southern families share things." It became a stare down.

The wet, joyous nose of Tater vaulted up into their faces and broke it up. Helen blessed the pet's intrusion. The Virginian, Butch, and Thad followed behind with the attack pack and an African-American Army Regular as prisoner. "The perimeter is secured, sir."

"Take the nigger inside," Tumult ordered.

Helen was the last to come in, and found a crowded room of Mountain Boys around the black Army Regular seated on the floor. "Why'd you bring the monkey in?" Tumult asked him.

"We pinned him down and he gave up." The question seemed odd to the Virginian, then he remembered hearing about the gang member's crucifixion. A warm rush that started at the top of his neck raced down his spine. It dawned on the Virginian that this part of the Triad didn't take prisoners. Chaos had his rebels shoot prisoners in the leg and leave them.

"We can get information from him," Butch chimed in.

"Niggers don't know nothing to tell us, boy," Tumult declared. "We shoot white Feds in the knee, but niggers, we just shoot 'em. Pop! Pop! Pop!" In one motion, Tumult had whipped a gun out from his shoulder holster and placed three rounds in the man's face. He turned to the Virginian, "You're new in this group, but we don't take prisoners. No place to put 'em."

It even stunned the Mountain Boys watching, most of Tumult's group were from the North Country. Butch and Thad just stared wide-eyed as the soldier quivered, squirting blood. Helen walked through the group and latched onto the boys; she took them to the little room where Chaos' wounded rebel lay and closed the door behind her. She leaned against the door and looked at the floor stupefied.

Butch, still dazed from the incident, "That ain't fair, shootin' 'em like that."

Helen put her arms around the Rousell brothers. She was nearly in tears. "Now listen to me, Tumult is an evil man. It doesn't matter who it is, you don't murder people because of their beliefs or color. We'll get out of this, but don't think for a minute that that man was justified murdering someone like that." She jolted as the door opened.

The Virginian and Tater came in. "Are you all right?"

Helen nodded and swallowed, "I guess I shouldn't have been surprised. That man is the Devil." Helen looked at the wounded man she had worked so hard to save. "What's going to happen to him? Does Tumult take his own wounded?"

"I have to stay with him," the other Virginian uttered. "Tumult said he wouldn't let me return to Chaos' unit."

"But why?" Helen asked.

"Either Tumult likes me because I routed out that sniper," he said, "or it's just another way to annoy his brother. He won't let us go back with you; Tumult's keeping my wounded friend with his group so I don't bolt. That man is diabolical, all right. Don't worry though, when he's better, we're going back to Chaos' group. I can't put up with this."

"God, I can see now why Chaos didn't tell me Tumult was his brother."

"Tater and the boys can go back with you. Do you have a gun?" Helen nodded yes with a look of concern--the 22 she had gotten from Butch earlier. The Virginian pulled out his Glock Autopistol from his belt to demonstrate. "Make sure your safety is always off so when you go to use it, it will work," he continued. "Always pull off three rounds at a time if you want to be sure of hitting something." He took the ammo clip out of the handle and held the gun with both hands, "Bam, bam, bam. Always pull off three rounds at a time." He put the clip back in the gun and placed it back in his belt. The rebel's demonstration had Butch and Thad's full attention.

"You're scaring me," Helen confessed.

"Tumult's taking you back to Chaos' triad, isn't he?"

Helen thought about his statement as she looked at him. Neither one blinked. She knew what he meant by the question: From all appearances, Tumult hated his brother, and anyone associated with him.

Helen went out the door to the main room. The Virginian gave a thumbs-up sign to the boys, the jagged scar on his thumb visible.

Two attack packs followed, Tumult armed with a motor-gun.

They headed down the west slope of Bunker Hill into the tight, narrow streets that bordered it. The whole area around the Hill was nothing but townhouses, packed together so tightly that concrete choked off greenery of any significance. Fire would have ravaged the area. And the historic colonial homes, as run down as they were, would have been gone with only their brick shells and foundations remaining. It occurred to Helen that the people of Boston were lucky to have young men of character like the Virginians. Even the gruff, burly Wolfenstein had a kinder side, she had come to realize.

While hiking through the suburban maze of crowded homes, one attack pack gained a lead of two hundred meters. This was deliberate: If Feds or gangs hit the lead pack, they would whistle back enemy numbers and location so the following team could flank them. The Mountain Boys had it down to a science. Using the laser sights on their weapons, attack packs had scrimmaged constantly in their off-hours in the North Country, a sport very similar to paintball but with better range and without the sting of a high-speed ball.

After leaving the residential section they traveled below an elevated highway that hid them from possible spotters; cloud cover remained, making for an unusually dark night. Helen found it difficult to follow the rebel in front of her. No one spoke; only random, dull footsteps were heard down the desolate highway.

Visual and sound deprivation heightened other senses. Varied, damp smells rose from the Charles River, some odors natural, some oil residue. But Helen knew something was going on among them. Tater's ears twitched and perked, trying to recognize whistled commands. They spoke a language of their own, an invisible dialect of another species, in a world they knew all too well. The regimented movements of Mountain Boys peeking around corners with readied autopistols and sprinting from cover to cover gave Helen a sense of security, knowing these assassins were there to protect her. Despite that, the sense that something was about to happen nagged at her. Though the Rousell children were not her own, she had an urge to hold them, particularly Thad. The boy had gone through so much, yet still continued to try and right the wrong put upon them at Dixville. Though mortified by events around him, Thad continued; courage is nothing less.

Tumult told the lead pack to scout ahead and wait for them at the warehouse. Brandishing a motor-gun, he stayed behind at Quincy Market to meet the second group. Members of the pack forced open a door in one of the buildings and took a break from the hike. Helen waited inside the structure with Tater.

Quincy Market was a complex of small shops and restaurants, an open mall of sorts with long continuous buildings on each side of a closed-off street. Years ago specialty shops dominated the mall--some of the best dining in Boston could be found there. Small vending carts with blue canopies dotted the square in those times; people of many colors crowded the square to browse.

Helen roamed though the halls of the abandoned complex and found herself in a glass atrium watching Tumult talking to members of the pack under a shredded canopy in the square below. She could see the shadowy Mountain Boys take the Rousell brothers toward the elevated interstate and counted to herself: one, two . . . eleven. She jolted. *Oh shit!* Tumult was the only one remaining. Even in the shadows she could see him look her way.

She raced down the hall checking for open doors. Tater pranced behind, not understanding the urgency. Finally, on the third level Helen found an open door, closed it, and hid behind a counter inside.

With her weapon drawn, she waited quietly for what seemed like hours. She could feel her own heart pounding, her breathing seemed rapid and loud.

The shop door opened and closed. Helen decided to confront him. She stood up, sending one round into the ceiling to let him know she was armed, "Pop."

"Hold it! Hold it! We were just looking for you. Where did you go?" Tumult had left his motor-gun in the hall. He hadn't known she had a gun.

"We? I saw the attack pack move off," She could hardly keep the gun from shaking.

"The first group is looping around to secure the area. They're coming back."

"Yeah, right," Helen commented sarcastically. "I'm going the rest of the way alone. It's only about five blocks. Why did we stop here in the first place, so close to our destination?"

"Like I said, to secure the area."

She wanted to believe him but knew better. "Thanks, but I'm going the rest of the way alone. How did you find me?"

"You left your dog outside the door."

Helen shook her head realizing her stupidity. "Just get out." She extended the gun.

"Okay. I'm leaving." He eased out of the shop, letting the dog in as he closed the door behind himself.

Helen waited a minute before going to the door. As she turned the knob it burst open on her, the door slamming her in the forehead. A hand reached out from the darkness and grabbed her gun hand, yanking her into the hallway.

Tater did not misread this sign. She lunged at Tumult. By then, he had twisted the gun from her grasp and shot three rounds through the darkness at the animal. Tater hobbled backwards and collapsed in the hall.

"You bastard! You shot my dog," shrieked Helen, incredulous.

He yanked her back into the shop and closed the door. "You shouldn't have had the thing jump me. Besides, that mutt would have interfered with our intimate moment, unless you're into the animal thing."

"What's your brother going to say?"

"Like I said: Our family shares. Even if he did mind, we don't exactly get along anyway."

Helen kept backing away from him, groping around in the dark for something to defend herself with; she knew he couldn't see any better than she could in the murk. She found a table lamp and swung at him. The lamp struck him on the forearm. "You bitch!" he swore, but the strike also knocked the 22 revolver out of his hand. He grabbed Helen's wrists and spun her to the floor. Tumult clumped both her wrists into one grasp and pressed them down above her head. His remaining free hand unzipped her jacket and in one motion stripped all the buttons off her blouse.

Helen, with clinched teeth, "Get your damn hands off me! I'm warning you!"

He opened her jeans and wrestled them down to her thighs. "*You're* warning *me*? You're in no position to warn me." He unhooked the front of her bra and began massaging her breasts. "You know, I've always appreciated these. They're the first things I noticed about you. I see they're perky from the cold."

The shop's showcase window exploded as Tater burst through it. She dove for Tumult's throat with all her teeth bared. During the struggle with the beast, Helen groped about the floor in search of the 22 revolver. Finding it, she called Tater off. The animal staggered to the edge of the room and lay down. Much of the blood remaining on the enemy, belonged to her.

Helen tugged up her jeans with the other hand as she approached her adversary who still lay on the floor. "Your rule, as I recall, is shoot African-Americans and maim whites. I can live with that." She leveled the 22 at his crotch and fired.

"You whore." The bullet missed his genitalia and struck the edge of his upper thigh.

"Let's go, Tater." Helen quickly pulled her clothes together and left. The dog didn't follow. "Come, Tater." Tater lay motionless on the floor, her eyes glazed. She had used every ounce of strength to rescue Helen; none remained for herself. "Oh, Tater." She went over to her dog and looked. Tumult began to move toward her. "Hold it right there, buster! Another move like that and I'll empty the rest of this gun on you."

That stopped him, but Tater was wrecked: One bullet had caught her in the neck, another in her lower rib cage.

Helen lifted her pet with a grunt, and left. Forty meters down the hall the unmistakable vroom of a motor-gun revving up echoed through the empty corridor. Helen realized she had forgotten to dispose of his weapon before leaving, and maybe she hadn't maimed him. *I should have shot the bastard three times.* She picked up her pace. Her arms began to burn already from carrying Tater. A hail of motor-gun balls sprayed the corridor, stray ones shattering showcase windows on both sides of them. Helen and Tater turned the corner as balls whizzed by into the shop at the end of the hallway.

Helen scurried across a glass-enclosed walkway that led to the shopping complex on the other side of the square. She checked for open doors--finding none. Her arms sagged with the weight of the dog. Helen gave up looking for an open room and frantically bolted down two flights of stairs and left the building onto the street. Her first intention was to race to the warehouse. *Think this time*, Helen said to herself. *That bastard knows where I'm going.* More cautiously now, she prowled up Chatham Street and circled back to Quincy Market. She waited on the glass walkway she had crossed before. From that vantagepoint she could view any shadows moving in the courtyard or hear Tumult approach from the corridor in either building.

It was a relief to put the dog down. Her arms hung limp by her side as she rubbed each elbow in turn. Helen kneeled over Tater. She felt overwhelming sympathy for her pet. It crossed her mind that if she wasn't carrying the dog she could have outrun Tumult to the warehouse. After all, he was shot. She knew something kept her clinging to the animal: Tater was the last vestige of her son's life; she was another being with a shared love for Barry.

Helen stroked Tater's head, "You're a good pup." The dog only blinked but she had heard it. Helen took off her jacket and girdled Tater's midsection. She wrapped the animal's neck with her blouse and hugged her bloody pet. "You'll be all right. I'll take care of you now." As she said it, from her crouched position with arms about the dog, Tumult appeared at the end of the courtyard. He followed her trail, scanning the ground for sign. Helen looked down the hall and saw the drops of blood. "He trailed us," she whispered to herself.

Tumult stood just below the glassed walkway. The man looked at the pecks of blood leading toward the stairway to the side. Helen raised the revolver and clicked off three rounds through the glass just as the Virginian had instructed her. "Pop! Pop! Click. Click."

After the shattered panel fell, Tumult stood below in the opening holding his face; a bullet had struck his nose. To Helen, the rest happened in agonizing slow motion. Tumult pulled his hand from his bloody face and yanked the starter cord to his motor-gun. The stream of balls began shattering the entire glass enclosure, strafing back and forth across the walkway.

Nuggets of glass hailed down on woman and dog, engulfing them in a shower of pointy teeth that pricked with every hit. Helen leaned over Tater to shield her from the rain of glass as she crawled and tugged, staying low to the concrete floor that provided refuge.

The only remaining garment Helen had on her upper body was her bra. Tiny lacerations tattooed her back. The shower of glass that pummeled her paralyzed her. Finally, small hands grabbed her and tugged her forward. Thad had run off from Tumult's attack pack and circled back.

On hands and knees, pulling Tater, Helen crawled toward the main building. Crystal nuggets cut her hands and knees. The glass enclosure gave way to cool, fresh air. Helen felt the warm blood from the plethora of cuts as they pooled together and oozed down her side in streaks. The shooting had finally stopped when Tumult emptied his ammo hopper. He clutched his face as he headed back in the direction of Bunker Hill.

In the hollows of the building, Helen patted Tater's head and rested against the wall. Thad began taking his jacket off to put around her. They were about five blocks away from the wharf.

"Ya found her!" Butch declared. He had made his escape from the attack pack by claiming he had to go to the bathroom and sneaking off. When the rebels had gone to look for Butch, Thad ran away to distract them. Legmen from the pack raced after him. When they saw they couldn't gain on the boy, they dropped their guns and ammo to lighten their load. It was still no use,

Thad knew he could outrun the larger legmen. And he did.

Now, with lacerations of his own on the back of his head and neck, Thad stood over Helen; she was shaking from the encounter. He had overcome his own fear to save her. Helen knew that. She got up and hugged the boy. "Thank you." He looked away and responded with a jittery smile; she had very little on.

Butch picked up Tater with a grunt, "Gotta go." They headed toward Union Wharf.

At Union Wharf, Chaos, Max and Captain Thomas of Regular Army discussed the possibilities of getting out of the city. The Wizard had set up the meeting with Thomas; unbeknownst to Chaos and Max, Thomas had been the officer in charge at the Dixville site.

"We've got a ship in the harbor loaded with supplies and munitions," said Thomas. "If you can get it out of the harbor and back to the North Country, you can have it."

"It's not that simple," Chaos corrected. "If we all get on that ship it would only take one missile to take us out. A pilot with computer-enhanced imaging could fly in this stuff. They only need to launch one missile."

"You're right," the Captain replied. "But the boat is loaded with top-of-the-line weaponry and an array of hand-held missiles. Not only that, but there are eighty-seven Guards on that boat who know how to use the stuff and want to join your resistance. Most of them are from the North Country. We've been able to get information, even with the communication blackout that the military imposed. There's *more* Guard who have gone AWOL and would like to join. It's just a matter of locating them and letting them know."

"I still think we should split the munitions up in a bunch of different boats," Chaos persisted.

"Agreed."

At that point Max had only listened in on the discussion. He spotted Helen entering the warehouse, now carrying Tater. The boys and one of Chaos' scouting packs followed. "Helen!" He ran over and offered to carry the dog but she refused. With Thad's jacket around her shoulders, she defiantly staggered in with blood-streaked hair. She saw Chaos but continued to a table where she placed her pet. The stunned group encircled her, all asking questions at the same time. Helen ignored them. "Somebody get me a medical kit. I've got to fix her."

Chapter 13

Helen sat in an office just beyond the warehouse. She had washed her hair and cleaned up, finally finding time to sit and relax behind a large desk. She instinctively reached to her shirt pocket to find the picture of Barry. It was gone. She remembered the photo was in the shirt left at Quincy Market in the struggle. Helen had an uncontrollable urge to return to the site. She would be without a picture of her son until she returned home. If she made it home. Helen got up from her chair to see Chaos. As she opened the door, she was surprised to find someone opening it at the same time. It was Captain Thomas. A rebel had told him Helen's son was at Dixville.

He fumbled, trying to find the words, finally telling her about his part in the massacre. Captain Thomas' pathetic apology wasn't the way she envisioned her first meeting with the murderer of her son. Oh, she knew it was an automated ambush, but some soulless son-of-a-bitch set it up. Helen couldn't look at him; she was uncertain how to feel and still numbed from her ordeal with Tumult.

"I just wanted to give you this." Captain Thomas handed her a memory disk. "I copied the imaging off the AutoMan. Do as you wish with it; it's about time everyone knew what really happened that day." His hand shook as he held it out to her.

"What is it?"

"Compressed imaging of the Dixville Massacre."

"Compressed imaging?"

"It shows what happened that day."

Helen held it with both hands and just looked at it. She didn't know if she wanted to see it.

"How are the boys who survived?" Thomas asked.

The question jolted Helen from her trance. "What boys?" She didn't know what to tell him; that had been secret.

"There were two kids in the roots of a fallen tree. I didn't see a blood trail so I presumed they were not hit."

"Ah--"

"You don't have to say anything. I understand." Captain Thomas lowered his head and backed out of the room, "I'm truly sorry. I just wish it could all be undone."

Helen looked up from the disk, "So do I." The Captain closed the door, wiping his eyes with the heel of his hand as he exited. "So do I," she repeated. Helen hadn't noticed it earlier but her eyes had tears too. She saw Wolfenstein's backpack on the edge of the desk. She opened it and pulled out his pocket computer. After loading the disk, she viewed scenes through the Toshiba graphic interface. The entire display couldn't have lasted more than two minutes from start to finish: The first Scout that triggered the device stuck his face in death's mouth, the constant strafing from side to side, then the pin-point single shots that either finished children off or targeted kids hiding behind trees and rocks. "Jesus, God!" She saw Barry. She didn't see her son actually but recognized his shoes extending out from a boulder. Helen put a hand to her mouth and stared at the screen as AutoMan pummeled away at the legs that extended beyond the stone. Her eyes winced with every flinch of her son's legs. Butch could be seen on the edge of the screen trying to go after him but an overpowering hand yanked him down. And then came Mr. Ronolou's heroic act that allowed the Rousells' escape. She replayed it over and over.

"What's that?"

Helen raised back upon hearing the words, and nearly hit Steve Morrison in the face with the back of her head. She hadn't heard him come in. "That's Dixville Notch, isn't it?" he queried, incredulous. His chewing gum fell out of his open mouth as he looked down.

The question stirred her from the nightmare. Helen nodded yes. Steve walked around her and saw the tear paths that marked her face. "I'm sorry. But you see, this can end it. This disc would hang the President. He had to know. It was at least a cover-up on the part of the White House. They knew it wasn't smugglers."

Tater woke from her anesthesia and began to stir. The new surroundings confused her. She recalled the same overwhelming stench of disinfectant at Barry's death, and in her own limited capacity, wondered why she was there. There could be no transfusion for her. On the floor beside her, Butch reached over, "Shhh, it's okay. Stay," he whispered and began stroking her head. Thad nudged a bowl of water closer to her. They appreciated the companionship of their mascot beside them. Tater accepted the solace but roamed the room with her eyes to see if Helen was somewhere among the shadows.

People moved about the ward quietly. Steve Morrison searched for Wolfenstein, scanning carefully from side to side. He found him asleep and nudged his shoulder.

"Look," demanded Morrison. Dixville images from the computer glared into Wolfenstein's eyes.

"What is it?" Wolf could hardly see. "Hold on, give me a minute." He turned his wristwatch up to the screen's light. "It's almost one o'clock!" Wolfenstein caught himself speaking too loud, "Okay, okay." They moved to the open part of the warehouse away from others. "Now, what the hell is so important?"

"AutoMan had a digital imaging system. Look." Wolfenstein watched the glaring scenes with squinted eyes. "I need you to help me get it to a news affiliate just outside Inner Boston. I want to send it tonight. We have a satellite link. There's someone there twenty-four hours a day."

Chaos noticed Wolfenstein and Steve acting peculiar and walked over to check. "Is this Dixville?" inquired Chaos looking over Steve's shoulder. Both Steve and Wolf nodded. "Where did you get this?"

Steve spoke slowly, "Captain Thomas brought it."

"How'd he get it? Never mind. I'll go ask." said Chaos. "If he was there, I want to know what he's doing here." He started to leave but turned back. "Wolf, would you make a bunch of copies of that and get them out to all the pack leaders to keep in their red disk case."

"Me too," Steve added, wanting a copy.

"And make sure Helen doesn't find out about this." Chaos could tell by their faces his warning was too late. "What?"

"She's seen it, sir," Steve confirmed.

Chaos shook his head and stomped toward the office where Helen was. Steve turned to Wolfenstein. "Did I just call him 'sir'?"

"I think you did."

Chaos found Helen seated behind the desk in a doleful state. "You all right?" He walked over slowly and pulled up a chair. Putting an arm around her, he said softly, "Steve showed it to me."

"I knew it was pretty horrible up there. I overheard some of the dads talking about it. Half the kids were gut shot and then hit a second time trying to drag themselves to cover. And what Butch said about Charlie Ronolou was true. That tough old bird did sacrifice himself to save those boys. Old Charlie, a Scout to the end."

"What was Thomas doing with the imaging from Dixville? I wonder if we can trust the guy."

"He asked about Butch and Thad," said Helen. "Well, not by name but he asked about them. He said he knew they were there hiding. He feels bad about the whole thing and wants to do something," she sighed. "The bad guys aren't what I thought they were. I don't know who to hate."

"You don't have to hate anyone." He held her in his arms. "Get some rest. We'll be leaving here within the hour." Chaos didn't want to question her at the time, but her story about being chased by a Boston gang didn't jive. "You know, the dog wasn't hit with motor-gun rounds like you said earlier. They were 22 slugs."

"Well I guess I must have accidentally hit her myself when I was shooting at them. It was dark, you know." Helen hadn't told him the truth. She was afraid of what Chaos might do, or rather, what Tumult might do to him. "And I think you already know your brother's a jerk. He just left me there."

Chaos didn't believe her, but nodded yes. "Just try to get some rest." He left to find out more about Captain Thomas.

Helen left the office, found a mat, and cuddled beside Tater, stroking the animal's head until they dozed off.

Chaos devised a three-part escape from Boston. The first strategy was to leave quickly to take advantage of the fog and darkness. Conditions made it difficult for aircraft to fly. Secondly, they would leave a radio jammer at the dock with automated Masadas fending off Seal teams that might try and silence it. All-band jammers had a radius of fifteen miles. That would put the Mountain Boys out of the Federal radar radius. If the weather stayed bad they could be well into Maine by the next day. Chaos' final ace: They would divide the munitions between many boats and make a shell game of it. They had a second jammer they would turn on in case of attack; pilots would have no communications system. The low altitude under cloud cover would make the pilots easy targets for smaller hand-held missiles from the many boats, and then they had the anti-aircraft batteries on the ship Captain Thomas had brought. Chaos was hoping the Feds' attempt to take them in Boston had been hastily thrown together and that they could just leave without a hitch.

For the past three hours attack packs had been pillaging the harbor and commandeering boats of all sizes. They found a cargo ship loaded with cigarettes stamped Taxes Paid to the Department of Alcohol, Tobacco, and Firearms, waiting in the harbor to be off-loaded. Chaos ordered the cigarettes dumped into the harbor. It was all too easy: The all-frequency jammer atop Hancock Tower still mangled radio signals for a fifteen-mile radius. And within that communication blackout, the Feds were unlikely to do much offensively. On their way out, the Mountain Boys had booby-trapped the Hancock Tower three floors above and below the jammer; they used motion detectors as the triggering device. The only way to get by the devices was to have someone go in and detonate them, or wait until the batteries in the motion sensors drained. Chaos hoped the Feds wouldn't destroy an entire building like the Hancock just to take out a radio jammer.

"I'd like some answers about why you are here," said Chaos to Captain Thomas as Mountain Boys moved supplies and gear around them.

Captain Thomas welcomed the interrogation, hoping it would clear the air and allow them to work together: "The truth about the Dixville tragedy has been withheld from the American people long enough. We were assigned to stop the smuggling in the North Country by any means necessary, the *any means necessary* emphasized. The White House wanted to make an example of the smugglers. After months with little success halting the smuggling of medical supplies, and a number of soldiers hit by locals in the hills, the AutoMan came strongly recommended. They claimed it had been thoroughly field-tested and would be perfect for blocking mountain routes in outlying areas. It had sensors to detect weight and weaponry. The thing should never have fired on those kids." He shook his head. "It just should never have happened. I'm not the only one who feels this way. There's a lot of messed up men and women in my unit trying to deal with this tragedy. As an added precaution afterward, they split up our unit and scattered us all over; we were ordered not to talk about it."

If the Captain was acting, he was very good at it. Chaos believed his story. Being a soldier of a different sort, he understood the predicament of battle, the possibility of the innocent getting hurt. "So the White House has known all along about this?"

"From the day it happened. Not everyone is in agreement: there's dissension at the top. But a direct link to the President and the Dixville Massacre isn't likely. Nothing was in writing. Besides, as tough as it is to accept, I screwed up by allowing a technician to turn off one of the sensors. It was my task force that did it. Exposing the truth about Dixville would only ruin the soldiers in my unit, at least that was my rationale for not saying anything for awhile. It won't touch the White House; they'll claim it was a military cover-up. But it might stop the bloodshed that's about to happen.

Three weeks ago, I found out about AutoMan's imaging system from our technician. He kept the disc to himself all this time; evidently the guilt got the better of him. Hardly anyone knows about the disk. Not even President Winifred."

"I guess I'm wondering where you stand," said Chaos. "A number of Guards are deserting with possibly more on the way here. Where is the Army in all this? When we get back to the North Country, is the rest of the Army going to move in and take us on?"

"There's a lot of unrest within the Army, particularly at the top. Secretary of Defense Kyle Paz believes he will be replaced by Colonel Greely."

"Greely." Chaos recognized the name from his encounters in the Tobacco uprising.

"Yes. I'm reluctant to join your side to fight my side; I've been Army all my life, but this has got to stop somewhere. I'm hoping you people can release the imaging to the public and put an end to the casualties in the North Country. This country's breaking up. There's uprisings like this going on all over the place. I don't know what the answer is."

"The Feds will just have to back off," Chaos avowed. "If they expect to regain the loyalty of the Northeast, they'll have to give in to the needs of the rural folks. When we control the land, we control the food supply. I know we're not alone in rebelling, but in this case, you have some pissed-off mothers behind it and it ain't goin' away."

Mountain Boys paraded past with stretchers of wounded, the last to be carried to the dock and loaded onto boats. Helen walked by lugging Tater, looking away as she went by Captain Thomas. The Captain sensed her coolness; old wounds he had received that day at Dixville re-opened and began to bleed once more.

The Wizard arrived at the warehouse at Union Wharf. Other than Max and the Rousells, this was the first time anyone in the Colebrook Covenant had seen him. Six-foot-one and lean with short kinky hair, The Wizard had delicate features; he was younger than anyone had expected. He carried a small backpack that housed a pocket computer, electrical parts, and tools. The Wizard had become a legend in the North Country, known primarily through his CB broadcasts. Only a handful in Vermont knew he was African-

American. If that knowledge had gotten out about The Wizard, he would have been an easy pickup by the Feds. There were few dark-skinned ethnic groups in that region.

"I've got bad news," The Wizard announced to Chaos. "I'm staying here." He noticed the Southerner's expression. "I'm sorry, but I have to stay. We're starting a Boston Covenant.

The Rebels had gained a lot of respect for The Wizard. He had helped recover Max. He was also the man responsible for their exclusive communication. While all other radio frequencies were jammed, the Mountain Boys could talk to one another. That was a tactical edge.

"We can't leave you like this, not after all you've done to help the North Country." Chaos knew they would suffer major losses if they even postponed leaving. "We've got to go tonight if we're going to escape from the city." He also understood the chance The Wizard was taking by staying in Boston to start a Covenant.

"I can't just leave my home, not with gangs running the city."

Steve had been at the edge of the group listening in. He recalled words spoken by the young man at the campfire days earlier. He blurted the phrase aloud: "You know you're home when your willing to fight for it."

Chaos recognized his maxim, words he had said to rebels in training earlier. He smiled at Steve, pleased to see the slogan returning to him through someone else. It sounded good.

The Wizard shook his head, "I guess that's true. That's why I've got to stay, despite the gangs."

One of the Virginians, spoke up from the group. "I could stay and help." A second Virginian added, "I'm in."

"Me too."

"He saved our asses on the tower," Der Dutchman stated. "I can't speak for my pack but I could stay until Boston has attack packs of their own." Others in Dutchman's pack nodded yes.

"I don't know what to say," The Wizard responded. "A couple of attack packs could take on any gang. I sure appreciate the help."

"If three fully armed attack packs volunteered, would you be able to hide them from the Feds in the city?" It concerned Chaos that his men might be getting caught up in the passion of the moment. "These white faces will stick out in Inner Boston."

"There's no problem hiding them," Wizard declared. "We'd love to have them stay in our apartment complex. We wouldn't have to pay extortion money to the gangs anymore. The thugs wouldn't be hanging around recruiting our kids either." The Wizard buttressed that line, "We could create a perimeter of lookouts to laser in and warn of any Fed movements in the city. That would give the attack packs time to shift to more secure locations if the Feds did locate us." The Wizard realized that with a couple of experienced attack packs, pushing gangs out of the city would be easy. The prospect wasn't exclusive to The Wizard, all the Boston natives would glow with the idea of restored liberty.

A short time later, Butch and Thad approached The Wizard as he spliced into a fiber-optic phone line to send the Dixville imaging to Spectator News for Steve Morrison. The Wizard noticed them staring. He knew them from Max's deer camp and had regularly corresponded with the boys by E-mail. "Hi, boys. How is your Scout group holding up?"

"Good, but we want you to have this Scout book. We want you to help us expand the Ghost Pack in Boston." Butch handed his Scout book to the Black man. "The Oath and stuff is in there."

The Wizard stopped his task to receive the book. He could tell the boys were sincere. "Thank you." The Wizard looked bewildered. "So what do I do to recruit for your pack, read the book or something?"

"There's more to it than that. They have to hear the story of the Dixville Massacre to be a member of the Ghost Pack. Ya know, me and Thad are the last of the original Pack 220." The Wizard nodded his head; so he had heard. But Butch began telling the story of Dixville. Like a relay baton passing, the lore of the massacre was re-told. The legend passed on.

Gloucester, Massachusetts (March 18)

Tumult's heel stepped squarely on the back of the starfish, forcing the yellowy innards from its carcass oozing out around the edge of his shoe. "Piss! Where the hell are we anyway?" He felt the slippery goo underfoot. "Piss! I stepped in dog shit or something." He rubbed his heel off on a clean section of the beach. Fog enveloped everything, limiting visibility to a mere fifty meters, only the bluffs of the narrow beach could be seen beyond the immediate area.

He found out about his brother's escape from the city. A guard from the remaining attack packs under The Wizard had contacted one of Tumult's patrols and informed them of recent happenings. Tumult was irate on hearing that his brother left three fully geared attack packs under the command of an afro. He sent five packs back to recover the group but Tumult's Mountain Boys found them untraceable.

Tumult's injury ached as he scanned the shoreline; he held the dressing over what was left of his nose. Even with his facial wound he had led his men out of what appeared a hopeless situation. The man had tenacity. Following his brother's lead, Tumult had boarded his attack packs onto the USS Constitution and had commandeered the nation's oldest commissioned warship out to sea. A diesel engine in its stern had navigated the sailing ship into the deeper waters of Boston Harbor, through the narrow channel of President Roads, eventually merging into the vastness of the dark gray Atlantic.

The USS Constitution, known as Old Ironsides, veteran of numerous engagements with pirates, and victorious in multiple battles against the British in the War of 1812, was now wrecked on the rocks in view of Gloucester's Fishermen Lost at Sea memorial. On behalf of the cause, Tumult shipwrecked it.

Two Mountain Boys returned from Gloucester and reported to Tumult and Glitch that phone service was out. "I don't understand," said Glitch.

"We don't need to understand," Tumult directed four attack packs with concealed Glocks to secure trucks and buses for transport. "If this outage is around for only two hours it will put us out of reach."

Washington, D.C. (March 18)

Colonel Greely sat impatiently in one of the seventh century, rosewood chairs facing the President's desk. Perched in its cage near the window, the falcon ominously surveyed the skies with apprehension. The Boston Fiasco, as Greely referred to it, was unresolved. If some of the Mountain Boys were still in the city, he wanted to isolate them and extract them.

The Colonel knew for certain that they had left in the night; enough ships were stolen in the harbor to transport a small army. Another disturbing fact: A Navy, ZF-4 Pursuit had been downed by a hand-held rocket, a U.S. model. But what really threw the nation into a tizzy was when a group of Mountain Boys from outside the city severed the fiber-optic trunks of all the larger cities throughout New England. They were more than just severed, they were blown out, leaving behind a melted tangle that would prove difficult to restore. All monetary transactions ceased throughout the East. It impacted financial markets nationwide, not to mention worldwide. The Colonel was not pleased to be called in, "I don't have time for this dog defecation, Mr. Bennett. What are we waitin' for? I got things to do."

"We're waiting for the President of the United States, Colonel," Chief of Staff Lucas Bennett said soundly as he rubbed his tattoo with a finger. The Colonel's very presence irritated Lucas. "I think that's reason enough, don't you? If you hadn't screwed up in Boston we wouldn't be having a strategy meeting."

"You Federal Boys are into meetings, aren't you?" Colonel Greely jeered.

"We're into getting things right."

"Why is it someone always has to be at fault? Can't things just happen? Couldn't the other guy have done something right? or doesn't that work in politics?"

"You had them on the tower, Colonel, and you blew it!" the Chief of Staff criticized. "We have to take out that Tobacco Bunch before the fall elections. At any cost!"

"So this is about getting you reelected. Well, I wasn't about to blow up an entire skyscraper and damage other buildings around it to get you reelected. And they aren't Tobacco Boys, as you like to call them. We ID'ed some of their dead and they're from all over the country. Some from Missouri. The gangs in Boston referred to them as Ghost Pack 220. That was the pack number of the Dixville group of Scouts killed, wasn't it? I need to know the whole story, Bennett. Are all the rumors about Dixvil--?" The Colonel stopped in mid-sentence to stare at a speck in the sky over D.C.'s downtown. "That's not a real plane." He squinted and leaned forward. "It's a scale model of a bird."

On the White House rooftop, special agent Ron spoke in monotone as he lowered his binoculars, "It's just a freaking model plane." He pinched his cigarette by the stub to put it out in a small metal container he used as a portable ashtray. Ron found the concealment a necessity with smoking prohibited on White House grounds, "Don't get all torqued up about it." His partner Paula began flipping switches on the Stinger HHR, preparing it to fire. "I'm tellin' you, Paula. You're gettin' torqued up for no reason. It's just another freaking kid fartin' around." He turned back to see the model plane bearing down on them faster than expected. "Shit, Paula, got that thing ready yet?"

The plane launched a flare. A split second later Paula fired the rocket, which zipped past the model plane, following the heat of the flare. It found the flare just beyond the walking mall on Pennsylvania Avenue.

Greely watched it all from the Oval Office, the best seat in the house. In awe, he uttered, "Those clever bastards."

Lucas ran to the door when he realized what was happening, but only got halfway there before the craft crashed into the top of the bulletproof glass with a resounding boom. Though the three-inch glass didn't break, the explosion forced it from its mounts, toppling the four-hundred-pound pane inward on top of Greely. His skull was instantly crushed, along with the seventh century desk and chairs.

The impact shook the entire West Wing of the White House. Seconds later, President Winifred opened the side door that joined his office, and saw the devastation. Chief of Staff Bennett looked back at him in horror from the other side of the room, turning his stare to Winifred's unzipped trousers and open shirt. Nancy Atherton, with an unbuttoned top, poked her head over the President's shoulder to catch a firsthand glimpse of the damage. *What a scoop*! She frantically put herself back together and attempted to call in the event on her cellular phone.

"The phones are still down!" Nancy shrieked. She turned back to the President, "Can't you do something about that?"

Security personnel flooded the room with drawn Uzi machine-guns; the woman in charge hustled the President back into the adjoining room, "You have to stay out of sight. We're open to snipers now, sir."

Winifred stared in disbelief at the mess: the seventh century desk and chair crushed, the French Savonnerie pile carpet spattered with Greely's blood. And then the falcon, feathers were flared and mangled beyond recognition.

Colebrook Congregational Church (March 19)

Helen said her peace at the edge of the First Congregational cemetery. They buried Tater beside Barry's plot in a private funeral ceremony. The animal had died from internal injuries. Twenty-four boys and Helen encircled the animal's grave in the damp night air. A chilled moon in the east illuminated gravestones marking the Scouts who had died in the Dixville Massacre.

Earlier as they rode home from Maine, Helen found out from the rebels that Butch and Thad's mother had left in the fall. She also learned that throughout the winter the Rousell brothers, with Tater, had camped with the

Mountain Boys, or at Max's deer camp, or in their own secret hideout. As Helen watched Thad, in tears and without voice, place his cherished Arrow of Light Award on Tater's grave, she realized someone had to take responsibility for them. She would do it.

Ever since the Dixville Massacre, Butch had been busy rebuilding Pack 220. Most of the new recruits were Thad's age or younger. Sam Larson, one of the larger boys in the Pack, sobbed through the ceremony. All of them had lost a brother or relative in the Dixville Massacre; and Tater was considered another one of the pack to die. "She was a good dog," said Butch in his eulogy, "and did everything we asked her to. She was as much a part of Pack 220 as anyone. Now, she's with her best friend, Barry. Don't worry though, girl; we'll get 'em back. No one murders a Scout without payback."

Helen looked from face to face as Butch spoke. Now their grim expressions didn't look like those of children.

Chapter 14

The group met at their regular spot on the edge of town in Mr. and Mrs. Philbin's cellar. Segments representing the Mountain Boys and the New Hampshire Covenant packed the room.

Time ceased in the drab underworld. Though mid-day, the room was black beyond the glow: a tight beam of sunlight crept between sill and stone, and arced across the void. Mrs. Larson sat with her massive shoulders hunched, listening to every word Reverend Thoreau spoke. The large woman didn't like what she heard and seared through the minister with her dark, beady eyes. Out of respect for his position, she refrained from saying anything. Also present were Max and Helen. Chaos and Wolfenstein represented the Mountain Boys. Others of the Colebrook Covenant besides Helen and Max were Mr. and Mrs. Philbin, Mrs. Noel, and Harvey Madison. Captain Thomas and Steve Morrison waited outside.

Reverend Thoreau came to speak to the group on behalf of the prudent population of Colebrook, who wanted a common-sense solution. "This movement has gotten out of hand. You're not considering the consequences on the rest of the community. Everybody's worked up and going along with it, but what are you fighting for? Secession? Is that it? You want to start your own country? You people have got to sit down and figure out where you want to end up. The Feds will come in here to put an end to this like they did in Utah and in the Southwest--as they did in the Carolinas."

"Like they did in Boston?" Chaos added. "What about Boston? The Feds sent the best they had against us. We got what we wanted and got out anyway. On top of that, The Wizard is starting a sister Covenant in the city with a secure communication link. And, sir, the Feds stopped nothing in the Carolinas. It simply moved here. I don't know you, but I respect your position; however, this struggle is about representation. Bad urban policies the Feds pass to gain votes, should not be placed on the backs of the rural working folks. And the very fact that uprisings happened in Utah and in New Mexico and in the Carolinas only illustrate the problem. The Feds can stop an uprising, but they can't put out the fire inside us called liberty."

"Yes! Yes!" Vanessa Larson stood and towered over the others seated. "Yes! That man is absolutely right. Someone's got to do it and it's going to be us. My little boy didn't die for nothing. There's no compromise while that crook is in the White House." Chaos' statement struck a cord with Mrs. Larson. She spoke passionately about family and community . . . as tears seeped from the corners of her eyes. She pointed one by one at others as she spoke, her tiny eyes squinted and peered beyond them. "That bastard in Washington might as well have signed his resignation in blood the day those boys died. I want him out of there. There's no room for compromise! No room!"

Helen's jaw firmed up with the recollections Mrs. Larson conjured up; her squinted eyes held back tears of rage. Reverend Thoreau spoke out before Helen could react, "Fundamental change can take place through the system. We should at least work out a truce and start a dialogue."

"No way," said Helen. "No way." Mrs. Philbin and Mrs. Larson joined in. The three women began talking at once, stating their opposition to Thoreau's idea. Vanessa Larson's statement the last definitive voice in the mêlée, "And I don't think you have any business telling us what we should or shouldn't do. Who did you lose?" Mrs. Larson taunted the Reverend.

A pause. Chaos and Wolfenstein looked at one another realizing the dynamics of the situation. Harvey Madison had no idea how militant the New Hampshire covenant had become. His vision of the Covenants as that of a benevolent, self-help organization had turned into a violent uprising. He looked to Max. Max stared ahead expressionless as he sucked his teeth; he was unshaken by the suggestion of armed revolt.

Chaos broke the silence, "Well, there you go, Reverend. I think we're going to prepare for a fight. If you wish to contact the Feds and set up a meeting and talk with them, that's fine, but we have to prepare for the worst. They can't be trusted."

Reverend Thoreau sulked as he nodded and collected his things to leave. Turning to Mrs. Larson, he said, "I *have* lost something. A whole town. And a way of life." Putting his hat on, he left.

"We're meeting down here for obvious reasons," the President stated flatly as staff members sat around a large oval table and looked back at him expectantly. The Map Room in the basement of the White House was small but today it seated Secretary of Defense Kyle Paz, Chief of Staff Lucas Bennett and Secretary of Human Concerns Darwin Combs comfortably. An additional member to the group sat away from the others, Commander Serrac, an obvious stranger. Kyle glanced his way and wondered what function this young commander had at the meeting.

"This is what we have." President Winifred grabbed the portable computer below the wall-sized, view screen and moved it to the head of the table where he sat. He flicked on the screen and the entire wall lit up with a live satellite view of the Earth. Winifred moved the track-point to the North Country and clicked. The room lights automatically faded. "It's not a big area to go into. Not nearly as bad as Utah and the Southwest were." Clifford clicked the Colebrook area and the big screen zoomed in again. "Without cloud cover we can look at everything." The greenery of the village park and the grassy patch behind the Congregational Church could be seen, but the sixty-five rectangles of fresh grass behind the Church went unnoticed. The President clicked a drop-down menu and chose the MAPPED GRID options, which changed the screen to a computer diagram of the village. He found the Philbin house and clicked the pre-marked structure. The screen switched back to a close-up, satellite view of the house and surrounding area. "It isn't just the Tobacco Boys anymore; there are some Army and National Guard deserters." Captain Thomas, with several others of his group, could vaguely be seen under a scant cherry tree on the viewing screen, their military uniforms visible below the clusters of blossoms. Two Chipping Sparrows nervously fluttered from branch to branch near their nest in the same tree, unwilling to leave their home despite the impending invasion. "The so-called Covenant is meeting in this place right now."

Lucas turned to Secretary of Defense Kyle Paz, "Do we have anything like the Israeli satellite with a Masada?"

"I think you know," said Paz, "we signed an agreement with China, Korea, and Japan not to develop space weapons of that type. Israel held off signing. Getting nuked changed their perspective on things."

"General Paz, I know damn well that our satellites could direct a missile right through the door of that house." Lucas pointed at the wall monitor. "And I question your loyalty, sir!"

"You *should* question my loyalty because I'm not inclined to use the United States Military to assassinate its citizens. We're not allowed to do that in other countries and we're not doing it here."

"Attacking the President of the United States was an act of war! Knocking out the communication system of the entire East coast is an act of war!" Chief of Staff Bennett flared.

"Hold on here," said Winifred. "We're getting nowhere with this."

Secretary of Human Concerns Darwin Combs confirmed the statement, "General Paz is correct, you know. Something like that is legally baseless. We can't just circumvent the law that way, even if they did attack the White House."

"If?" Lucas reacted. "The Tobacco Bunch used those little kamikaze planes on the Prudential Tower. The very same kind!"

"Lucas! Please!" The President's tone was more insistent this time. "I'll have none of this." He collected himself. "I asked Commander Serrac to join us. He flew in from . . . . "

"The Amur River Region of East Russia," Serrac filled in the President's awkward lapse in memory.

"Thank you. The Commander has had a lot of experience fighting guerrilla forces in that region. Their terrain is similar to the North Country, as is the weather. What's your insight on this, Commander?"

Serrac rose and walked over to the screen. He was six-foot two and sharp looking. Commander Serrac was part Mexican, thick chested with a slender waist--the stuff diehard novels routinely portray. There was not a hair out of place, every pleat of his uniform pressed, every wrinkle ironed to a crisp edge. "Sir, could you zoom out to the immediate area, please."

As the President looked for the drop-down menu to pull the satellite view back to a wider scan, Reverend Thoreau could be seen on screen coming out the front door of the Philbin house. He walked directly to the tree where Captain Thomas and Steve Morrison stood. The viewing screen zoomed out to a regional map.

Reverend Thoreau spoke to Captain Thomas, "You started this thing. You should be in there trying to stop it!"

"I don't think there's anything I could say that they would want to hear, sir."

Reverend Thoreau continued, "If the town could just have more time to get over the tragedy. You could propose some type of strategy that would provide more time. We're going to try and arrange a meeting with the Feds but we need someone from the Covenant to be there. The Covenant might listen to a soldier such as yourself. Just talk to them."

Commander Serrac pointed to the Dixville region and surrounding area. "Unlike the Amur region in East Russia, the North Country has a network of back roads. We can make our perimeter along these roads, using line-of-sight or sensors. If our satellite sensors show them concentrated around Colebrook and Dixville Notch, we can tighten our perimeter around that immediate area. The smaller the perimeter, the more tightly compacted we can keep our forces. Limiting their territory is paramount." He pulled his hand down from the viewing screen and paused to give thought. "Another factor is time. We have a large number of Guards going AWOL. If they're headed to the North Country we have a big problem, your earlier photo of the soldiers under the tree is evidence of that." Winifred zoomed in on the Philbin place again to see the figures blurred by the limbs and flora of the tree.

"This is all wrong," stated Darwin Combs. "Constructive dialogue should be our first wave of attack. I'm disturbed by the unstated assumption that this has to end in violence. And what particularly disturbs me, is Chief of Staff Bennett's notion to use a satellite to assassinate American citizens."

"I didn't say anything like that. I only asked if we had them!" Lucas nearly yelled it out.

"Of course you didn't, Luc," Winifred consoled. "And Darwin, dialogue *is* our first option, but we must prepare. Like Commander Serrac stated, the time factor is important. No one in this room, including yourself, really expects anyone in the North Country to turn themselves in for what they did in Boston, or for the murder and attempted murder at the White House. You are right though, and I want you to make contact with them. Arrange that dialogue."

"I want to start right away."

The President nodded.

Darwin Combs closed files on his pocket computer and left the room.

"Where do we start?" asked Mrs. Larson after Reverend Thoreau had left. The group looked back toward Chaos and Wolfenstein.

"Are we talkin' tactical strategy?" asked Chaos. He got up from his chair and asked for something to write with. Mrs. Philbin went for paper and markers. Chaos looked shabby; he was unshaven and dressed in dirty blue jeans and a red flannel shirt. He wore a Mail Pouch Tobacco hat. With his chiseled physique and folksy attire, he looked like a local farmer.

Mrs. Philbin returned with her grandson's large drawing pad and a fat crayon. She opened the pad and leafed through it for a blank page, stopping on a picture her grandson had drawn; she moved on and tore out a blank piece. The awkwardness in the moment muted everyone. "Here." She handed it to Chaos and sat down, clutching the drawing pad to her chest.

Chaos taped the sheet to a blank section of the wall just beyond the light. "Three things are critical: time, territory, and the support of the people. That support may be willing or forced support, preferably willing." He drew a big circle on the paper, splitting it into sections like a piece of pie. "The center is Dixville Notch. It's rough terrain, and if the road through the Notch is blocked then they have to go out around. This is how the *Pie Tactic* works: Twelve attack packs are assigned to each sliver of the pie. As the Feds locate and attack Dixville, attack packs engage and down troopers from behind, within their sliver. If one sliver of the pie is having trouble, attack packs from nearby slivers flank the Feds. Within each sliver, attack packs engage in typical bait and bushwhack tactics, getting Federal units to chase a pack into unsecured woods, so waiting groups can ambush them.

Packs also need places to wait undetected, so they can drop back to their sanctuary if they begin to get flanked. Concealment is critical. We have to build vented bunkers below ground that can't be detected by heat scopes from a satellite or plane. Our biggest advantage is communication. When the radio jammers go on, their patrols are isolated. We can signal with laser from mountaintop to mountaintop and with line-of-sight from pack to pack. The Feds should experience utter confusion within their ranks. Their casualties will be very high following their initial attack."

Harvey Madison raised his hand. "Can I ask a question?"

"Sure."

"Are you counting on the Vermont side to come into this big battle, because unless things have changed drastically, I don't think we're ready to take on the most powerful nation in the world in a civil war?" Harvey had worded his comment carefully.

Chaos looked at the group. Other than Wolfenstein and Max, they didn't look like much. Helen and Mrs. Larson looked up with interest as though they would be the ones in the bunkers. It was hard for Chaos to envision anyone other than Mountain Boys running about the woods executing attack pack maneuvers. "We could use the help but I expect the other two parts of the Triad to come in on this, at least my brother Snake from the Vermont side. Snake must have been the one responsible for knocking out the phone service in New England by severing the optical trunks. And I suspect he arranged the attack on the White House, too. Snake can be reasonable, as well as resourceful."

"Reasonable?" Helen wondered allowed.

Mrs. Larson spoke up, "You're missing something here: The Wizard. He helped start this whole Covenant thing in Vermont. We would be crazy to do anything without bringing him in on this." Other people from Colebrook's Covenant commented in support of Vanessa's suggestion.

"The Wizard is in the process of organizing their own covenant in Boston. I don't know if he's in any position to help us," Max commented.

Harvey was determined to defuse the crisis, "I just want us to agree that we will not initiate any more attacks on Washington until Reverend Thoreau has had a chance to work out a deal."

"I'll contact my brothers and let them know our intentions," Chaos answered. "I warn you though: I can't control what my brothers do."

General Paz had heard enough of Serrac's plan. "May I add something to this discussion?" He seethed with the notion that the President would bring in a military specialist without his knowledge to undermine him. "Is Commander Serrac here to replace me as your adviser?"

"Oh, no. Of course not, General," the President assured. "Colonel Greely mentioned using the troops in the Amur region so I called him in. Greely set it up before he was murdered."

Tension thickened in the room. The small alcove suffered from 20th century ventilation and the body heat from the people present added more dankness to an already muggy chamber. Serrac cut in, "Sir, I'm sorry. I didn't know."

General Paz turned to Commander Serrac, "At ease, Commander. It isn't you. It's them." Luc's mouth trembled out to a sneer at Kyle's comment.

"Kyle, you're taking this personally," said the President. "Don't let the imaging of the Dixville Massacre that Spectator News published get to you. The public will understand that Captain Thomas was to blame."

"Negotiations are fine," Chaos continued, "but we have to prepare in the interim. Wolf, anything to add?"

"Well, I think they're going to bomb us at the Notch. I think they may even use the Israeli satellites to pick off individuals they recognize. You know, those satellites in orbit with Masadas. If everyone stays under the trees as much as possible, they won't see us. And we could use decoys to let their heat sensors focus in on the Notch as a target."

"There could be more to it than that," said Chaos. "They've come out with a new type of automated weapon that is mobile, kinda like a roving AutoMan. Captain Thomas could verify this I'm sure; the Army Regulars are training with these Armdroids. They're like little tanks with heat, motion, and metal sensors to detect any booby traps and ambushes. They are sent remotely, ahead of the troops. They look like a fifty-five gallon drum on tank tracks. Arms help it climb stairs and such; it can climb most anything. You should see them."

"Would a radio jammer stymie them?" asked Max.

"Nope. They work off a fiber-optic line, or on auto. If the line is severed, they just sit there and shoot anything that moves until the proper infrared signal is shot at it to shut it down. I don't think a Masada can even shoot through it. A hand-held rocket might damage one. We have some of those."

"It is personal, Mr. President," said Kyle. Commander Serrac didn't understand the meaning in Kyle's statement, or how the General's contingent set up the Dixville Massacre. "No disrespect to Commander Serrac, but Colonel Greely was your best shot at taking down this bunch with little bloodshed; and they got him first. Your second best option was Captain Thomas." He turned to Lucas Bennett, "I think you remember him," he said sarcastically in reference to the chewing out Thomas got from Bennett in the Oval Office. Turning back to the others, he went on, "He's familiar with all the top weaponry, and the region. He was with Greely in the Carolinas. This is no longer just Colebrook and the Tobacco Boys: we have some intelligence that Boston has their own Covenant with a force made up of both whites and African-Americans." He stopped and stated resolutely, "They call themselves 'Ghost Pack 220,' and they pledge their allegiance to someone called the Akela. How do you fight ghosts, gentlemen?" General Paz turned to Commander Serrac, "Pack 220 was the group of boys slaughtered out at the Dixville Massacre."

General Paz picked up his hat and overcoat as he rose to leave. On screen behind him, Wolfenstein and Chaos came out of the Philbin house to meet Captain Thomas, Steve Morrison, and Reverend Thoreau under the flora of the cherry tree. "I'm resigning, Mr. President," General Paz declared. "I've had enough of this charade."

"Kyle," Winifred stopped him. "What will you say to the press?"

"Don't worry, Mr. President. Captain Thomas has gone AWOL. You have

your scapegoat. Besides, there's nothing I've done that I would care to repeat."
Before exiting the door, he paused and turned sideways, "A word of caution,
Commander: This is nothing like the Amur River Region. Not one bit."

Chaos was the first out of the covenant meeting to join the Captain and
Steve Morrison under the blooming cherry tree. "Captain Thomas, we could
use your expertise," Chaos said. "What do you know about the vulnerability
of Armdroids?" Morrison listened in.

"An HHR will knock it over but it won't necessarily down the machine
unless it hits a port and tears it open. It can get back on its tracks with its
arms." Other Covenant members came out the Philbin's front door. When
the Captain looked up, Helen turned away. Mrs. Larson glared at Thomas
with contempt.

Thomas returned to his conversation, "I've seen the Armdroids tested.
They're tough-skinned with three centimeters of hardened alloy. A Masada
won't touch it unless you can hit a port, and that's difficult."

Chaos narrowed his eyes, thinking. "How about satellites? They got any
sitting above us by now? Any Israeli types?"

"You mean for shooting people from the sky?" the reporter chimed in. "I
thought they couldn't do that."

"They're not supposed to," Captain Thomas replied to Steve. In his
response to Chaos, "I don't know about an Israeli version but if it wasn't for
the tree we're under they would be counting the buttons on your shirt as we
speak,"

Chaos stepped out from under the tree and turned his head up to look
under the bill of his hat. He lifted his hand and raised his middle finger to the
sky.

"Must be a local," said Lucas in reference to the man on screen flipping
them the finger. All the others had left the Map Room; Lucas Bennett and
the President Winifred were the only ones remaining. "What happens here is
critical in this fall's election, sir."

"I realize that. I think I'm going to make a trip to Colebrook and actually
take part in the negotiations. It will look Presidential. Turning over Kyle as
the culprit behind the Dixville Massacre should also help defuse things a
little. You see, Lucas, a President needs to show leadership in a crisis like
this. I might even take William fishing while I'm up there. Makes for good
press." Winifred had frozen the scene of the scruffy dark-haired man with

the baseball cap. He walked up to the big screen beside Chief of Staff Bennett and stared at the figure. An eyebrow raised as the President said, "We'll see who screws who."

Max's deer camp near Colebrook, New Hampshire (May 10)
DEER WIZARD,
THIS IS THAD-

"No, stupid," his older brother corrected. "Write: *THIS IS BUTCH AND ME*. He won't know who it is that's written it." Thad nodded and backspaced to the beginning.

WE NEED YOUR HELP. WE HEAR THE FEDS HAVE AN AUTOMAN THAT MOVES AND THEY MIGHT USE IT ON US. CHAOS SAYS WE NEED A TECHY LIKE YOU BUT THEY THINK YOUR TO BISSY IN THE CITY TO HELP US OUT.

"You spelled TECHY with a Y," Butch noted. It should be with an IE. This E-note won't go through unless everything's spelled right." Thad went back and changed it. "There. That's better. Now send that son-of-a-bitch." Butch whispered his order as though they had entered forbidden territory. In truth, the boys huddled around the glow of Max's laptop in the black, desolate deer camp on Van Dyck mountain.

Thad moved the track-point to the drop-down menu of addresses and found The Wizard's E-mail address. He clicked and sent it.

"There." Butch felt satisfied that a message had been crafted and sent out under his direction. Both boys waited for the mystical machine to respond.

Got your message, boys. Where's Max? The Wizard replied within the minute.

Wide-eyed and anxious, Butch and Thad read the message as it came on screen. Butch nudged his brother, "Say somethin'." Thad pecked out: *NOT HERE NOW*. They sent it and waited at a blank screen for a response.

How did your dog do? The Wizard wrote.

The Rousell's responded: *TATER DYED*.

The Wizard replied, *I'm sorry to hear about that boys. But I need to talk to Helen or Max. Are they there?*

Thad looked up at his brother before pecking out the reply, *JUST BUTCH AND ME. NO ONE ELSE. GHOST PACK 220 NEEDS HELP. . . .*

Butch had told The Wizard the Dixville story in Boston. He wore the scar. The man from Boston had taken an oath to recruit more pack members, and Butch would hold him to it. "That's good Thad. And tell him he made a promise to the Ghost Pack."

Thad punched the period key hard and sent it.

The Wizard replied, *We'll send help. By the way, your Ghost Pack has taken off in Boston. Congratulations.*

The mute boy at the computer keyboard turned to face his older brother and beamed a look of satisfaction.

Chapter 15

Eastern sunshine captured her, and wrapped her, exposing every curve that made up Helen Conrad. The woman looking down at Balsams Resort from Table Rock had transformed into a butterfly, but only in body. Trauma had hardened her soul. A life she created, a spirit she had loved more than anything, had been snuffed out. And the worst of it was watching President Winifred's brown-haired son standing on the same rock where Barry once stood.

Chaos understood her tragedy; he had lost loved ones in the struggle for freedom. But watching Helen at the bluff, he didn't see the pain, just the woman. He approached her from behind and tried to see what she was looking at through her binoculars. Chaos stood beside her with two coffees, peering down at the resort. He noticed something dripping from the eyepiece of Helen's binoculars. "Something's leaking."

His comment startled her. Chaos saw she had been crying; even Helen hadn't realized it. She lowered her binoculars and paced toward the tree line to be alone. Chaos looked closely at William Winifred, William with fishing pole in hand standing on a rock in the water. He shook his head, *I'm so stupid!*

William Winifred spotted the Rousell brothers standing side by side in the gully where the stream fed into the pond. The three boys stared at one another from fifty meters away. William looked at the Rousell brothers, then turned to see if the security person on the lawn was watching. Thad offered a conservative wave. William glanced up at the guard to make sure he wasn't looking and returned the greeting.

Chaos found Helen seated on a rock just beyond the pines. "I'm so sorry." He put the coffee down and held her, stroked her hair. "If you need someone to talk to, I'm here." No response. He started back, "Or maybe you want privacy."

"No." She patted the rock beside her. Chaos walked back over and joined her. "You know, I don't know if I'll ever get over this," uttered Helen. "After viewing the imaging of the massacre, I realize the horror Barry must have gone through."

"Well--"

"Even if both of us make it through this thing alive, you won't want anything to do with me," she continued. "Some days I can't stand anyone. God! I can't remember the last time I slept through the night. I have nightmares. I swear, I'll never get over this."

Chaos considered launching into an oration about oppressive government but thought better of it. Her struggle was not political. He put his arms around her, squeezing tightly. The embrace wrapped Helen in a cocoon where she wished she could hide. "You're the best thing that's happened to me, Helen. I'm a patient man; I can wait until you're ready. What about the *good* memories of Barry?" He looked in the direction of Balsams Resort. "I bet Barry was a good fisherman."

"Fisherman? I'm thankful he wasn't, I'd have had to clean them. He spent a lot of time trying at that pond at Balsams though. Barry and those Rousell boys were all over the place--Tater too." She reached down for her coffee. "You know, I miss that dog. I've been shot at and chased; Tater was there when I needed her." She took a sip. "Barry loved that mutt. I guess I did too. Another part of him died with her."

Secretary of Human Concerns Darwin Combs succeeded in arranging a meeting between the regional Covenants and Federal negotiators. The peace talks took place in the Balsams Resort. Army Regulars occupied Colebrook and the Resort for security.

As planned, President Winifred seized the opportunity for a photo op. In a campaign year, with gossip of his role in the Dixville Massacre spread throughout the country via CB radio, Clifford had some damage control to do. Captain Thomas and Secretary of Defense Kyle Paz had been made the scapegoats, but the illegal CB broadcasts proclaimed the President himself had known all along. As tradition dictates, Clifford huddled his family around him in a desperate attempt to stay in power. As William fished at the pond in front of Balsams Resort, the President swung a few rounds of golf for the media. He was surrounded by his wife Patricia, Chief of Staff Lucas Bennett, and dressed in a spandex one-piece with bulging genitals, the latest urban rock sensation, Ravenhelm.

Digital recorders from major networks whirled about the President, asking questions, adding cursory comments against the rebels. Nancy Atherton was, as always, among them.

Meanwhile, the gasoline tanker, driven by Captain Thomas turned into the lane toward Balsams Resort. He stopped in front of a truck loaded with concrete ingots parked crossways to block the road; it served as an impenetrable gate. A man waited in the cab of the truck, his tanned drivers' arm dangled out the window. He waited for a signal from the two security people on the ground to let the tanker pass.

One of them approached Captain Thomas, "Sir, we need your clearance code." Thomas didn't stir; the Captain mindlessly gazed forward. "Sir." The guards looked to one another. One of them climbed to the window to check the Captain, and found him dead. As Captain Thomas fell forward, the guard noticed the seat cushion smeared with blood.

Captain Thomas served a purpose for a radical faction of the Colebrook Covenant, as a corpse to drive the remote controlled truck. Despite Thomas' desire to rectify what he had done at Dixville, some Colebrook residents looked for more immediate revenge.

The guard looked back and saw that the truck loaded with ingots had begun to move off the road. Simultaneous bullets penetrated the skulls of the security personnel and the truck driver. Snipers fired from atop Sanguinary Mountain, northeast of the resort. Obeying an infrared signal, the tanker truck started forward again, picked up speed, and raced headlong toward the resort. The tanker plunged deep into the Balsams structure and exploded. Filled with gas and nineteen pressurized oxygen tanks, the tanker laid waste to the entire area. Intense blue flames erupted; the fireball destroyed everything in its wake. Remnants of building jettisoned away from the main structure were quickly eaten by fire. Burning flesh filled the air with death, as vapors hovered above flaming bodies before drifting off. Secretary of Human Concerns Darwin Combs, Reverend Thoreau, and the peace delegation were cremated by an oxidized ball so intense that vehicles blown away from the site landed in a melted heap. Burning tires added volcanic-like soot to the holocaust.

President Winifred saw it, *and* felt it from the golf course. The shock wave knocked everyone off balance. In stunted horror, the President and

First Lady watched the blast mushroom rise to the heavens. Security personnel shuffled them into a nearby tandem copter and took them out of range from any snipers. From miles above, Mr. and Mrs. Winifred looked down on the burning site in disbelief. Nothing recognizable could be seen. Their son could not have survived.

"Jesus, God! Who did that?" Helen had run back to the edge of Table Rock and viewed the burn pit that was once Balsams Resort. "Did you know anything about this?" she asked Chaos.

"Helen, what do you think I am?" It surprised Chaos she would ask such a thing.

Helen peered down at the resort to locate the boy at the pond. "I don't see him! Oh God, I think they killed him!" The surrounding trees were aflame, the rock where little William stood was vacant. "Do you think he's in the water?"

She raced down the slope toward the pond. Chaos stopped her. "Now, stop. Even if you found him in the water, it would be too late. It would take too long to get down there."

Helen was in tears, "This is all wrong. Children aren't supposed to die."

After hearing the blast, other rebels had come from the encampment on the mountain and looked out from Table Rock. There were no voices of glee. The hope of compromise was gone.

Colebrook, New Hampshire (May 28)

Junco Willis came to Colebrook by boat past Nova Scotia, down the St. Lawrence, through Quebec eventually to Sanguinary Mountain overlooking the wasteland that was once Balsams Resort. "What the media said was true. The President's son had to have been killed in the blast," Junco uttered in amazement. To this point, no one knew who was responsible for the bombing. Everyone in the North Country suspected Tumult. The Federal Government blamed all rebel forces and covenants in the area.

Der Dutchman and seven fully geared attack packs stood behind Junco. Four of those attack packs were African-Americans from Boston. Der Dutchman had worked closely with the newly formed Boston Covenant. The attack packs had devastated the gangs. New packs were formed made up of Bostonians. The Ghost Packs, as they were called, developed the reputation of invincibility; that attracted street kids. Gang members switched sides to be a part of the mystique. If Ghost Packs moved into an area, gangs simply moved out. Any resistance by a gang was dealt with by crushing force, attack packs aggressively shooting to the source and taking no prisoners. The benevolent hand of the court system wasn't there to pander them and return the gangs to the streets. Junco Willis, an African-American, found himself at the forefront of his new cause as a leader.

Ironically, Butch had had something to do with Junco's conversion. The Wizard had given Butch's Scouting book to Junco and told him about Butch and Thad--and about the Dixville Massacre. The word spread. Inner city youths found direction in the values promoted in the Scouting manual. Through the efforts of Junco Willis, the moral codes within that Scouting manual became a beacon. Young black men without direction, found purpose. After extensive training by Dutch, the Boston packs were as good as any unit in the Vermont and New Hampshire Covenants.

Since receiving the E-mail message from Butch and Thad, the Wizard had been working on the motor-gun to improve its penetration and range. He asked a chemical engineer he knew at MIT to help out. The Wizard came up with a ceramic ball for the gun made of nitrogen-oxide, some lead for weight, and carborundum--all bound together with clay and baked in an oven to harden. The range of the guns hadn't improved because of the lighter ball, but the balls burned and exploded on impact. Not impressive shot one at a time, but a stream of balls would blast a hole through anything. Junco came to Dixville to deliver the goods, and to fulfill an oath for the Wizard.

Dixville Mountain, New Hampshire (August 4)

Rain pummeled the region. Lightning snapped the earth like a jagged whip; the crack shook the ground beneath them. The deluge would befuddle the Armdroids guarding the Army compound. Thick cloud cover shielded rebels from the satellite's eye. The weather was perfect for the mission.

Chaos was not about to wait for the Feds to make the first move. Seven attack pack leaders huddled around him in a small, underground bunker. "Their command center is just this side of Colebrook." He pointed at the topographical map on his laptop computer. Helen listened from the edge of the room. "We'll penetrate the sensors at this location," he pointed. "Wolf's packs will take out the Armdroid sentry, here. Once inside the security ring, designated packs will cut the optic cords that allow communication among the other Armdroids. Then all hell will break loose--at least for them. We need to remember to leave the way we came. Except for the Armdroid we take out, the others will still be active as stand-alones."

Understandably, there had been no attempt by the White House to renew negotiations. Killing the President's son had provoked congressional sympathy, turning representatives against the rebels. It licensed Winifred to do as he pleased. Within three and a half weeks, an overwhelming force of Army Regulars had amassed. Satellites, redirected to new coordinates, would seek out the rebel forces through their heat signatures, and could direct bombs and artillery rounds to referenced locations when the attack began.

Helen had insisted on going with the detachment that night. She cared for Chaos and decided to go with him whether he wanted her there or not. And they could use her medical training; the rebels idea of a medic was someone with a roll of gauze and duct tape.

She approached Chaos after the tactical briefing. Other rebels moved in and out of the bunker. Chaos was aware of them, "Once the battle starts, this thing takes on a life of its own. You don't have to go with us."

An anxious sigh followed, "I'm going. I'm obviously needed." She forced a smile, "And you macho guys will have to get over the girl-boy thing." It had been nearly a year since the Dixville Massacre. Helen had stayed out of the fray as Butch and Thad built their Ghost Pack, as the Vermont and New Hampshire Covenants gained prominence, as the rebel attack packs absorbed disenfranchised Americans from across the nation to become a combat-ready army. She had awoken. The enemy hadn't been Captain Thomas or the Army: It was the White House. They had treated the North Country like the enemy. And they had found one.

Chaos continued, "We're not like the Feds: Their soldiers follow orders mindlessly--just like their machines do. Our packs are self-sufficient. They know the area; they'll keep fighting until the other guy stops shooting back--even after my demise. I must say, The Wizard's improved shot for the motor-gun helps my confidence. When their Armdroids are downed, their soldiers will panic."

Chaos could see she was uncomfortable. He put an arm around her shoulder. "We're all scared. It doesn't matter how much action you see, that feeling never goes away. You'll do all right. If this new motor-gun shot takes out the Armdroids effectively, you might find yourself patching up more of them than us."

"We probably should have listened to Reverend Thoreau."

"We did. We tried to negotiate but someone sabotaged it," said Chaos.

"Don't second guess. That does no good. I mean, what are our options: We could run or we could surrender. How would either one help Colebrook or the nation?"

"I know, but--"

"It's too late." Chaos softened his voice. "When this thing goes away, I'll still be here. I love you, Helen; understand that. I don't know what your feelings are for me, but I'll wait as long as it takes."

Helen didn't respond in kind. She wasn't sure how she felt about Chaos long term. So much was left unsettled in her mired life.

Rain, which began at dusk and continued through the evening, shot from the sky as large droplets. Small brooks gulped to swallow it all. Tiny streams were now rivers. Seven attack packs drudged solemnly down Roaring Brook toward Mohawk Creek. They tugged makeshift rafts wrapped in plastic, loaded with motor-guns and shot. Roaring Brook started at knee level at the source; by the time they got to Mohawk Creek they found themselves treading the liquid and hanging onto the edge of the rafts to stay afloat. The maneuver worked. By two o'clock in the morning, the advance team had collected at the edge of the Army Command Center located near Colebrook.

Helen hadn't seen Chaos the entire time. He led the group. With her backpack of medical supplies, she slogged along at the back of the detachment. She stopped trying to remain dry. Helen wondered if she could get lost from the group in this storm, at times holding on to the shirttail of the last young man in front of her. Unknown to her, it was his task during this mission to watch over her--Chaos' orders.

They readied motor-guns for the assault on the compound. Chaos worked with Wolfenstein's pack preparing the gun that would take out the Armdroid sentry. Their new motor-gun would be mounted on a tripod to improve accuracy. Mohawk Creek was at maximum distance for the Armdroid; the ceramic balls had to hit the same spot in succession to penetrate its skin. When everyone whistled the signal that they were ready, Chaos and Wolf lifted the gun onto the bank; Wolf whaled away at the Armdroid from seventy meters out. Luminous balls streaked out as a beam. The gray, potbellied Armdroid sensed them and rotated toward their position. Ceramic balls striking the metal gut flared sparks. When the contraption stopped to triangulate and fire, the consecutive balls burned a hole through its skin and penetrated its innards. Smoke oozed from its seams.

"You got it!" yelled Bird Dog looking through a night scope. On Chaos' whistle, four legmen from each pack sprinted across the clearing past the smoldering sentry into the compound proper to the computer trailer monitoring the Armdroid sentries. An Army Regular in the computer control trailer opened the door to see what might have downed their Armdroid. Bird Dog popped her in the face with three rounds from his Glock and tossed an incendiary grenade through the trailer door. From the cover of a neighboring trailer, Step-n-Time guarded the entrance until the explosive did its job. That maneuver took eight seconds.

At the same time, other legmen attacked the trailer housing the satellite link, as well as the motor pool; the mortar batteries had a strategic position near the officers' trailers. The ensuing packs lugged motor-guns. Though visual range was limited in the drizzle, three snipers for each team positioned themselves to provide cover fire.

Myriad tractor-trailer trucks made up the encampment; the inner walls of each trailer were lined with plate steel to protect occupants inside. Gunners of each pack who carried M-30 Strafers in the past, now brandished motor-guns; straps were attached to the weapons and looped over the shoulder to help distribute the weight. They squatted behind the legmen and began strafing the trailers. The streams of ceramic balls fluffed holes through the aluminum skirt and burst through the three centimeters of steel that lined the inside. Sometimes rear doors of the trucks would open with a soldier or two jumping out. Their M-30 Strafers spewed out flames into the night--but only for a moment, a motor-gun ran a stream of glowing balls into Army Regulars. More often, troops would crawl out of the trailer dragging friends, coughing uncontrollably in the mud beneath the truck.

Helen remained at the riverbank with a rebel. She couldn't see a thing, only muzzle flashes and motor-gun streams. When shot, the stream of luminescent balls looked like a white laser beam. "Can I go yet?" Helen was anxious to get into the compound and help with the wounded.

"No!" snapped the rebel. It was the third time she had asked. A flurry of Armdroid fire echoed across the valley, screams followed. "See." This time Helen went anyway. The young man scurried to catch up.

Chaos and Wolfenstein, with attack packs, raced through the middle of the compound. Legmen secured positions ahead of them and pinned down Feds by shooting at door openings. Within minutes the Mountain Boys secured strategic positions in the compound by shooting streams of motor-gun shot into trailers until the occupants surrendered or until doors remained fixed with smoke bellowing out the cracks. On hearing the attack with motor-guns, troops housed in the outer part of the compound ran toward the security perimeter to escape. Waiting Armdroids, detached from their optic link, shot anything that moved. Army Regulars who followed knew enough to return to the compound and surrender. The entire operation lasted ten minutes.

Wolfenstein approached Chaos, "Sir, communications and Armdroids on the perimeter are cut off."

Chaos nodded. Three other Mountain Boys brought Commander Serrac to him.

Random gunshots popped as rebels wounded captives by shooting them in the knee with small caliber pistols. Chaos turned to Step-n-Time, "Go around and make sure our boys aren't using rhino bullets to do that. We want to take them out of service not take their whole leg off." Step acknowledged and left.

"I wouldn't call this humane," Serrac remarked to Chaos. "Do you always shoot your prisoners?"

"You should feel lucky we don't randomly murder everyone like your weapon did at Dixville."

Step-n-Time checked the legmen who were doing the maiming. They were all using standard lead rounds. He came upon Bird Dog with a communications officer sprawled below him. Bird Dog aimed his pistol and lanced her with a bullet to the fleshy part of the calf. She screamed and clutched the wound. Step-n-Time reminded him in a whisper, "Bird Dog, you're supposed to shoot 'em in the knee."

Bird Dog held his gun out and stated glumly, "You want to do this?" Step-n-Time shook his head no, rapidly. "Then, shut-up!"

"Who's in charge here?" insisted Serrac.

"Are you the Akela?" Serrac asked because the name Akela seemed to be connected to the figurehead of the Colebrook and Boston Covenants. The name "The Wizard" had been linked to people from different regions. Somehow intelligence reports linked allegiance to the word Akela to two different areas. Serrac was hoping that by asking, some information might come out.

"No. I'm Chaos. I'm in charge of this raid."

"What are you going to do to me?" asked Serrac. "Shooting me in the knee won't do. I plan strategy around here."

"Not a thing," Chaos replied. "If I shoot you, your soldiers might respect you more. And I wouldn't want them to replace you."

"Stop shooting them!" Helen yelled to Chaos as she approached. Bird Dog and Step-n-Time followed behind her. They had already been scolded. Helen was livid, "I can't believe you're doing this. You shoot them up. I fix them up. I can't keep up with it."

Chaos pulled her aside to talk privately away from Serrac and the men. "What the hell is wrong, Helen? We're in a battle here. We have no way of holding them prisoner. If we just let them go we'll have to fight them again."

"It's wrong, that's why." She said it loud enough so the others heard behind her.

Chaos tried to reason with her. In a slower voice, "Then what do you propose we do to detain them if we don't maim them?"

Helen thought a moment. "Send them off naked and destroy the compound."

Chaos looked around and reflected. He didn't like having to maim prisoners, something immoral about it. He returned to the group, "Bird Dog and Step, with the exception of the people we just maimed, go around and tell the boys to have all the prisoners strip naked and send them out of the perimeter of the compound where we downed the Armdriod. We'll destroy everything here except for a place for them to keep their wounded. Start by stripping Commander Serrac and showing him the way out," Chaos said with a restrained grin.

Serrac stood indignantly as rebels yanked his clothes off. Before being tugged away by rebels, he pointed at Helen and asked Chaos, "Who's the woman?"

Chaos responded, *"That's* the Akela."

Chapter 16

Dixville Mountain, New Hampshire (August 6)

By midmorning, clouds moved off as excess moisture, smitten by sunlight, changed to fuzzy humidity that lingered on distant mountains. The plush, green hills around Dixville Mountain looked desolate. There was not a sign of human life in sight. Route 26 passed the Balsams blast site and wound through the valley to the notch. No traffic rode its back. The usual critters that scamper about the leaves in the forest, huddled in their lairs. The sparrow near Helen's medical bunker, who sang so freely earlier, could crouch no lower in her nest. Domesticated animals, cows, pigs, and sheep, waded ankle deep in mud. They dumbly munched on feed below the forest canopy, ignorant to a world of human predation.

Washington, D.C.

"Mr. President . . . Mr. President." Lucas had trouble getting Winifred's attention. He had Serrac on the phone and needed a confirmation from the Commander in Chief. Though weeks had passed since the bombing of Balsams, the President had not recovered from the loss of his boy. Winifred had led a superficial life, in his marriage, in politics; but Clifford genuinely loved his son William. He had become a dysfunctional man, reflecting on the past, often coming out of his daze not recalling the conversation going on around him. "Sir! Cliff!" The President looked up. "Serrac wants to know—"

"Yeah. Go ahead."

President Winifred hadn't heard the question but his answer agreed with Chief of Staff Lucas Bennett. "You got the go-ahead," Lucas told Serrac on the other end. "What! How many?" Serrac told Lucas about the surprise raid. "Well, how many did *they* lose?" Lucas asked. "Holy shit! Only two? They lost only two? Yeah . . . Yeah . . . Okay . . . No . . . No, From now on, report the numbers of dead and injured of both sides directly to me." Bennett listened to Serrac intently. "Yes. And whatever those numbers are, cut our casualties in half and double theirs . . . Yes . . . Yes. That's what officially goes down in the record. The media's *our* problem." Bennett's voice became stern, "You worry about your own ass . . . and Serrac: You'd better not screw up again today." Lucas hung up on him.

Bennett looked over and saw the President's eyes soaked. Reminiscing again. "Don't worry, Cliff. Today those bastards will pay for what they did to your son."

Dixville Mountain, New Hampshire (August 6)

Ankle deep in mud, a Holstein cow bit into a pillow of hay and shook a cluster loose. She chewed at it. Paused. Chewed some more. Paused. She looked up through the forest canopy at the whistling sounds. A small, heat-guided bomb whisked through the treetops into the underworld and struck the cow solidly in the middle of its back. Hide and body parts spattered in all directions, startling other nearby animals. More bombs hit other animals with a splat. The docile creatures, with swinging milk sacks, waddled away from the slaughter and stopped. Quickly and with little pain, they received the same blast to the back. The creatures exploded like melons, the forest floor became coated with a layer of gut and hide.

"Chaos, you should see this," Wolfenstein transmitted his signal to Chaos' bunker. The Colebrook Covenant had built a complex system of bunkers over the past three months. They used small backhoes to dig the tunnels and bunkers, topping that with logs, dirt, and concealing it then with leaves and brush. Unlike conventional bunkers, each hideout had a spider web of piping from its center to disperse the heat; the setup made them undetectable by heat-seeking bombs. They trimmed the forest undergrowth for line-of-sight laser communication from bunker to bunker.

"We've got the same thing here," Chaos said, responding to Wolf with a returning laser message. "Just sit tight. The plan is working. When this is over, expect some penetration bombing to go on for awhile; the Armdroids will follow with troops. Then it's our turn. They can't bomb their own positions."

Colebrook Diner (The same day.)

With every blast that shook the earth, anxiety struck. The penetration bombing had begun. And for Harvey Madison, every jolt shook him to his core. "Why aren't you up there in the medical bunker?" He asked Mrs. Larson. She was all for the fighting.

Her tiny eyes stared back coldly, "I have my reasons and it ain't none of your business."

"I see," he said.

"You don't see. There's six tanks rowed up outside my diner with just a handful of soldiers looking after them. Look at those Army boys out there; they're ready to wet themselves. They don't want to be here. If you hang around long enough you'll see the shit hit the fan. When the bombing stops," Vanessa winked, "if you get my drift."

"You mean, you're planning some kind of attack in Colebrook?"

"You got it. And if you open your big mouth, you'll find a blade in your back!" she spoke adamantly.

Harvey Madison turned his attention back to his bowl of corn chowder. He hadn't touched it. Just dipped up spoonfuls and ladled it back into the bowl.

Five Army Regulars entered the diner and seated themselves near the plate-glass window. They looked up toward Mrs. Larson for service. She stared back, her puffy eyes narrowed to slits.

Meanwhile, Butch and the boys of Colebrook's new Ghost Pack 220 squatted in a circle on the asphalt behind the Main Street drug store. Butch held a 400-gram propane canister with a three-inch pipe connection on the top. A drilled hole in the top housed a steel plunger used to detonate a shotgun shell inside. Some of the boys backed off, worried about Butch's bomb going off. Thad stayed, he knew better. "No. No," Butch explained, "there's no shell inside yet. "It won't go off unless it has a shotgun shell in it." The group moved back to the circle cautiously.

Twenty-four boys made up the huddle. They had all heard Butch's tale of Dixville and endured the thumb cut that sealed their loyalty to Ghost Pack 220. They were a proud lot, armed with kitchen and hunting knives; Sam Larson had a beer bottle stuffed with rags and filled with gas as an inflammatory device. They talked rugged as a group, but as individuals they were still boys. Their mission: To take a tank and to drive it through the Feds perimeter and deliver it to the Mountain Boys by dusk. The cannon on the Abrams could be used by the rebels to fire on Army positions in the valley.

Butch spit in the middle. The bubbly saliva jiggled as penetration bombing continued on Dixville Notch ten miles away. "Denny's pack is going to throw a football up by them," instructed Butch, "as me, Sam, Thad, Charlie, and Billy come around on the street side." Billy, the newest member of Pack 220 had a bur-haircut with singed eyebrows and scalp. "They're going to tell you to 'get,' but ignore it. They won't shoot kids. While they're looking at you, we'll do our thing."

The children glanced at each other for weakness. Stony-eyed, they rose slowly from their crouched positions and split up into groups to their respective locations.

Thad never looked up from the ground as he followed his older brother Butch. It had been a year since the Dixville Massacre. Gnawing anxiety tied his stomach in knots, but he felt he had to do this for his friends slaughtered at Dixville. Though he had gone to the bathroom earlier, he felt he had to go again. Thad's long, thick legs beneath his light-boned physique carried the weight of the Dixville Massacre--the guilt of surviving. Thad wondered if he could follow through with his older brother's plan.

Vanessa Larson put the fifth burger on the bun; she spit on it before capping it with a sesame seed top. Waddling out to their table, she tossed the plates on the surface. Sarcastically she said, "Here. Enjoy." She stared down on the soldiers as they sheepishly lifted their burgers and bit into them. Her attention turned to the window as a group of boys tossed a football in the village green inching toward the tanks. She turned to Harvey to see if he saw; the children's presence might mess up her attack plan. Then Vanessa looked back through the window.

"Hey, get out of here." The soldier's voice carried across the park and was faintly heard by everyone inside. The soldiers seated in the diner turned to see. "This is a restricted area. Get out!" repeated the voice from outside. The boy with the ball deliberately tossed it over his partner's head to bounce near the guards.

From behind, Butch and Sam raced up from the alley and threw their explosives at the unsuspecting soldiers guarding the tanks. Sam's gasoline bomb splattered at the feet of one soldier and caught the man's pants on fire. The propane canister Butch had tossed shook downtown Colebrook and sent the other two sentries flying through the air.

Immediately following the blast, Butch climbed the backside of a tank with Sam Larson following. The burning soldier saw Butch scrambling to the top of the tank; he lifted in M-30 Strafer and streamed six rounds at the boys. A bullet caught Butch on the thigh. A stray hit Sam in the stomach as he crawled over the top of the tank. Sam fell to the ground in a fetal position; Butch hugged the top of the tank moaning.

Billy and Charlie raced from the alley toward an M-30 Strafer a soldier had dropped in the blast. Charlie ran between the tanks and snatched the weapon up in a dead run.

Thad wasn't among them. He stood on the side street paralyzed with fear, and watched his brother's blood trickle down the side of the tank. The flaming guard caught sight of the boys running among the tanks with a rifle in-hand. He popped off several more rounds. One hit Charlie in the back. Billy continued without the weapon, glancing back only once in his dire race for cover on the other side of the green. Thad at last broke loose, streaking at top speed between the tanks. Adrenaline drove him, leaping over both dead soldiers and sprinting ten more meters, where he snatched the rifle Charlie had carried. Two soldiers in a nearby jeep lifted their weapons and took aim at the boy darting across the green. The rounds chased Thad and struck in the wet sod behind him. Thad caught up with Billy, and ran through the rest of the boys on the opposite end of the village green.

Soldiers in the diner sat stunned on viewing the scene through the window. One soldier remarked incredulously, "Why--they're shooting the boys!"

The fat lady's beady eyes widened from slits to golf ball size. "That's my boy!" She reached under her apron and pulled out a knife, wielding it into the back of the first soldier. As another trooper looked around, she caught him in the chest with the second strike. The third private, she paralyzed by a blade between the shoulders as he reached for his rifle. By then, the older Colebrook residents in the diner, overpowered the remaining two. Harvey Madison blocked the arm of Mrs. Larson as she tried to impale a fourth soldier. "Stop it Vanessa! For godsakes, stop it!" Harvey lowered his hand but stayed between her and the captives. He was no longer sure what she was capable of.

"They're murdering the rest of our boys." Vanessa was crying now. She stood hunched and in shock. Dark red blood dripped from the blade of her knife.

"What we have to do," stated Harvey, "is round up the boys and make sure they stay out of this."

Harvey had not realized Mrs. Larson's son was involved. She ran out the door and across the green, pushing a soldier to the ground en route to her child. Other Colebrook residents ran out to the wounded children. The village people scurried through the streets in confusion; boys were running through side streets every which-way as troops chased them to recover the stolen rifle.

Thad stashed the weapon under an outbuilding behind Sam Larson's place and darted back to the center of town to check on Butch.

The men from the jeep recognized him. "He's the one who had the weapon." They revved the engine and pursued him. Pulling up alongside of the boy, the soldier on the passenger side nabbed Thad's shirttail. Thad stumbled and was dragged beside the jeep until it stopped. In a flash, he slithered out of the shirt and ran barebacked through the center of town. Now two vehicles chased him across the green. The boy streaked into another side street and turned between houses. Soldiers honked in pursuit while women dragged their children out of harm's way. The jeeps crashed through fences to keep up. Thad knew the village. He cut through sections too cluttered for jeeps and doubled back the way he had come. Three times he evaded capture, cutting back through the center of town time after time. Infantry in the square tried to block his escape but found themselves outmaneuvered and nearly run over by the men in jeeps pursuing the boy.

The chase lasted nearly ten minutes, and ended when one of the drivers turned to circle back, but didn't; he backed up in front of the boy from a side street. At a dead run, Thad was looking back to locate the other jeep when he collided into the vehicle that pulled in front of him. His legs buckled under him; the boy slid off the door to the pavement.

On Dixville Notch, the Armdroid's wide tracks inched up the steeper slopes of the trail along Cascade Brook. Gorilla-like arms hung from the base of its barrel torso; they were used to dig into the steep embankment to pull itself up. To rebels watching it through the glazed bunker ports, the thing looked surprisingly homemade. Nothing fancy, just a fifty-five gallon drum on tracks, with arms. Sensory ports for radar, heat, and motion, dotted the armored skin of the contraption. A fiber-optic tether came off the back, its link to the infantry that followed.

Wolfenstein, and others in the bunker, pressed up against the small rectangular port to watch. "See that thing on top?" Wolf referred to the rounded receiver node at the very top of the machine. "I bet you that's an infrared node to receive a signal in case the optic line is cut off. If we could cut the line and shoot that node off the top, they couldn't control it either. It would sit there and protect us, as long as *we* stayed in the bunker."

"Rrrright," responded one of the rebels." It would also be tough getting behind it to cut the line. If the Armdroid doesn't get you, the troops on the other side would. They've tested this thing, you know."

An old camcorder strapped to a motor-gun sat covered with brush thirty meters away from the rebel bunker. Wolfenstein watched a digital monitor displaying an image of the Armdroid. Wolf used a joystick to align the barrel to target. "Here goes." He pushed a black starter button and revved it with a rheostat knob. The Armdroid rotated toward the heat of the engine. On pressing the joystick button, glowing motor-gun balls shot out the barrel toward the Armdroid like a garden hose. Wolfenstein held the stream of shot steady on one point. The Armdroid fired back, taking out the camcorder and some of the stepping motors controlling the gun. A second later, the potbellied machine began smoldering and stopped. Wolf shut down the motor-gun and grabbed his Masada. "Let's chase after their asses boys before they get a chance to call in artillery."

Three legmen with all-frequency jammers raced out the mud-covered hatchways and sprinted in different directions to set up a series of mobile frequency jammers. They synchronized each of the three units to turn on at different times for two minutes, every six minutes. Every two minutes, a legman had to race the jammers to a different location before a missile honed in their frequency source.

Other rebels sprinted down-slope with only Glock autopistols to intercept Army Regulars. They whistled location and numbers back to gunners and snipers who followed. Legmen baited the troops with pistol fire. Once the Feds trailed them into the ambush, motor-guns rained shot into the thick of them. Snipers with Masadas tediously peered through tree slits and popped enemy faces they viewed through their scopes. The same legmen who baited the Army units, returned to the bunker to reload their belts with ammo clips. Then they did an end run around to waylay the Federal soldiers. They ambushed anyone trying to retreat.

From satellite and low altitude drones, sensor readings showed what the Feds thought to be concentration centered around Dixville Notch; but those sensors actually read animal life and kerosene smudge-pots. Rebels waited undetected in bunkers. Commander Serrac had no idea they were concealed.

As Federal troops closed in on Dixville proper, attack packs came out of their hives--but to kill not to sting. Like the ghosts of Pack 220 seeking revenge, they would appear at will to assassinate their target, only to vanish without a trace to their secluded bunkers.

Chaos planned to inflict as many casualties as possible. Mountain Boys shot Federal Troops instantly unless the enemy waved a white cloth. Rebels gave no overture to surrender. Even after a Federal soldier hoisted the white cloth, rebels shot them in the knee with a lead bullet and left them without a weapon; they hadn't time to take care of prisoners.

Chaos didn't fair so well on the southwest side. In the initial duel between Armdroid and motor-gun, the Armdroid won. The distance was too great and the Southerner had trouble holding a stream of shot on target. The Armdroid took out the remotely fired motor-gun and kept them pinned down in the bunker. Artillery had already pounded their location. The tunnel leading up the hill that served as an escape had collapsed, eliminating their means of retreat.

Vanessa Larson's scheme to destroy the Abrams squad with a remote-controlled, gasoline truck was preempted by Butch and the Ghost Pack's attempt to take a tank. She and Max's group had used the same strategy to bomb the peace talks at Balsams Resort. This time the plan failed when Colebrook's Pack 220 intervened. Federal troops moved the tanks to an off-road location. Now, her primary concern was the children: Three boys lay dead, four wounded.

"The boys need medical attention. Right now!" Mrs. Larson was livid, forcing the captain against the wall as she screamed in his face.

Captain Jacobs shifted to the side to get more space between them. "God, lady, we're doing what we can. We can't find the medic. The last anyone saw him he was in the diner, and people there said he left." Captain Jacob shook from the incident. "God, lady. I'm sorry. We didn't want to shoot those kids but they took out two of my soldiers and burned another. We couldn't let them get off with the rif--"

Too late. Larson was off to the diner to see what Harvey and the others did with the captives. One of them might be the medic. She stomped through the diner and forced herself between two of the men in the back room. "Where are they?" she demanded.

Harvey stood between her and the door of the walk-in refrigerator, "You're not going to kill them."

"No. I'm not going to kill 'em. Get out of the way!" He stepped to the side. Vanessa opened the locker door and closed it behind her. She stared with a peripheral gaze at two young men in their twenties who looked back. "One of you peckers had better tell me you're a medic."

After Thad's capture, the Feds commandeered the Philbin home to use as a holding tank to question the boys. The captain in charge wanted that M-30 Strafer back before it was used on any of his troops.

At last, Thad stirred and rolled onto his belly, ending up face to face with Butch on the floor of the Philbin's living room. The floor puckered the boys' lips to a fish-lipped pose. Thad raised a hand and poked at his brother's shoulder with his index finger.

Butch blinked--and tried to figure out where he was. Butch could hardly speak, "Your nose?"

Thad felt his own face. His eyes widened on touching his nose. He had broken it. Blood covered the bottom half of his face and spread down to his belly.

Butch spoke carefully. "We need the Akela. She almost saved Barry and he was shot up a lot worse than me. You can outrun 'em, Thad. If you get in the woods, they'll never find you." Butch was unaware of the gauntlet his brother had run trying to evade soldiers the first time. The delicate-faced boy only stared forward as his older brother spoke. "You gotta do it. I don't know if I can make it for very long."

Hearing that, Thad got to his feet. He stood bloodied and bare chested, wearing only shorts and tennis shoes.

Tiffany saw him stand from the other side of the room. She had been in one of the jeeps chasing the boy, so she knew how fast the kid was. "Hold it right there!" She turned to the door behind her, "Mark, get in here." Tiffany needed help covering the exits, "Now don't move, kid!" Turning back to the door she hollered, "Somebody get their fat ass in here!"

Thad sidestepped to the right and looked around the room. The lady stood at the doorway. Billy was also in the room because his arms and shoulders had been cut when he had tried to jump through a window during his chase. He whispered, "The window, Thad."

Both the lady and Thad saw it at once. Thad took three steps toward the window and switched direction to the door. The woman tried to cut him off at the window, slipped in blood when changing direction, and landed on her side. "Get him, you idiots!" she shrieked.

"Gotcha!" Thad went limp when a powerful arm caught him as he zipped through the doorway--a short chase this time. "What's the problem, Tiffany? You can't handle a few wounded kids?" The strapping soldier held the boy in midair, "This little bantam ain't going nowhere."

Tiffany got up and looked around at the bloodstains on her backside. "Oh, jeez." She looked to Mark, now holding Thad, "That boy's got to be locked up. He can't be in a room open to the outside like this."

"There's people all around," Mark answered.

"There's people all around, but if that rabbit gets loose and into the woods, we'll never catch him. I've decided to keep him in the basement. So put him down." The man lowered Thad to his feet.

She took Thad to the basement and sat him on the same table the Colebrook Covenant met at. Under the single bulb, she coaxed him to tell the whereabouts of the rifle. "So you won't say a thing, is that it?" She got out an electronic notepad, flipped open the screen, and wrote down her name. "See, I'm Tiffany. What's yours?"

Thad cautiously leaned over and pecked out his name.

"Well now, Thad. That's a start. What's your mother's name?

"MOM'S GONE," he typed.

"How about your father, or guardian, or something?"

"JUST BUTCH AND ME," the boy kept it simple.

"The other boy you were talking to?" Tiffany asked. Thad nodded yes. "So no one watches over you?"

Thad pulled the memo pad closer. *"THE AKELA, AND THE GHOST PACK, AND THE MOUNTAIN BOYS WATCH OVER US."*

Tiffany watched the boy as he typed it out. "You can't talk at all, can you?" Thad looked away, not answering. Tiffany sounded more consoling now. "Okay, why did you boys attack us?"

"YOU SHOT US."

"We had to. You kids blew up two of our guys and were running off with a rifle."

Thad started pecking before she finished, *"NO. BEFORE. YOU KILLED OFF PACK 220. AND YOU KILLED MY FRIEND BARRY."* The boy's soft, brown eyes turned dark.

"Are you talking about the smugglers' attack at the Notch?"

Thad's finger moved swiftly over the keyboard, "YES. TALKING ABOUT THE AUTOMAN. BUTCH AND ME WAS THERE."

"You were--"

He hadn't stopped typing, *"MY BROTHER AND ME ARE THE LAST OF PACK 220."* Tiffany watched in stunned silence. *THE GHOST PACK HAS SWORN TO FIGHT THE FEDS UNTIL THEY GO, OR UNTIL THEY HAVE NO ONE TO RULE."*

"I'm sorry about your brother." Tiffany was guilt stricken. She had heard the rumors, but didn't really believe it. "I can let you see him if you promise not to bolt." Thad didn't respond. Tiffany continued, "Okay, but I'm going to have to keep a hold of you at all times."

She took him upstairs and led him to Butch on the other side of the room. The wounded boy hadn't moved. Tiffany checked Butch's carotid on his neck. No pulse.

"He's dead," Billy announced glumly from his prone position only yards away. "No one helped him." Speaking to Thad now, "I heard him call your name before he went. He said he saw Barry, that friend he talked about."

Thad dropped his head to his brother's back to listen for a heartbeat. He straightened up and just watched his lifeless brother.

"Oh, I'm so sorry," Tiffany said in tears.

Mark came in from the other room. "What's the problem?"

She went over to talk to him, "I think we might be making a big mistake here. You know those rumors on CB radio about the Army and Dixville?"

"Yeah."

"I think they're true."

"How can you be sure?" She pulled out her electronic notepad and showed him the comments Thad had pecked out earlier. "They're brothers," her voice cracked, "and now he's the last one." Her hand quivered as she showed him the pad. "This isn't about stopping a bunch of smugglers and tax cheats." She wiped tears from her eyes. "Everyone here hates us. The U.S. military murdered 64 of their children. We have no business being here."

Mark was ready to believe her. "I heard they're kicking the living shit out of us on the mountain. Son-of-a-bitch, I overheard the captain say he's never seen so many casualties so fast. Everything people have said about the combat skills of those Mountain Boys was true. And they have motor-guns like the ones in Boston, only these cut through armor."

"I'm going to the Captain with this," said Tiffany

"What about the kid?"

Tiffany looked at Thad. "Be kind to him, but don't lose him. He's the last survivor from the Scout Pack that was massacred."

After Tiffany left, Mark gently held Thad's arm and led him to the basement stairway. "I gotta do this kid. We can't just let you go. I have my orders. Were you really at the Dixville Massacre?" Thad looked away and nodded yes. "Look, if you promise not to run, I'll let you stay up here with the others." Thad gave no response. "Okay, then. I'll have to keep you down there." Before closing the door he said, "I'm sorry about your brother."

Thad inspected the basement for exits. The two, eight by sixteen-inch windows had been boarded up solidly by the Philbin's for privacy during their Covenant meetings. Light, cast by the single bulb, crept halfway up the stone walls and highlighted the bricked-up exit used to smuggle slaves during the Civil War era. Below it, a rat scampered along the edge of the wall and stopped to sniff an empty jar before it continued on. Thad grabbed a hammer from the bench and went to where the rat had stopped. With a burlap sack over the wall to muffle the sound, he began hammering the brick--the same exit to freedom used by desperate people over a century ago.

Chapter 17

In wonderment, Steve Morrison stopped recording the historic battle from Chaos' underground bunker, "We're going to die!" Their "back door," as Chaos called it, which tunneled up the mountain, had been severed by penetration bombing. The attack packs that had scrambled out earlier to take on the Armdroid, had been killed or wounded. Chaos' left hand had been injured. Only Chaos, Steve Morrison, and Al remained in the bunker. Al was a big, likable fellow from Missouri.

Optically controlled by a soldier from the rear using a virtual-reality visor and command pad, the automated Armdroid could be shut off at any time. The potbellied robot sat fifty yards down hill, holding Chaos and Al at bay. Army Regulars disabled the weapon so companion troops could launch hand-held rockets at the viewing ports. The blasts left gaping holes in the bunker the enemy could shoot into.

Steve Morrison couldn't take it any longer, "God, what if they put another rocket in here? Shouldn't we give up?" Chaos had learned to ignore Steve's perpetual whining, but the same thought had crossed his mind. "Hey! I'm still here! Can you hear me, Chief?" The reporter insisted, as he gnawed on his gum aggressively.

Chaos used a stainless steel mirror to look around the edge of the opening. "If they had the missile, they would have launched it by now." Al jerked his head in and out of the opening to get a fix on troop movement; he did it again for another look-see. "Don't do that," said Chaos, "that thing will trace your heat signature and lo--" A bullet reeled passed the edge of the opening where Al was looking. "See what I mean. If you don't have your mirror, get one off one of the bodies in here."

Al looked around at the corpses littering the floor. "Yes, sir." He began sifting through a man's side-pack.

"Can I give up? I'm just a reporter. This isn't my fight!" Morrison protested.

Chaos stopped and looked at him. "I thought you wanted to be in the thick of it?"

"But I don't want to die."

"Find something white and give it to me, but I can't guarantee you won't get shot surrendering."

Steve feverishly took off his pants to get to his underwear--the only white thing he had. The reporter was reluctant to strip the dead. Chaos placed the briefs on the tip of a Masada. He poked it out the opening for all to see. "You might want to put your pants back on," Chaos instructed Morrison. "There might be some females down there." The jittery reporter noticed and complied.

An Army Regular yelled up, "It's okay. The Armdroid is off."

Steve frantically gathered up his equipment in a knapsack. "You're not coming with me?"

The Southerner answered flatly, "No." Chaos turned to Al. "You're not obligated to stay."

"If you're not going, I'm not going," the chubby Missourian answered. He pulled a red memory disk from his side-pack and handed it to the reporter, "Give this to my niece, Chelsea. Her name and address is written on the disk."

"When you get down there," Chaos told Steve, "tell them we're going to stay and fight. Don't say how many of us are left."

"Reporters are neutral. I don't have to say anything." Steve stopped before leaving and put out his hand, "Good luck, guys." He shook Al's hand too. Then he added regretfully, "I'll see you on the Evening News."

"I hope you find what you're looking for, Steve."

"Oh, I have my story."

"I was referring to home," Chaos concluded. "You'll know you're home—"

"--when you're willing to fight for it." Steve finished the familiar refrain with a restrained smile, waved goodbye and crawled out the opening. That statement continued to haunt him. Always on the move, Morrison hadn't formed commitments. He had few friends. The alliance with the rebels had been bittersweet, mutual survival the skilled mediator that bonded them. Steve regretted walking out on them. He couldn't look back.

Two soldiers escorted Steve Morrison to the base of the slope where two other Army Regulars were bunched up, one of them the commander of the squad; the Armdroid controller was in a world of his own with visor and command pad.

"Hey, I know you, don't I?" The radio operator gawked at Steve. "I've seen you on the news." Morrison's red hair made him more memorable than other journalists.

"Yes. I'm a reporter." Steve cautiously pulled out his press card and displayed it to the officer in charge. The commander promptly found his electronic note pad and slipped the card in its slot; Steve's picture and statistics came up on screen.

"At ease, gentlemen. He's the real thing." The soldiers stopped pointing weapons at him.

"Are we ready to start up again?" the Armdroid controller asked.

The commander asked Steve, "They're not surrendering?"

"I'm afraid they're not," Steve muttered.

Two troopers huffed and puffed up the slope carrying an elongated, plastic crate. They sat it on the ground and flopped down beside it.

"How many up there?" asked the commander to Steve. He noticed the reporter's hesitation. "Doesn't matter." The commander unlatched the crate and pulled out a rocket. "Let's get 'em, soldiers." He ordered the women who had escorted Steve down the hill to take a couple of rockets to the front line and prepare them. Then he ordered the privates who lugged up the crate, "Get your asses over to each side. The rebels might be sitting back hoping for help from somewhere, I don't want to be caught by surprise."

Steve Morrison watched the two women pick up the missiles and lug them out of sight in to the thick undergrowth. Something gnawed at his stomach. He had been with the Mountain Boys for five months, through danger and ecstasy--through desperate times with seemingly no escape. He had always thought of himself as an unbiased reporter; yet familiarity tainted that self-image somehow. Steve had not found the Mountain Boys to be the bigots his colleagues made them out to be. Looking down at the red disk case Al had given him, he realized how real it was. He read the name to himself, *Chelsea*. It seemed as though everyone had someone but him. Steve thought a moment, then spit out his gum.

"The women got there, sir," the Armdroid controller reported to the commander, "I can see them out my back ports. They're setting up the rockets." The controller heard a thud and a grunt behind him, the words uttered, "You know you're home when . . . . " He turned to look. Steve cracked the controller across the side of the head with a rocket tube.

Steve Morrison's hands shook as he lifted the visor off the stunned

Armdroid controller. He studied the visor screen to see who encircled the Armdroid. The controls were so easy, a child could figure it out. He set the weapon to scan and shoot at the sloped side instead of the bunker. Then Steve pulled the headset off, yanked the fiber-optic cord from its housing and smashed the command pad. After a second of silence, the Armdroid began shooting Army Regulars behind it; the monster had turned on its own. Steve thought of the two women who delivered the missiles, *God, what did I do?*

Other than their skirmish with the kids, the Feds still thought Colebrook were residents neutral; meanwhile a group met at the American Legion Hall. Mrs. Larson's faction wanted to fight, even though the Federal troops in town had been alerted and had scattered the Abrams tanks.

Harvey Madison and the older veterans at the meeting still spoke out against joining the fight with the rebels. Harvey had the podium; the American and New Hampshire flags hung side-by-side on the wall behind him. Neither group really knew whether the Mountain Boys or the Feds had the upper hand in the battle. Government casualties flooded Colebrook's hospital-- now a makeshift medical facility for wounded. But the U.S. Government had the numbers to spare. Madison's argument went well. The bombing of Balsams Resort began the conflict; the Mountain Boys' preempted raid started the battle. And the resulting casualties brought the notion of mortality closer to heart. Mothers and older vets of the audience paid closer attention to Harvey's pleas to halt the fighting.

Vanessa Larson became impatient. She tramped up to the podium and took the mike from him. "Hold on here! Aren't we going to get to hear the other side?" Harvey leaned over to respond in the microphone. Vanessa elbowed him in the shoulder. "It's my turn. This isn't about God and Country, it's about community, the rights of communities across the country to live in peace without oppressive government keeping their thumb on us. It isn't just us. Communities have been fighting for freedom off and on for years--all over the country." She pointed toward Dixville Notch. "Those Mountain Boys up there aren't just from New Hampshire and Vermont, they're from all over: Pennsylvania, Virginia, the Carolinas, Boston, Missouri, you name it." Mrs. Larson stopped to take a breath. Tears ran down her face during her speech. "Those boys up there are fightin' for us." Her voice finally cracked, "I don't care what the rest of you do, but my Josh and my Sam didn't die to look down and see you folks sittin' on your asses."

Harvey Madison stood by, waiting for the right moment to intervene. He couldn't gauge the audience response; they sat looking beyond Mrs. Larson in stunned silence, maybe because of what she said, or possibly because of the events whirling around them, he couldn't tell. Some in the audience cried.

"Like I said," Mrs. Larson said as she stomped to the exit at the back of the room, "I know what I'm doin--" she froze when she turned around to finish her sentence.

Colebrook residents gazed to the front of the room. Harvey turned to see what everyone looked at: Thad stood in the door behind him, bare-chested and smeared with dried blood. He held the Pack 220 flag, a reminder of what had been lost in the Massacre. His very presence would sway the group to fight. Harvey knew that; the silent gesture convinced even him. There are things worth fighting for; community is one of them. He walked up and hugged the expressionless boy. "What have you done, Thad?"

A Volvo station wagon sped past the Abrams tank that sat in front of the Philbin house. Mrs. Larson hit the brakes and spun 90 degrees. Revving the engine, Vanessa drove the car head on into the front of the tank. She got out holding her bleeding forehead with one hand and pointed a 22-caliber revolver with the other. "Get out of there! Get out of there, now!"

Soldiers near the Philbin house aimed their weapons at her. A private in the tank uttered, "That bitch is crazy. Are we supposed to take this, sir?" he yelled to his Captain.

More townspeople followed, some by vehicle, some on foot. Harvey had grabbed the U.S. and New Hampshire flags from the Legion Hall.

Tiffany noticed Thad among the group. Astounded, she uttered, "How'd he get out?" She had already talked to the commander about her interview with the boy. "Sir, what are you going to do?"

Both groups pointed weapons at each other. The commander rubbed his stubbled face and tried to decide. "I know one thing: We're not going to shoot the people we came up here to defend."

Tiffany pulled the pad from her side pouch and held out the note for the captain to see. He had read the statement before but this time the stark print became an ominous threat: *"THE GHOST PACK HAS SWORN TO FIGHT THE FEDS UNTIL THEY GO, OR UNTIL THEY HAVE NO ONE TO RULE."*

Dixville Notch, New Hampshire

183

With the Pack 220 flag mounted in the corner, Harvey Madison drove the lead tank up Route 26 toward Dixville Notch, at times topping fifty miles an hour with the sixty-one ton Abrams. Vacant jeeps, left behind by officers and messengers, littered the roadside; victims of Masada snipers dangled from open doors--some sprawled on the ground.

A Mountain Boy stepped onto the road and waved down the tank carrying the Pack 220 Colors. A message had been lasered up from an earlier lookout describing the tank activity. As insurance, a motor-gunner sat in wait at the road's edge, ready to cut a hole through the armor of the Abrams. Harvey stopped and opened the hatch.

"What's going on?" asked the rebel. He looked uneasy standing in the open. With clear skies, they were easy targets for the Federal satellites to shoot down on them.

"I'm Harvey Madison. I'm in the Colebrook Covenant. We got these tanks for you, and we need to get to Max's deer camp."

The rebel was skeptical that an older man had captured a tank; most elders in the community hadn't been enthusiastic about the cause. "How did you get them?" He glanced at the motor-gunner hidden along the roadside.

"The troops in Colebrook just took off. They found out about the first Dixville Massacre and lost their loyalty to the military," Harvey answered.

The rebel still thought it looked suspicious--until Thad forced his head out the same hatch. The rebel recognized him. "Thad, you with them?" The boy nodded yes. The sentry finally waved a halt signal to the motor-gunner. Harvey's story about the Colebrook outpost of troops pulling out surprised the rebel, "Is their communications center south of town still up?" From the communication center, Federal troops could beam signals to a satellite for additional air support or supplies. Loss of that link would isolate Federal troops, transforming them into a less adventurous bunch once they realized they might not have backup.

"I don't know," answered Harvey. Thad tugged on Harvey's shirt as a reminder. "Listen," Harv continued, "Thad needs to get an important message out."

"Can you run that thing?"

"Somewhat. It's a little different from what I'm used to, but I'm learning."

The rebel climbed the tank. "I'm Bondo. We'll signal around and let everyone know you're in the area." To Thad he said, "Can you and your brother guide him up to Table Rock." Thad turned back to Harvey as Bondo spoke; he didn't have a brother to communicate for him anymore. "We'll laser in coordinates and use the gun on this thing to take out that communications hub down in Colebrook" Thad nodded yes and edged below.

Harvey said in a tempered voice, "Bondo, I think you should know, his brother's dead. Butch got shot trying to capture a tank."

"Oh." Bondo sighed. "That's a shame. Thad's the last one now." He became misty-eyed, and rubbed his scarred thumb with the index finger of the same hand; it had become a habit, a reminder of the cause. Bondo recalled the nights the Rousells spent at their campsites; they sat around the campfire telling stories or jokes. Butch recited the Dixville Massacre repeatedly, adding more flavor to it with every telling. Thad softly played his harmonica after fires burned down and everyone settled in for the night. The Rousell brothers and the dog became mascots of a sort, circulating from campsite to campsite, eating and sleeping there. After their mother took off with her boyfriend in the fall, the Mountain Boys became their only family. Anyone seeing the Rousells' approach, instinctively smiled. "Thanks for letting me know. I'll pass the word. If for some reason you come under fire, give up the tank. We can't let anything happen to Thad."

"We've found the system to be compromised, sir," explained the Network Security Advisor to President Winifred. "The note we received from the alleged Ghost Pack earlier was put through by somebody's password within the system. We followed up on it and believe the security of the network has been breached. The message today was under an anonymous login, and addressed to you. Very few people know your Fednet E-mail address. The note signs off as Billy, your son."

"What?" Winifred yelled. "If this is somebody's prank, I'll hang the bastard. Hook me up with this so-called Ghost Pack."

The Network Advisor turned the President's portable computer around and set it up for Fednet mail.

Lucas Bennett had only watched until now. He had many questions for the Network Advisor: "Jim, at the very least we have a major security breach. I'm not all that familiar with these systems, but if this guy has used two different passwords already, what makes you think he doesn't have access to all messages in the system. Hell, Jim! We don't know what they know. They must have known when we were coming and what weapons we were using. How could you let this happen? You stupid shit! You stupid, stupid shit!"

Jim's neck and face turned red, "Wait a minute! We don't know who this is. It could be just a hacker."

"Trace the damn call!" Lucas was livid, now face to face with the Network Advisor.

Jim, calm but angered, "It's going through Quebec. And thanks to your sanctions on that country we're not getting along with them right now. It can't be traced."

"Luc," said the President, "let's get on with this. I want to talk to this guy."

An unspoken truce was declared as Jim pulled up the message sent earlier. The President read it. Winifred typed in:

Subject: *THE FIGHTING*
Date: Tue, 6 Aug. 2024 04:15:03
From: President Winifred <cwinifred_999@fednet.washington.dc.us>
Reply-To: BILLY WIN <billy_op_440@kidmail.com>
Attachments:
Ghost Pack??????:
We're talking. What do you have to say?
"Do you think they're still waiting on-screen?" asked Winifred.
"It's only been fifteen minutes," Jim answered.

Billy looked over Thad's shoulder as he read it. "Tell him that I'm okay, and ask him if he can do anything to stop the Army at Dixville." Thad typed in what Billy had dictated and clicked send.

Lucas, watching over the President's shoulder, "Ask him how we can be sure he's William?"

Thad looked at Billy for a response to the request for verification. "How can I prove that?" Billy thought aloud. "Tell them the rotor is the weakest part of the model copter I have. Check it."

After reading the treasured reminder from his son, President Winifred focused on the model helicopter resting in front of him. He lifted it by the rotor blade. The copter separated and fell to the desktop. "Shit!" Winifred began typing feverishly, hitting backspaces, retyping. "Shit, shit, shit!" The President got up and pointed to the chair, "You type, Luc."

Lucas sat down and rested his hands on the computer. "What do you want me to say?" Lucas suspected that they were being set up, "You know, this so-called Ghost Pack could have had the informa--"

"Shut up and ask William where he is." The President started pacing. "Ask him if he's in danger, if there's any shooting around." He walked back to look at the screen. "Tell him to stay put. I'll send in Special Forces to rescue him." While the Chief of Staff typed, the President picked up the phone connected to his private secretary, "Shelley, arrange to have Air Force One prepared immediately, and have them set a flight plan for the North Country with a helicopter waiting there to take me to Colebrook, New Hampshire." He listened a moment, "Yes! Right now!" Winifred hung up.

Lucas Bennett had prepared the message as Clifford arranged his flight. "I got it. Send it?" asked Lucas. The President nodded.

After reading the White House note, Thad turned to Billy for a response. Billy looked away. He didn't know what to tell his father.
Subject: *THE FIGHTING*
Date: Tue, 6 Aug. 2024 04:15:15
From: BILLY WIN <billy_op_440@kidmail.com>
Reply-To: President Winifred <cwinifred_999@fednet.washington.dc.us>
Attachments:
CAN'T COME BACK. WE'RE FIGHTING THE FEDS. THE FEDS KILLED SOME OF MY FRIENDS TODAY. I'M IN THE GHOST PACK NOW. WE TOOK A TANK FROM THE FEDS AND GAVE IT TO THE MOUNTAIN BOYS.

"I don't understand this," a frantic President looked back at his Network Advisor, "You say we can't trace this because their line goes through Quebec?" The Advisor nodded yes. The President picked up the phone to his secretary again, "Shelley, get me Prime Minister Merrique on the phone, right now." Winifred motioned for Lucas to get out of the seat so he could type. "Luc, if we still have a satellite link to Serrac, ask him if some young school boys were shot and if a tank has been captured." President Winifred typed out a letter asking his son who the Ghost Pack was. He begged William to let them know their location. A few minutes later, a message appeared. Thad had authored much of the response.

Subject: *THE FIGHTING*
Date: Tue, 6 Aug. 2024 04:15:20
From: BILL WIN <billy_op_440@kidmail.com>
Reply-To: President Winifred <cwinifred_999@fednet.washington.dc.us>

Attachments:
THIS IS THAD. BILLY'S FREIND.
PACK 220 WAS THE SCOUTS KILLED AT DIXVILLE LAST YEAR.
BUTCH AND ME LIVED. FEDS DON'T NO THAT. WE REBUILT THE
PACK AND NOW WE ARE GHOST PACK 220 CAUSE THE GHOSTS
OF THE MASSACRE STILL LIVE TO FIGHT. BILLY TOOK AN OATH
AND JOINED THE PACK. BILLY SAYS HE IS NOT LEAVING TIL THE
FEDS GO. SO SEND THEM HOME. WE ARE KICKING THERE ASSES
ANYWAY. WE GOT TO GO. BYE.

Winifred turned to Lucas, "Is this true? Are they beating us?"

"I think it's a ploy," said Lucas. "The battle is taking its toll on them, too.
They must be ready to break."

"How many casualties did you say we have so far?"

"About twenty-two hundred."

"Is that the actual count or the figure we give the media ." President
Winifred was losing confidence in Lucas Bennett's judgment.

"It's the actual."

Winifred sighed and turned to the newly replaced window, "This is no
longer an uprising. This is a civil war and my son's in the middle of it. It's
like they were ready for us." He turned to Luc, "And their casualties?"

Lucas lifted his hands, "It's so hard to say."

"Just a guess!"

"I would say, maybe half as much. I don't know. We sent our troops in
there from all sides and motor-guns with balls that cut through anything ate
them up. The units fighting up there just haven't come back. They're jamming
all frequencies so our troops are fighting blind. We have to use handwritten
messages to communicate, and sometimes they shoot the messenger."

The President had closed his eyes and shook his head no through Bennett's
entire report. "Is that a joke? 'Shoot the messenger.'" The Network Advisor
had been standing to the side quietly the entire time. Winifred lashed out at
him, "And what the hell's wrong with you?" Jim reacted with a stunned
look. "Go trace the damn call! Trace the damn call!" The Advisor scurried
out of the Oval Office, chased by the President yelling, "What the hell's
wrong with you? I don't care how you do it, just do it!"

Chapter 18

Blood soaked the front of Helen's surgical gown. Except for the white surgeon's mask and hat, she looked more like a butcher than a doctor. "Oh God! Oh God! I don't know what I'm doing. Deb, give me a clamp," Helen instructed as she pinched off the artery with her fingers. "That thing on the end." She pointed to the instrument, paused, and took a breath. "Deb, can you look at this? I'm not sure."

Deb Philbin stepped over and looked at the opened thigh. She was frazzled too from the daylong siege of mutilated bodies they had to patch up and send back to their packs. The unspoken verdict was, salvageable rebels received treatment. Rebels more critically wounded didn't make it to the medical bunkers. The packs wanted as many fighting men as possible, even if they could only sit in the bunker as a guard. That policy put enormous pressure on the men and women staffing the medical bunker. Though not doctors, they functioned as such. The less experienced volunteers served as support staff. Deb Philbin looked at the gore and said, "All you can do, Helen, is stop the bleeding, take out the debris, and stitch it up."

Helen had made a large vertical incision, laying the skin back on each side of the upper leg. "This will take an hour. We're so backed up. Rrrrrah!" she shrieked to no one in particular.

"Sorry. This is all we can do, Helen." Deb went back to her table.

Max's condition exacerbated Helen's state of mind. A penetration bomb found his bunker and mangled his left side, taking off an arm and part of his leg. Her older brother clung to life in a gully just outside the medical bunker. Helen's worst nightmare would be fulfilled if Chaos lay on a slab as her next patient--to find love after such a tragic event as Dixville only to have it slip away.

Then Chaos walked into the ward looking for able-bodied medics to form a new attack pack. He stopped by Helen, and whispered in her ear, "How's it goin'?"

"You startled me." She turned back to her patient, "Horribly. When's this thing going to end?"

"You should see the other guy."

"How do you know?"

"You don't see any of them here. If they broke through our perimeter you would see some of them here." He yelled across the room to Al, "Run a signal to Wolf's bunker and tell him to figure out a way to make the Armdroids work for us. We got one holding up my sector right now." Without hesitation he informed them: "I'm taking some of your medics to make a new pack. I only have one guy left."

"How are the wounded going to come in?"

Chaos looked around as he left, "I think you have enough to keep you busy for a bit. There's no laser signals from the Boston packs on the southwest slope. I think that section's been breached."

"Chaos, don't go!" She finally noticed his wrapped hand. "You need attention."

"It isn't that bad. This thing is almost over. We've held the mountain. And Snake and Tumult have just gotten into the fight."

"How's that?"

"The Feds have almost vanished completely on the north and northeast sides. We haven't received any communication from them yet, but I know my brothers. They're there."

Myriad vapors oozed upward from Boston rebels and Federal troops scattered along the southwest slope, vapors hovering at times above warm corpses. Motor-gun fire burned off shrubs and weeds, replaced by skeletal plant stock; lingering smoke limited sight within the tree stand. Boston's Ghost Packs had held the southwest sector until four o'clock in the afternoon--until an overwhelming number of Federal troops took out what they thought was the last motor-gunner. In a rocky crevice just below the summit of Baldhead Mountain, an African-American man still clutched an idling motor-gun as three Federal Troops looked down on him.

Private Clyde Jackson graduated from Colonel White High School in Dayton, Ohio. After receiving a two-year degree from Wiberforce College, he enlisted into the Regular Army to avoid getting drafted into the Guards. Until Dixville, his military stint served him well. Though he'd seen some action in Middle East and the Amur Valley of Russia, Clyde had never been in a situation so blind: no communication, no artillery, no air support. "Shit! I didn't join this white man's army' to be killing my own kind," he said, looking down on the Boston rebel. "There could be another nest of them just ahead, for all we know. Our Armdroid's out. We're on our own. For all we know, the rest of our people around this mountain are all shot up too."

Another soldier added, "I don't think we should stay. These guys fought to the last man. They were waiting for something. There could be another group of them coming over that rise at any time. This isn't what they told us it was. These aren't the Tobacco Boys. They're all African-Americans. They lied to us, Clyde. We're killing our own."

Clyde Jackson glanced over at the third soldier. As Clyde began talking to him, the soldier vanished before his eyes. From up slope Junco Willis had shot the soldier with a Masada, hitting him squarely on the Kevlar vest. The impact tossed the man thirty feet down the hill. Without another word, the remaining two Feds sprinted down the mountain. Other soldiers noticed their hurried retreat; they too turned and fled the soil they had so ardently fought for.

"Hey! Get back here!" Sergeant Janet Davis hollered. "Are they deserting, Corporal?" The corporal had been right beside her. Davis turned and saw him headed in the opposite direction. "Hey, Corporal!" The corporal continued on as if not hearing her. Sergeant Davis turned to ask an adjacent soldier, "What's going on here? Is everyone deserting?"

"We're not even near the top of Dixville Mountain, ma'am," answered the private. "And we ain't got another Armdroid to scout ahead." He waited anxiously for a response from her.

Frantically, a tiny voice echoed back from the distance, "There's more up there! There's more up there!" Everyone dropped for cover as the soldier on point sprinted down the slope, ten-foot strides with every bound. He ducked behind a tree trunk near Sergeant Davis. In a breathless voice he went on, "There's more up there. They got motor-guns and Masadas."

"How many?"

"Maybe five or six packs with perhaps a dozen rebels in each pack. It was hard to tell."

"That's about sixty." Commander Davis hesitated to continue, but she did: "Were they African-Americans or whites?"

He jerked around the edge of the tree, peering out from binoculars for only a second before shifting to another point along the tree's edge. He was fully aware that at any moment a bullet from a Masada could pop him in the face. "I'm not sure," he said, still bobbing and peering through the lens.

"What? You're not sure! You said they had Masadas and motor-guns and you're not sure of their color? Why, you lying little coward! Is there anyone up there, Private?"

The skulking private yelled back, "They were camoed up, okay? They were green and brown and black, bitch! All right? Get off my ass!"

The whole unit was on edge. Janet knew if there was anyone ahead, her squad was in no position to take them on. She ordered her remaining group to provide cover as they backed off. The squad leapfrogged down the slope, leaving what Janet suspected was empty ground.

"I could pop one of them, sir. Like threading a needle." Junco Willis had a member of Janet's squad scoped in with his Masada, looking downward through hundreds of meters of tree trunks at a face peering around a tree. There were only two other men left from Willis' Boston Ghost Packs. They had held their side of the mountain: at great cost.

"Naaa. Hold fire," replied Chaos. "I wonder what spooked them? For all they knew, they had open ground to the top."

Junco scoped out the surrounding area. "There's your answer, sir. Boston's Ghost Packs held their sector while we held back their main advance." The two other men who survived the ordeal nodded in agreement. "Our guys shot the shit out of their guys." Bodies pummeled with multiple rounds littered the slope. Blood-spattered trees and rock surrounded the corpses. "Wanna look?"

"No. I'll take your word for it," the Southerner replied. "I guess if I found out that only a few packs were the cause of so many casualties, I'd turn tail and run too." Chaos turned to the rest of his group taken from the medical bunker, "I think it's over for now, boys. They could always go back to penetration bombing but the hands-on stuff is done."

"Listen!" said Junco. "What's that? It sounds like Glocks and Strafers, there's a Masada." The rest of the group listened.

"Our boys must have ambushed 'em. Use your whistles so they know it's us up here," Chaos instructed. "We're going down to check it out."

Rebels cautiously moved down the slope. By the time they got to the edge of the clearing where the ambush took place, only the Army Regulars' bodies remained. Other attack packs had strafed them with M-30s; legmen had run down strays, taking them out with Glock autopistols.

"This was done by Snake or Tumult." Chaos pointed to the corpses. "Do you see any motor-gun clusters with burn holes in any of them?"

Junco, "No, sir. But why don't our guys come out?"

Chaos held his hand up and stood still. A laser beam signal hit his stocking hat, relayed from a line-of-sight atop Baldhead Mountain. "Listen. This message says they called a cease-fire an hour ago. Junco, run a beam back and tell them to have everyone shut off their scramblers so Federal troops can let their people know to stop fighting." Chaos told two nearby legmen, "Go find Snake or Tumult, whoever the hell it is that did this, and tell them it's over for now." Except for the rifle Tumult took from Chaos in Boston, to his knowledge, Snake and Tumult did not have laser communication yet. The rebels nodded and jogged off. The Southerner directed the surrounding gunners, "Let's see if anyone can be helped around here."

"Well, would you look at that shit." From a mile off, Tumult scoped in his brother from Godwah Notch through the Masada with the laser transmitter. His nose had healed up into a scabby, jagged nub. "We shoot those afro Feds and my little brother's runnin' 'round trying to keep 'em alive. That turd." In reference to Junco, " Look there, he's got afros in his own attack packs. What do you think about that, old man?"

Glitch finished a deeper-than-usual suck of his cigarette. Smoke came from his mouth and nose in his response, "I don't know as how that's proper, sir."

"Proper. It's downright asinine. And there they are standing out in the open for a satellite to shoot 'em. Stupid turds." Using the stepping motor control pad near the trigger, Tumult sighted in the rifle on his brother's hat.

"Sir, what are you doing?" asked Glitch, dropping his cigarette.

"I've got to tell my little brother to get the hell out of that clearing before the eye-in-the-sky sights him in." He looked around the rifle stock for the speaker switch. "Here it is." Speaking into it, "Little brother, it's not real smart to be standing out in the open."

Chaos scanned the hills for the possible transmission point. He looked right at Godwah Notch.

"Yeah, that's right, it's me, little brother. You've done a lot of stupid things before, but this takes the cake." He pulled the trigger. A bullet screamed out the barrel at a velocity of Mach three and sprinted the distance in a fraction of a second.

Glitch watched Chaos fall through his field glasses. "You shot him! You shot your brother!"

"Piss, no! I shot that negroid beside him. A satellite must have got my brother. Piss! I told that turd to get the hell off open land. You'd think he'd know better by now." Tumult quickly collapsed the tripod of the weapon and carried the unit off. "Those queers and negroids are going to pay for this."

Glitch stood mortified. He knew better: A satellite hadn't shot Chaos. Tumult was just talking to him when he pulled the trigger. He had been focused on his brother's hat. Glitch still found it unbelievable. Shooting his own brother?

The medical bunker at Dixville Mountain

"Stay still! Someone help here, *please*," Helen yelled out in the medical bunker. Deb ran over and held Chaos down. A third nurse connected belts together to strap down the rebel until someone could prepare anesthesia.

Chaos had been skimmed along the side of the head, his scalp laid open just above the ear. The Southerner struggled to get up, finally saying, "It was Ray. It was Ray."

"Hurry up with that hypo." A nurse handed Helen the hypodermic needle, which she immediately used to inject Chaos.

He made one last statement before he lay back and gave in to the sedative: "Just tell Wolf about Ray. Tell him."

"What do you think that meant?" Deb asked.

"I don't know and I don't care," replied Helen. He's out of the fighting. She took a better look at his head wound. "Praise God! I don't think it's as bad as it looks. I think he'll be okay." She unwrapped his hand and inspected it. "We'll have to wrap it up tight for now." Helen finally sighed. *The fighting's over for him at least. I'll keep him unconscious 'til this is over, if I have to.* Helen began shaving his scalp so she could staple it together as Deb cleaned and stitched Chaos' hand.

Helen had just finished mending Chaos when she noticed Thad and his friend across the crowded operating room, Thad was shirtless with dried blood caked on his chest. She had never seen him with such a pathetic expression. The Rousell brothers had always been hardened survivors; Helen knew something was wrong.

Keeping her bloodied hands overhead, she approached the boys. Thad buried his head in her stomach. "What's wrong? What is it?" She turned to Thad's new friend, Billy, "Is it Butch?"

The boy nodded, "Feds killed him," Billy answered.

"What were you boys doing down there?" she flared.

Billy broke into tears, "He was my friend, too," a ridged lip quivered out the words.

"I'm sorry." Forgetting her sterile hands, she reached out and pulled the second little man into a group hug.

Harvey Madison, stood over them in a somber gaze. When Helen looked up, he said, "I just heard: Max didn't make it."

Helen returned to her hug, resting a cheek on the new boy's bur haircut; it made her itch. "I know." Helen hadn't surrendered the hugs through the verbal exchange with Madison; the clinging arms soothed her. Things were winding down; the wounded were being cleaned. They hoped to take back the Colebrook medical facility after the truce set in. It would get the men more extensive treatment once all this was over.

"Helen, you have to come outside, *now*," said Wolfenstein in an urgent tone.

"Ah--"

Deb heard the exchange from the operating table: "I can finish, and there's other nurses to help me."

Helen left the bunker with Wolfenstein peeling off her surgical gloves. A moment later he stopped her in the tunnel. "It's Tumult. He's outside. He says he's in charge."

"Why, that bastard! Chaos would have something to say about that."

"But he can't, the way he is now," said Wolfenstein, "not after getting shot by the satellite."

In a strained voice, Helen asked quickly, "What makes you think it was a satellite?"

"We were the ones using the Masadas," he replied. "Chaos was in the open because there was no reason to believe they'd be shooting from the sky during a truce."

"Okay, okay," said Helen. "I guess what I don't understand is how a Masada on a satellite could shoot sideways." Wolf looked at her oddly. "He was shot across his head, you know," she continued. "If it means anything, Chaos said to tell you something about a ray doing it."

Wolfenstein's eyes widened, "What did he say, exactly?"

"He said *a* ray did it," Helen answered.

"Did he say a ray, or Ray did it?" Wolf questioned.

"I'm not sure. I presumed he was talking about a laser sight."

"Ray is Tumult, that's his real name," Wolfenstein stated. Now Helen understood. Wolfenstein continued sternly, "We don't want Tumult in charge. He started the whole movement in the Carolinas; the Tobacco Boys who came up with us won't forget that. They might go with him instead of me.

We're in no position to fight Tumult's attack packs. They only came into this thing near the end. They're fresh and we're in bad shape."

"What do you want me to do, Wolf?"

"You're the Akela, Pack 220's leader."

"The what?" Helen put both hands on her head in dismay.

"You heard me. A lot of the men in Tumult and Chaos' forces are from the North Country. The all know who you are. I'm just another pack leader to some of them. They also take the Ghost Pack Oath seriou--"

"Did Butch run around cutting everyone? You men are like a bunch of little boys. God!" When Helen had decided to get involve with the Colebrook Covenant, she had never sought a position of authority. Leadership had found her. The responsibility Chaos had had of sending rebels in to battle and possibly to their death was unthinkable for Helen at the time. This was different. It was personal now. Tumult had shot her lover. "I'll talk to him!" She reached into Wolf's belt and pulled out his Glock. "I'll talk to him," she repeated with more conviction and headed out the exit.

"Hold on, Helen," Wolf caught movement out of the corner of his eye. Thad and Billy had been listening in behind them in the tunnel. "You boys get your asses back in that bunker and stay there!" He turned and went after Helen.

Chapter 19

It was nearly dark, the gray light made steely shadows of everyone. Odors from the damp forest lingered. Much of the mud had dried except in pockets where water once stood. Milder, dank air brought out mosquitoes; they chased warm flesh, or gorged in the open wounds of the dead.

Helen stuck the gun in the back of her belt as she walked through the clusters of attack packs. The Virginians noticed her moving through the groups and joined in. They found Tumult with his back to them, talking to Glitch and several pack leaders. Junco Willis knelt off to the side; one of Tumult's men held an autopistol to the back of his head. Though Junco fought bravely for the covenants, he was still an African-American. Tumult would tolerate none of that.

"Let him go!" Helen ordered the rebel guarding Junco. The man didn't respond. He just looked to Tumult.

Tumult turned around on hearing her. At first he just stared, his stub of a nose the focal point on his face. Wolfenstein caught up and stood beside her.

"Wolf, you ran off to find a skirt to hide behind?" Tumult razzed. "That slut gets around." He looked about, "Where's the mutt? I'll put a bullet in that dog's head if you don't control it."

Helen and Tumult stared at one another. Tater's death--another reminder of why she hated him. "We won't be needing your help, thank you," she spat out, "so get out."

"Is that the gratitude I get? Snake and me were shooting the Feds up from behind. That's the reason they didn't overrun this bunch of queer, afro lovers. Piss, the Feds had a pit bull on their ass."

"So, you're not leaving?"

"Let's say, I have some unfinished business," Tumult grinned lecherously.

Helen looked at Junco, then to Wolf. She turned back to Tumult and spoke in a low, possessed voice, articulating every syllable for all to hear: "You shouldn't have shot Chaos. And you shouldn't have killed the President's boy."

"I have no idea what you're talkin' about, bitch," Tumult sneered.

"You know what I'm talking about, *Ray*. Chaos told me himself," Helen accused. "You killed the President's boy at the Balsams, and you shot your brother." Attack pack leaders began looking at one another. They knew that only those closest to Tumult knew his real name.

"The Balsams blast? I wish I had." Tumult struggled to turn the subject away from Chaos. "The fact is, I had nothin' to do with the bombing." Gesturing around him, "These boys can back me up on that one."

Wolfenstein saw her hand move to the butt of the gun in her belt. "Be careful, Helen," he whispered.

"It doesn't change the fact that you're not welcome here," Helen stated resolutely. "Now please, leave!"

Tumult put his hand on the grip of his Glock autopistol holstered on his side. "You can go back to changing bedpans, bitch." He looked around himself at his pack leaders; "I'm in charge. My will decides."

Ferman stood beside Tumult. He was one of Tumult's most loyal pack leaders but he could tell that not everyone was in favor of going with Tumult. A large group stood beside and around Helen, some of them with their hands on their guns. Glitch even moved around closer to Helen's side. Ferman whispered to Tumult, "Look around you, boss. Don't pull that gun, boss."

Glitch, the old and weathered techie for Tumult's triad considered his stand as he rubbed his scarred thumb on his forefinger. He relocated to Helen's side. "Tumult shot Chaos," Glitch spoke out.

"Oh, come on, Glitch" Ferman retorted "a satel--"

"No! I was there. He *told* everybody it was a satellite, but I was there. He was talking to Chaos through the laser when he pushed the button. I saw it, Ferman. Snake will believe me."

"Piss, Glitch. You old fart," Tumult scoffed. "You don't know when your tellin' the truth."

The pack leaders loyal to Helen began to slowly spread out to the sides for better position. Both Virginian rebels stepped up the hill to higher ground. Everyone held a rifle or had their hand on an autopistol butt. Wolfenstein placed his hand over Helen's, which she now had on the gun grip behind her. "Hold it, Helen," he whispered. "Don't start it."

"We got to let them go, boss, or there's going to be a shoot-out," Ferman whispered to Tumult in a nasal voice.

"My will decides!" Tumult boomed. The adrenaline was flowing. He could see it might come to a gunfight.

"Tumult won't back down," Wolf murmured to Helen. "I know him. You've got to give him a way out. He won't."

"Jesus, Boss! I don't want to get shot over this," Ferman whined softly. "The rest of our attack packs are over the hill. Let's back off 'til we get the rest of them. We can come back here later."

Tumult grew tired of Ferman's whimpering, "Ferman, this is why I'm the leader. You never understood the teachings of the master race: 'Strength lies in attack.' My will decides." Tumult pulled his gun and leveled it at Helen, pulling off two rounds as bullets from all directions bombarded him. One of Tumult's bullets went wide and hit a Colebrook Mountain Boy in the ribs. The second bullet skimmed Wolfenstein's shoulder and struck a rebel standing behind them squarely in the chest.

Ferman and the pack leaders surrounding Tumult tried to back away in retreat. The swarm of bullets shot at Tumult struck some of them; he died before he hit the ground.

"Hold it! Hold it! Hold it!" A number of them yelled. The Virginians stepped in front of Tumult's pack leaders, "No more shooting!" They yelled repeatedly.

Helen pointed her gun at Junco's guard. "Now, let him go," she ordered. The man guarding Junco backed off into the crowd.

"I don't understand this. You guys are pointin' guns at us?" Ferman spoke out in his high nasal voice. When Snake finds out, he's going to be pissed. Covenant leader or not, he'll shoot her ass for this. And you, Glitch, what's with you? You're on the wrong side, buddy. You can take care of this with Snake. I'm not tellin' him. You're going to have to talk him down."

Before leaving, Ferman approached Helen, "Ma'am, I just want to clear something up. I don't know about Chaos getting shot but we had nothing to do with that Balsams bombing that killed the President's kid. We were in Vermont at the time. You gotta believe that."

Helen stared him off as the packs collected their gear to head north. Junco got up and thanked her before heading to his bunker. Wolfenstein stuffed gauze under his shirt to stop the bleeding; it wasn't serious. What was serious was the direction they chose from here. Helen looked around herself at the rebels, a force that had held off an advance of the United States Army. Somehow through Butch and Thad's Ghost Pack activity they had vowed an allegiance to her. From the surrounding slopes, her ragtag Mountain Boys looked to her to say something.

Without the clamor of battle, breezes could be heard stirring the trees, catching the fragrance of pine, and casting it to the wind. The vapors that had ebbed and flowed in still air so freely throughout the day, had been pushed away. And the sparrow near Helen's bunker that had ridden out the shelling of day, now slept.

The White House (later the next day)

Billy Winifred walked into the room. "Say, Champ!" said the President "No, I'm sorry. Now I should call you 'the rugged one,'" Clifford Winifred hugged his boy. Ever since his son had returned, that urge to hug Billy was always there.

When the Colebrook Covenant realized that the President's son was in their midst, they reserved seats on a flight out of Montreal and delivered the boy the next day. Not only did the Covenants want to demonstrate good will by bringing back Billy Winifred unconditionally, they also wanted to discuss a more permanent solution to the crisis.

The Feds were in an awkward position: The Covenants controlled northern Vermont and New Hampshire. When the fight began for Dixville Mountain, the newly formed Boston Covenant launched raids on the Guard Armories in eastern Massachusetts. The Wizard's Ghost Packs now controlled the city; the gangs had been driven out. Winifred feared that other cities would form covenants, the White House scheme of controlling the population hubs to stay in power was fading.

Billy smiled, "Did you meet The Wizard yet? He's slick. Butch used to say he can do just about anything."

His father looked puzzled. "So you and Butch think The Wizard is slick."

The President's physician entered the room: "He's fine. He was singed pretty good and there was a cut on his thumb; that's healed up. But other than the scratches and bruises of being a boy, he's fine."

Lucas joined the group around Billy. "So how did you survive the blast?" Lucas asked.

"That's how I met my friends Butch and Thad. See, the blast blew me off the rock into the water. They were in the gully nearby and came and pulled me out. I thought I died. See, they kept me in their hideout and fed me and everything."

The President turned and smiled at the others with unrestrained pride, "We'll have to give those boys a special award for bravery. Maybe we can get them out of there, too."

"Can't do that, Dad. Butch was murdered." Billy's comment startled the men. "See, we tried to take a tank and Butch got shot. Two others in our attack pack got shot and died too. Thad is the last survivor from the Dixville Massacre."

They all looked at one another confused. The note they had read from Thad mentioned the Massacre and Ghost Packs; they assumed the boys were being held captive. President Winifred was compelled to clarify, "Attack packs? Tanks? Who were you boys fighting?"

"The Feds." Billy's voice lowered, "We hate the Feds. They captured us, but Thad escaped; he's the fastest runner in the Pack, you know. Thad rounded up the town, and we got those tanks in the end. Thad and me rode up in it to show them where to go. Thad's rugged." Excitement beamed from Billy. "The Feds got their asses wiped that day." The statement widened the onlooker's eyes. Some Rousell lingo had invaded his speech.

Lucas Bennett said it without thinking: "Billy, we *are* the Feds."

The glint in Billy Winifred's eyes changed to confusion. Then to disappointment. The look of shame Bill shot at his father would haunt the President for decades to come.

Balsams Pond, New Hampshire (August 11)

Thad stood on a boulder above Balsams Pond, fishing. Helen and Chaos sat on a grassy knoll overlooking Thad, with the resort's charred remains in the background. Though the structure made by mortals lay desolate, traces of bright green speckled the scorched woods surrounding the resort, life's eternal ability to start anew. High sun of late August baked Helen's bare legs as she propped herself up with both elbows to soak her face with the remaining rays of summer. Breathing deeply, she took in the fragrances of hemlocks and goldenrod before fall kills and winter covers nature with her blanket of snow.

Chaos' head was still wrapped. He relaxed flat on his back with his black, Mail Pouch Tobacco hat over his face. They sat on a large blanket, a cooler and picnic basket beside it.

Helen watched Thad from the other side of the pond. "Do you think Thad will ever talk again?"

"I expect so," said Chaos with his baseball hat still over his face. He lifted his hat and sat up to look at the slender, brown-haired boy casting into the water. "Is he a keeper?"

"He is a keeper. His mother abandoned him, and I plan on adopting the boy." Helen had realized through the ordeal that she must get on with her life. Barry would always be with her in sleep's brighter scenes; inexplicably, the images of the Dixville horror faded in the shadows. Another child needed to be taken care of.

"Thad will make a fine son." Chaos shifted his eyes toward Helen to catch her expression, "But he needs two parents who love one another."

She understood, and reached for his hand. Helen continued to be attracted to Chaos, but events whirling around her made it difficult for Helen to know when infatuation changed to love. The philosopher, the poet, the patriot, Chaos was all of those. He had been her friend and lover, enduring her tirades, her frustrations, and her torment of outliving her child. He had given her an unconditional commitment; he had been patient; he had been thoughtful. The characteristics in a man as charming as him were hard to find.

"You've got what's left of me." He rubbed the side of his head; the wound itched during the healing process. "Did you have to shave my hair off?"

Helen smiled, "You look good to me."

The fighting was over for now. The disillusionment from Winifred's son had toppled the Presidency. He resigned from office shortly after the Dixville battle. Of all the weapons, the love of his son had proven the most powerful. Margaret Sorenson had taken over as President. Her first act had been to fire Chief of Staff Lucas Bennett. Sorenson had always hated Bennett, she vowed to investigate his antics. Sorenson also reinstated General Paz as Secretary of Defense. She announced a plan to initiate a less centralized government. She had always been sympathetic to the cause. President Sorenson wanted to meet with the leaders of the covenants; Helen was now the head of Colebrook's Covenant.

To Helen's disappointment, Max had set the Balsams Lodge bombing. It was believed, but not established that Vanessa Larson might have also been involved; Captain Thomas had died of knife wounds in his back. If proven, the Covenant agreed she would be turned over to the White House. They never found out who launched the model plane attack on the Oval Office. Snake claimed that their part of the Triad had had nothing to do with it. Evidence pointed to a militant faction in Island Pond, Vermont. They might never know. One thing for certain, there was no turning back. Sorenson knew that compromise was a must to hold the Union together. Once Steve Morrison's channel aired in-depth, covenants formed across the nation. The blood spilled in the North Country and Boston had been the catalyst.

Steve Morrison remained in New Hampshire, taking over the communication hub at Max's deer camp as a means to get his stories out to Spectator News. He walked up the knoll to deliver an E-mail note from Billy Winifred to Helen. Steve waited for a response as she read it.

The story pulled out a sigh from Helen. "Billy wanted to tell me he is sorry about his dad being behind the Feds. He asked if the Akela would write him back . . . and he wondered if he was still part of the Ghost Pack."

Chaos spoke up, "He must have been with the Rousell boys at Max's computer and remembered the E-mail address."

"You bet I'll write him," Helen continued. "None of this was his fault. I'm sure he'd appreciate a note from Thad, too." Helen shook her head, "The boy must have given his father the Rousell's version of events. It had to have been an eye-opener for the President to learn his own son was one of the rebel forces."

Chaos added, "Butch and Thad's role in this whole thing has been grossly understated. Butch and his oath secured the loyalty of my triad when Helen stood up to my brother. And of course, the Rousells' rescued Billy Winifred." The Southerner appreciated Butch and Thad's role in securing the loyalty of the rebels: The Mountain Boys had a special place in their hearts for the families victimized by the Dixville Massacre. Helen was the embodiment of that tacit alliance.

Helen directed a question to Steve, "Are you anxious to get back to the newsroom?"

"Well," Steve hesitated as he looked past Helen to Chaos, "I'm staying here. If you'll have me?"

"Of course." But Helen had to ask, "Why have you decided to stay in Dixville, Steve?"

Steve recalled the campfire conversation with the young rebel Crucible, "Someone once told me 'You know you're home when you're willing to fight for it.'" Morrison discovered that objective reporting was a euphemism. If something is wrong, if something must be done, merely taking pictures of the event is as immoral as participating in the act. Ultimately, he had chosen sides for the first time in his life.

Morrison turned and started walking up the slope. Chaos yelled out and stopped him, "Steve!" the Southerner gave him a thumbs-up. "Thanks." Morrison smiled sparingly and returned the gesture.

Chaos told Helen about what Steve had done with the Armdriod unit back at the bunker. "He can't go back, they'd convict him." Chaos rubbed his eyes; he was tired.

Helen looked down at the pond and watched Thad standing on a boulder above the water. He reeled up his line and held up a tiny Bluegill for Helen to see. Helen and Thad smiled at one another as though they had always been family.

"You know, some of the Scouts in town swear this pond is haunted, but the rumor doesn't seem to bother Thad." Her comment caused a lull in conversation.

After all the turmoil, Thad was back on Balsams Pond taunting fish as Barry had a year ago. In the sun's glare, he was the spitting image of her son.

Fall's twilight glow softens the reds and golds of distant hills, as still, chilled air works its way into the longer shadows beside buildings and trees. Embedded in a fresh granite gravestone, just beyond the shadow of the Colebrook Congregational Church, an Eagle Scout medallion glistens in the autumn sun.

If you asked Butch what he wanted to be when he grew up, he would tell you: an Eagle. An Eagle Scout is the highest honor one can achieve in Scouting. Former President Gerald Ford was an Eagle. As was every astronaut who walked on the moon. Few boys attained such a level in Scouting, and those who did became successful leaders. Butch knew that. And though at times he didn't do so well in school, he excelled at what he loved, always finding time to filch trout and crawdads from the pond at the Balsams Resort.

And within the morning vapors rising off the water, before the sun rises over Dixville Notch in the east, three figures can sometimes be seen at the pond below Balsams' charred remains: One wading in the gorge, looking for crawdads beneath the rocks; and a boy and his dog on a boulder rising out of the pool; they stand motionless in the vapors--above the water, swimming in innocence.

THE END